THE BLUE GEM

THE BLUE GEM

Clash of the Aliens

M. B. WOOD

WFP
WordFire Press

EBook ISBN: 978-1-68057-052-6
Trade Paperback ISBN: 978-1-68057-051-9

Cover artwork by Michael J. Canales
Kevin J. Anderson, Art Director
Published by
WordFire Press, LLC
PO Box 1840
Monument CO 80132
Kevin J. Anderson & Rebecca Moesta, Publishers
WordFire Press eBook Edition 2020
WordFire Press Trade Paperback Edition 2020

Printed in the USA
Join our WordFire Press Readers Group for
sneak previews, updates, new projects, and giveaways.
Sign up at wordfirepress.com

❄ Created with Vellum

THE STORY SO FAR

Middle Eastern fanatics paralyze Western Civilization with massive EMPs, creating a post-apocalyptic world that is a sea of chaos and near-anarchy. Refugees create a society under a primitive rule of law. Proud, fierce, and free, Taylor MacPherson and a tight-knit group of survivors known as the Clan take their first steps to restoring law and justice ... as a race of hermaphroditic aliens, the Qu'uda, arrives to find a post-apocalyptic Earth.

As the Qu'uda ship orbits the Earth, a leftover missile-defense weapon fires a shot that hits the ship's drive. When the Qu'uda attempt to restart the ship's drive, it explodes and puts the disabled vessel into a decaying orbit that will ultimately spiral into the planet. The shock of the explosion and the crisis triggers an abrupt gender change in many of the alien crewmembers.

Needing a new propulsion tube to complete the desperate repairs, the Qu'uda disguise one of their crew, Bilik Pudjata, to look like a human and send him to the surface. In reality, however, they make Bilik into a caricature of a human. It takes Bilik a year to learn the

English language by eavesdropping on the natives using a language-learning algorithm in his personal biocomputer. Bilik makes contact with a humble farmer who turns his name into "Billy Potato." The name sticks.

Conflicts with humans convince "Billy" to kill those who oppose him. He takes over the Fed, a small city-state headquartered in Defiance, Ohio. He uses a fusion-powered drive unit from a wrecked shuttlecraft to generate electricity for a foundry to cast the needed parts for the necessary propulsion tube. The Fed expands into Taylor MacPherson's Clan territory south of Cleveland, starting a border dispute, which deteriorates into series of bloody battles.

The arrival of a Qu'uda shuttlecraft causes a crisis in the Clan, because they fear that the Fed has a terrible pre-Collapse weapon. Taylor persuades the Clan Elders to negotiate a solution to the crisis, but unfortunately the solution fails. A larger war becomes inevitable. After a series of battles, a Clan attack catches the Fed without a full complement of guards in Defiance, and Billy has to summon the alien shuttle to pick up the last castings. In only a matter of days, the giant spacecraft will plunge from orbit. During the attack, Billy is injured, and a woman, Joyce Vargas, drags him to safety. The noise and flash of the shuttle's beam weapon and the purple color of Billy's blood makes Joyce believe she has gone insane.

The Qu'uda shuttle picks up the last parts and takes off. Heavily laden, it flies low across Defiance. Fed guards panic and fire their muzzle-loading rifles at the craft, damaging it. The damaged shuttle limps back to the alien ship with the parts for the propulsion system, but it cannot return to the planet. The Qu'uda are forced to abandon four crew members on the surface, on Andros Island in the Bahamas, where they are guarding eggs sent down from the ship.

The humans' violence angers the military faction of the Qu'uda. They vow to build battle craft and return to Earth, where they will remove all technology from the violent "dry land vermin" and bomb the land into ruins.

Meanwhile, Taylor questions the wounded Billy after he regains consciousness, and then he examines the Qu'uda drive unit that powers the Defiance generators, which makes Taylor believe Billy is an alien. Billy learns from his biocomputer's communications module that the Qu'uda on the orbiting spaceship no longer need or want him. Betrayed by his own kind, Billy turns to the humans and reveals everything. Taylor and the others learn that the Qu'uda plan to return with advanced weapons to wreak havoc on Earth.

CHAPTER ONE

A scream woke Suh-Joh.

Once more, a cry echoed through the tunnels. It was a death cry, like a baby wailing for its mother.

It's a guard, Suh-Joh realized. He'd sounded the alarm with his last breath.

She ran toward the sound until she caught a glimpse of unknown Chosen-Male warriors racing into the bowels of the Hive.

She stopped, stared, and sniffed. *Unknown,* she thought. *I must warn Lok-Nih, my Hive-Mother.* She raced back to her sleeping quarters. "Intruders."

"Who violates my Hive?" Lok-Nih asked.

"Blessed Hive-Mother." Suh-Joh flexed low. "I know not. They came without warning. They use naat-jii juice to hide their spine markings and they mask their odor with glik-lee. They're in the food stores."

"Do they use energy weapons?" Lok-Nih, like all devout worshippers of the Spirit-of-the-Mother, feared the energy weapons of war that had been used in the time of high technology. There were no defenses against heretics who violated the bans on weapons of mass murder.

"No, blessed Hive-Mother. I saw none."

"That's one mercy," Lok-Nih said.

Lok-Nih gave her paat-kli a quick poke with a spine. The tiny creature squeaked and folded into its articulated shell and scurried under Lok-Nih's klut-shi, the mating-skin flap.

"Rouse more warriors." Lok-Nih gestured to Suh-Joh.

"Now help me," Lok-Nih said. Attendants rushed to her assistance, keeping clear of the klut-shi. With ponderous bulk, she moved slowly onto her spindly rear limbs, using her mid-limbs for balance. Her deadly spines could either ripen them to Chosen status or kill them instantly. Now erected in anger, there could be only one outcome.

The intruders' attack had come in during the middle of the sleep cycle. Once the intruders found the Hive's food stores, they fell into a feeding frenzy, their discipline disintegrating.

The war-chant of the Hive's warriors grew louder.

"They remind me of Zak-Joh and the battles he fought on my behalf." Lok-Nih sighed. "Oh, Spirit-of-the-Mother, I do so miss him."

The chant changed to a cacophony of squeaks and cries.

Lok-Nih moved quickly to a growing melee near the main entrance.

"Hoo-Lii," she screamed. It was a challenge to the intruders. The word "Hoo-Lii" meant Mother-favored. "I am here. Protect me." She pushed forward.

At these words, her Chosen-Male warriors redoubled their efforts against the intruders.

The tunnel reeked with the odor of glik-lee and the metallic stink of spilled blood and guts.

Warriors twisted with acrobatic fury, flicking and slashing with their long cutting spines. Whenever a spine touched the skin between the armor-like plates of the invader's hide, muscles ruptured, and blood spewed forth. The Hive's warriors tightened into ranks, sweeping forward against the disorganized intruders.

Suh-Joh watched Lok-Nih advance with her Chosen-Male warriors, urging them on. Even the unripened May-be-Chosen joined the fight, wielding domestic implements as weapons against the out-numbered intruders.

Some of the May-be-Chosen fought well, Suh-Joh thought as the warriors continued to drive the intruders back. The Hive's warriors surged forward, and the intruders broke and ran, fleeing into the darkness of the tunnels carrying their stolen food.

Bodies of intruders and defenders lay scattered around the entrance to the Hive. Pools of blood and coils of guts gleamed darkly on the time-polished stone floor under the pale yellow of the emergency lights. The wounded twitched, unable to rise.

I wonder who was behind this raid, Suh-Joh thought.

Four squared of the Hive's warriors were dead. Some lay paralyzed, their hind limb muscles cut. Others called out in agony. They fought well, for there were more bodies of the intruders than the Hive's warriors. Suh-Joh stooped to examine the corpses of the intruders, wiping the naat-jii juice from their spines.

CHAPTER TWO

From within the Hive came a coterie of sterile Chosen-Male priests singing the prayer of death. Its familiar and comforting cadence brought a soothing note to the chaotic scene, calming those present.

"... From Life to Death,

Death to Life,

As ever, the cycle repeats ..."

"Now." Lok-Nih's voice rang out. "I must ripen more males. It is time for more offspring." She touched eight May-be-Chosen who abased themselves before her.

"Blessed Hive-Mother, may I speak?" Suh-Joh asked.

"Yes?" Lok-Nih emitted an odor of irritation.

"I cleaned the spines of the dead intruders. They had the markings of the Af-Gih and the Jan-Dil Hives." Suh-Joh flexed low in abasement.

"So, my precious offspring, Af-Gih, grows bold." Lok-Nih erected her breathing flaps in annoyance. "Prisoners?"

"There are thirty-two uninjured captives. As I speak, the dead and maimed are being fed to the food-insects."

"Condition of the prisoners?"

"Emaciated, smaller than our warriors. Many show signs of malnutrition," Suh-Joh said. "It looks like their attack was an act of desperation."

"Hmm, unfit for breeding. Pluck their spines and neuter them. Send them to the surface to replace the weak and worn-out crop workers. Feed the discards to the insects."

"Yes, blessed Hive-Mother."

"Those two Hives produced many of the Disobedient." Lok-Nih paused. "They've lost so many of their young they must be weak. Raiding them would garner little, if anything." Her voice was soft, barely audible. "They do have a strong gene pool, perhaps a female—"

"Blessed Hive-Mother. You can't leave us." Suh-Joh crouched low, touching her head to the ground. "Please."

"No. I'm just thinking out loud. Don't repeat that." Lok-Nih released an odor that showed her frustration "So, my offspring Af-Gih seeks to steal from me? Send her the spines from her dead warriors with this message: She must ripen a daughter and send her, with a levy of Chosen-Males, to the planet Kamah as colonists."

Lok-Nih rippled her spines. "This will ensure the survival of my bloodline even if Hool continues its decline. If she chooses not, tell her to expect a visit from my Chosen-Male warriors. As for Jan-Dil, she deserves something special."

Lok-Nih scratched her plate-like skin and raised the fringe of spines along the edge of her klut-shi. The paat-kli cautiously extended its head out from its shell. Lok-Nih tickled the paat-kli gently and it chirped. It resumed grazing on her skin, feeding on the dead flakes between the plates on Lok-Nih's hide. She stroked the paat-kli, encouraging it to rasp its tiny tongue on her skin.

Our richness in food makes us the target of every starving Hive, Lok-Nih thought. *I've balanced my Hive's population with the supply of food-insects and crops from the surface. My populace is healthier and more energetic than most. Still, we could use more food.* She knew she could only mate when the Hive needed replacements or conquest expanded its resource base.

"Follow me." Lok-Nih gestured to the eight unripened ones she'd raised to Now-Chosen status. Her arousal grew as she went through the tunnel leading to her quarters. She always enjoyed ripening males.

Suh-Joh could hear the Now-Chosen twittering and smell their arousal. *Yes*, she thought. *They are ready to breed with Lok-Nih.* The emotional state of the Hive-Mother controlled the toxins or hormones produced by her klut-shi. She had to be aroused to produce the hormones that turned unripened males into warriors. If not, the klut-shi produced poison. *If I were a Hive-Mother*, Suh-Joh thought. *I too, could enjoy ... No. I'll never be a Hive-Mother.*

"Hoo-Lii, you," Lok-Nih uttered the blessing and pointed to the first Now-Chosen, gesturing he should come forward.

"Hoo-Lii. Immediately, gracious Hive-Mother," the young male twittered in a voice pitched high with excitement.

"Take the position," Lok-Nih said.

Suh-Joh found the mating aroused feelings of envy within her. She could not draw herself away. Fascinated, she continued to watch.

The young male moved in front of Lok-Nih and flexed into a position of abasement as demanded by his status. He exposed the tender connective skin between the armored plate-skin, thus presenting her with many vulnerable locations.

Lok-Nih moved behind him and draped herself over him, enfolding him with her mating-skin flap. She flexed the edge of the mating-skin flap inwards, hooking the klut-shi into the delicate membranes connecting the plate-like sections of his hide. She held him in a grip from which there was no retreat.

"Closer, still closer. Here, let me feel you," Lok-Nih said to the hesitant male who assumed a raised position. "You know what is next?"

"Yes, gracious one."

"Are you ready? When you are, call my name."

"Lok-Nih—"

As he spoke, Lok-Nih slid the spines of the klut-shi between the plates of his hide. They bit into his flesh and flooded his system with hormones that catalyzed his transformation from a juvenile to a mature state.

Lok-Nih pushed against him.

The male shuddered as hormones sped throughout his system, triggering his instantaneous arousal. He shuddered and sagged.

Lok-Nih relaxed her grip. "Ah, good." It was over. "Males," she said. "They have so little capacity for this. Mate once and they are done."

The male collapsed to the floor, exhausted.

Lok-Nih made a gesture. Attendants carried the newly ripened Chosen-Male away, who was limp from exhaustion.

Suh-Joh remained to watch. She knew that seven more would be ripened.

Lok-Nih gestured for the next Chosen-Male to approach.

Each time Lok-Nih ripened a young male, she received a fresh charge of juvenile hormones from the Chosen-Male. The Hive-Mothers' longevity came from ripening young males.

CHAPTER THREE

That was the beginning of a series of events, which completely changed life on Hool. It seems like a long time ago when the priests of the Shrine-of-the-Mother asked me, Kot-Nih, to write the history of our encounter with the Others. I am a priest and not a very good one at that. You see, I spend too much time in the archives, which may be the reason this assignment was given to me. It was not an easy task, for it required I travel to other worlds and pore over alien records to find the truth. Though their archives were most fascinating, I was thankful to return home and be among my own kind again. Yet I have been told I have a talent for teasing out the truth.

There are those who will not like what is written here, for they would like to assign blame for what happened. The investigation lasted many years—yes, it took that long for the truth to reveal itself.

The truth is strange because it showed there were no real villains in this encounter, contrary to what may have been passed down. You see, once the actions of all parties are examined closely, it becomes clear that most acted in what they believed to be a logical and reasonable way. Perhaps some of the actions taken were self-serving, but who doesn't look to protecting one's own kind first? Some say I am too forgiving to think this way, but look at the consequences of doing otherwise.

Certainly, mistakes were made and the motives of many may be called into question. It is now quite clear no one set out with a deliberate and preconceived plan to destroy a world. It was a situation that got out of control. The subsequent events brought us together for a fateful meeting, a meeting that was both a horrible nightmare and an impossible dream.

Many things have happened since then, but that's another story for someone else to tell. My assignment is to relate the events up to the encounter with the Others.

Where and when did it all start?

Since Suh-Joh played a major role in these events—she was a catalyst, you see—it should start with her. To understand her role, you must also understand her origins. How she too, was shaped by history. You must forgive me if I include some history; it is one of my weaknesses.

The events of several hundred years ago, on our dry and dusty world, where in spite of the great technological achievements of our golden age, had reduced us to a hardscrabble existence. It was out of those difficult circumstances a dream was born, a dream of a most unlikely individual, a Chosen-Male warrior by the name of Zak-Joh, consort of the Hive-Mother Lok-Nih.

So, with a few exceptions, I'll let Suh-Joh and her Chosen-Male warrior tell their own stories about those fateful events and what came to pass.

Later, Suh-Joh learned Lok-Nih gave birth to only three tiny babies instead of the normal eight from mating with the eight newly ripened males.

So few, Suh-Joh thought. *Her time draws near.*

Suh-Joh watched and said naught. She knew Lok-Nih loved her babies, but she would keep them only a short while before transferring them to a partially ripened female who served as brood-mother.

Demands of ruling the Hive eclipsed her desires and duties as a biological mother.

Suh-Joh knew custom required Lok-Nih to ripen a female from a different Hive to maintain the diversity of their gene pool. Hive history had the account of how Lok-Nih killed the Hive-Mother who ripened her. *It is the Way-of-the-Mother*, she thought. *It will happen here, soon, in this Hive.*

Suh-Joh recalled the legends of ancient Hool when it was beautiful and verdant before fusion weapons and bio-engineered plagues poisoned its surface. Details kept in the archives that lay beneath the Shrine-of-the-Mother told of a nuclear winter that drove the survivors underground and away from the surface radiation. They also contained technological secrets of the once-used weapons, but the horrors of the high technology war led to a prohibition on bioweapons. These bans prevented even the use of genetic engineering to strengthen the gene pool.

～

Suh-Joh watched Lok-Nih drop two of her newborns into the pit. Even in the dim light of the cavern, she could see the seething mass of voracious white grubs tear into the soft, pink bodies of the two deformed offspring. Out of her litter of eight, she'd dropped just three, two of which were only good as food for the insects.

Lok-Nih crooned a fragment of verse from the Song of Summer over and over while clutching her pouch where the last one of her litter suckled on a teat.

Declining fertility has caught up with her, Suh-Joh thought. *This means change.* She knew Lok-Nih, as a devoted defender of the Way-of-the-Mother, would put duty to the Hive above all else. *Where will she get a successor? Who will it be?* She'd heard whispered stories of new Hive-Mothers, young and erratic, who killed randomly and without mercy until they dropped their first litter.

Especially those who carry the odor of the previous Hive-Mother. *Like me*, Suh-Joh thought.

Suh-Joh shivered as she followed Lok-Nih back to the great hall through narrow rocky passages. *And it will mean no chance of another Hive seeking me to be its Hive-Mother.*

Ovals of amber light from the overhead sunshafts illuminated the rich brown floor coverings decorated with the Hive's motif of stylized crossed quills. Glow globes on the yellow sandstone walls of the cave focused on the decorated and colored quills that had been plucked from defeated enemies as battle trophies. They were proof of the Hive's proud history, of its fight to preserve the Way-of-the-Mother even as war had weakened every Hive on Hool.

Lok-Nih remembered Zak-Joh, her favorite Chosen-Male who had died a generation ago. *So wise and patient, he was my savior when the Disobedient rose to challenge the Spirit-of-the-Mother and the rule of the Hive-Mothers.*

She remembered more.

In four thousand nine hundred and ninety-two, year of the Mother, Wod-Jur preached the heresy of "Disobedience." He infected many of the vast underclass of the May-be-Chosen who became Disobedient. Expelled from their Hives, they set up decadent communities dedicated to the selfish, wanton pleasure of illicit breeding in violation of the Way-of-the-Mother. It outraged the Hive-Mothers that so much juvenile hormone was lost to casual sex. That was a threat to their longevity.

Zak-Joh used his considerable diplomatic skills to change the Council of Hive-Mothers from a forum of useless bickering into a real alliance. He led the Council's Chosen-Male warriors in battle against the Disobedient. Even after several victories, Zak-Joh realized Wod-Jur's Disobedient had grown strong. Zak-Joh recognized the need for compromise.

Zak-Joh persuaded the Hive-Mothers to retrieve technology from the archives under the Shrine-of-the-Mother on how to build a ship with the capability to enter the portals that led to distant stars. He offered a treaty to the Disobedient with a home on the long ago discovered but never inhabited planet of Chud-Loo in the "Daughter" star system.

Wod-Jur accepted the treaty along with a commitment from the Hive-Mothers to provide resources to settle on the new planet. It took a great effort by the Disobedient to build an orbital space station and years later, two interstellar ships. These ships had the long-forgotten technology that opened the strange cubical gate leading to a gravity string that crossed the gulf of space-time to Chud-Loo.

Lok-Nih remembered with a trace of amusement when the Disobedient discovered upon their arrival, the vast plains of Chud-Loo on its single continent weren't vegetation like they'd assumed, but an endless expanse of windswept sand and rock, colored by a thin coating of a slow-growing lichen. The icy polar oceans, bounded by huge, barren sand dunes, teemed with marine life that competed for survival with a vicious ferocity.

The Disobedient settled on the equatorial mountain range, which reared up out of the desert-like continent. Within the frigid mountains, they found three circular valleys that had water and plants. A complex of narrow canyons joined the basin-like valleys through which small streams drained, to finally disappear into the sand sea on the leeward side of the mountains.

Once the Disobedient settled on Chud-Loo, the Hive-Mothers found it a convenient place to send those who fell from favor. Chud-Loo's unrelenting harshness convinced its colonists they'd made a mistake. However, when they petitioned the Hive-Mothers on Hool to return, they found they had taken a one-way trip.

A partially ripened female, seeking metals in a tiny spaceship among the outer asteroids of the Hool system, discovered another portal through space-time. When opened, it led to an inhabitable planet orbiting the dimmer of the two stars in the "Sister" binary system. It was a warm, watery world with three large islands. This world, called Kamah, quickly became the privileged destination for newly ripened females sponsored by Hive-Mothers. Too soon, its best living areas became filled.

Having promised to supply the Disobedient on Chud-Loo for a generation as part of the treaty, the Hive-Mothers found the commitment was a weighty load. The need to send a ship once a year to Chud-Loo cost them dearly. This too contributed to the Hool's privation. Shortages came from the supplies needed for the Disobedient's settlement on Chud-Loo.

It was worth it, Lok-Nih thought. *For it had eliminated the threat to our way of life.*

It amused Lok-Nih to learn Di-Nah, Af-Gih's beloved daughter, had accepted exile in Kamah. As a new Hive-Mother, she would have to eke out a living in a marginal area on the planet Kamah. The economic burden on Af-Gih's Hive to send out colonists would bring it one step closer to ruin.

Lok-Nih cared not.

CHAPTER FOUR

Lok-Nih rotated her head and rippled her spines. "Bring me a data terminal." She waved a limb and flared her breathing flaps. "Then leave. All of you."

"Including me?" Suh-Joh asked. This was most unusual.

"Yes," Lok-Nih said. "Now."

"Yes, blessed Hive-Mother." Suh-Joh rushed to comply, then hurried from the hall to an alcove, which had a terminal. She drew the privacy curtain and traced the files Lok-Nih called up. *Odd*, she thought. *It's only history. Lok-Nih was spending time on the records of how the Hives lived long ago.*

Suh-Joh preferred science and technology, even though the priests of the Spirit-of-the-Mother discouraged study of those subjects, especially for anything that could be used for war.

Yet war was all their society now knew.

ᘓ

Lok-Nih summoned Suh-Joh at mid-day. "Prepare me a meal. I want a feast." Feasts were usually reserved for celebrating the Day of the Mother.

"Yes, blessed Hive-Mother," Suh-Joh said.

"Music. I want to hear the Symphony of Summer."

"Immediately, blessed Hive-Mother." Suh-Joh scurried out.

After the senior food attendant arrived to learn her specific wishes and preferences, they left.

The music servant aroused the insects.

The go-lik insects started their gentle wail, an almost hypnotic, undulating sound heard during the warm days of the crop season. The purple maa-li flies began to click their mandibles and provide a counterpoint to the droning tempo. More tiny creatures joined the chorus with their clipped wings adding a high-pitched hum until the Symphony of Summer filled the great hall with its rich and complex sound.

As Lok-Nih listened to the music, she tickled her paat-kli. The tiny creature chirped with pleasure and stretched its head from its shell, presenting more of itself to her touch. Satisfied, it resumed grazing on her wrinkled flesh.

The senior food attendant and two unripened females arranged the meal on an eating platform. It was a platter of red, green, and brown food items adorned with a spicy yellow puree made from stinging naad-luu insects. When the senior food attendant finished the last detail of arranging the food, she touched her head to the ground before Lok-Nih. "Your food is ready, blessed Hive-Mother."

"Stop the music and leave." Lok-Nih selected a lightly braised dak-li, cracked its shell, dipped it in the sauce, and sucked out its pale green flesh. She spat the shell to the floor and laughed at the antics of the naat-jii as they scurried to it, looking for something to eat. The spicy puree brought water to her eyes. "Good." She ate in a slow, methodical fashion. Finished, she pushed away from the eating platform, stretched, and discharged a movement of small fecal pellets. As the pellets hit the floor, naat-jii scrambled after them.

Lok-Nih heaved her bulk to her favorite resting-rock, a smooth mound of pink granite, polished from generations of use. Her armored exoskeleton clicked as each plate slid over the rock as she spread her four rear hind limbs on it. The rows of breathing flaps along her torso opened and closed in a regular fashion. The hall grew quiet, still.

She stared at the holograph of her favorite Chosen-Male. "Zak-Joh," she said in a quiet voice. "Give me the strength to do what I must now do. I need your strength now more than ever." She closed her eyes and settled lower on the resting-rock. Soon the only sound in the great hall was the sigh of the ventilation system.

"Priests," she called. "Bring me the priests. I want absolution. I must make my peace with the Spirit-of-the-Mother."

♻

"Suh-Joh, come here." Lok-Nih waved her wrinkled fore limb and pointed to the place of honor before her resting-rock. Attendants twittered formless concern. She rippled her breathing flaps. The hall became quiet.

Suh-Joh hesitated. It was rare for an unripened female to be so honored. She also knew that position was sometimes used for executions.

What is she up to? Fear slowed her limbs.

"Well?" Lok-Nih's voice echoed in the hall.

"At once, blessed Hive-Mother." Suh-Joh crawled into position. "Hoo-Lii." She bent to the posture of submission, presenting vulnerable openings in the plate-like armor of her hide. "What is your wish, blessed Hive-Mother?"

"Hoo-Lii. Come closer, I want to talk to you, daughter of mine from the seed of Zak-Joh. It's time I told you how I feel."

"As you wish, blessed Hive-Mother."

"You've grown more like him. You make me proud."

"You honor me in ways I don't deserve."

"My child," Lok-Nih said. "You remind me of Zak-Joh when I first met him." Her eyes closed. "I too, was thin, and none of my connective skin showed. Yes, there's a lot about you that reminds me of when I was your age."

"Blessed Hive-Mother, you flatter me. I'm not worthy."

"Please, grant me the right to judge my get. By the grace of the Mother, I've done enough of it, and some of those I've judged are no longer with us."

Yes, Suh-Joh thought. *You found them unfit and fed them to the food-insects without hesitation.* Fear made her flex lower in the posture of abasement. "I'm just an unripened female and destined to remain that way. I'll always be a lowly servant, if it pleases you."

Lok-Nih leaned forward and touched Suh-Joh with one of her long quills. It was a formal acknowledgment of her abasement. "Perhaps. Do you know what I liked about Zak-Joh?"

"No, blessed Hive-Mother." Suh-Joh raised her head to a more comfortable position and swiveled it to watch Lok-Nih.

"He was my equal."

"How could he be your equal?" Suh-Joh straightened slightly and held her breath momentarily. "He was but a Chosen-Male, good only for fighting and fertilizing."

"My child, in this, you're wrong. He had a brilliant mind hidden within a humble shell. He saw the truth clearly. He had the ability to solve spiny problems. His words rang true and clear, convincing even the most intractable Hive-Mother of the wisdom of his ways. He did things of which I only dared to dream. Do you understand what I mean?"

"You mean that he solved the problem of the Disobedient when the Hive-Mothers could not?"

"Yes. Still using computers to read history as well as watch others, eh?" Lok-Nih lowered her head and stared from a pair of unblinking eyes almost buried behind folds of fat-filled flesh. "Zak-Joh did much to unite the Hives against the Disobedient."

"Yes, blessed Hive-Mother." Fear rippled through Suh-Joh. *Does she know? Did I leave tracks in her files?*

"Tell me, how many of our unripened ones read history? Or secretly study the sciences contained in our archives? Or tap into the terminals of others? Well, answer me that?"

The cold mandible of fear gripped Suh-Joh. "Oh, blessed Hive-Mother, please forgive me." She crouched lower. *She knows. I'm done for.* "I mean no harm. I've never neglected my duties."

"My child, my child. You're so like Zak-Joh that I feel his presence. You've inherited his keen mind and humble ways. I sense your ability to see things clearly. Come here, nearer to me." Lok-Nih pointed. "Perhaps your scent will bring back the feeling of those glorious times when Zak-Joh and I were together, when we overcame the threat to the Way-of-the-Mother." Her breathing flaps opened slowly in unison.

Suh-Joh winced and looked at the ground. She could only bring herself so close before fear stopped her.

"Here, next to me." Lok-Nih beckoned with her wrinkled digit to indicate the base of the resting-rock.

Suh-Joh moved closer, reluctant to touch her. Up close, she saw how loosely the skin hung from Lok-Nih's bloated shape.

Lok-Nih opened her breathing flaps and sniffed. "Tell me, Suh-Joh, do you ever dream?" She closed her eyes and exhaled.

"I once dreamed ..." Suh-Joh looked at the floor.

"Yes?"

"I wanted to be a Hive-Mother, but that is not possible."

"Why not?"

"No Hive wants me." *Especially after you are gone*, she thought.

"Come, my child." Lok-Nih motioned her to come closer. "This," she said to no one. "Is even better than I could have wished."

Suh-Joh hesitated before moving within the reach of Lok-Nih's mating cloak. She flinched when a quill or two found their way between the plates of her skin to prickle her delicate connective membranes. But they penetrated no further. She relaxed slightly; the quills did not have their deadly sting. She could smell the pheromones associated with sex on Lok-Nih's mating-flap.

That too, she thought, *is forbidden to an unripened one such as me.*

"I used to have many dreams. Now I'm old and my time has passed. Zak-Joh and I once shared a dream long ago. It has long haunted me." Lok-Nih paused and her breathing flaps flared in unison. "Now you shall fulfill it for us. You know I must soon choose a successor? One who will kill me so I may join the Spirit-of-the-Mother, is that not right?"

"Oh, blessed Hive-Mother, you're not old." Suh-Joh flattened her small quills, for this was a dangerous topic. "You bring forth young each time you choose to breed—"

"My dear daughter, the whole Hive knows deformed ilk came forth the last time I bred. My day has passed. A successor must send me on my way, and soon. Does not the Way-of-the-Mother demand it?" She rippled her quills.

Silence filled the great hall.

Suh-Joh hesitated. "Yes, it is the Way."

"My dear child, you're the best of my offspring from Zak-Joh, of those I gave his name. Thanks to the Spirit-of-the-Mother, you've turned out to be more like him than any of the others. You have the best of both of us." Air whistled through her breathing flaps. "I've chosen you to succeed me."

"What?" Suh-Joh wanted to flee. This conversation sounded like the forbidden subject of ripening between relatives. "I don't know what you mean."

"You will be my Hive-Daughter."

"That cannot be." Suh-Joh stopped breathing. She felt her spines rise to a defensive position. She could not believe what she had heard. "I'm your true daughter. It is not allowed." She held her breath.

"I shall ripen you. You will succeed me."

"No, you can't. That's a perversion." Suh-Joh felt her breathing flaps snap closed in unison. "It's against the Way," she whispered. "It would violate everything in which we believe. I'd be an abomination."

"You are mistaken." Lok-Nih spoke in the voice of one accustomed to obedience. "It is but a custom to seek a daughter from another Hive. It is our way we preserve genetic diversity. During the time of the great dynastic families, Hive-Daughters succeeded their Hive-Mothers. I believe it was a better strategy."

"It was abandoned because it was wrong."

"Not true."

"It's against the Way-of-the-Mother."

"Again, you are mistaken. During the time when Chosen-Males could move about freely, Hive-Mothers sought out the strongest and added their gift to the Hive's gene pool. And they ripened their best daughters. That was the golden age of Hool. That was when we made all our great advances. That was a time of peace and wealth."

"Wasn't it stopped because it violated the Way?"

"No. We grew too many. Competition for food and resources grew fierce. Heretics came forth who polarized our society. War became our way of life. The indiscriminate use of weapons poisoned much of the surface of our world. And now Chosen-Males only visit another hive to kill or be killed."

"You mean the only reason new mothers are sought from Hives other than their own is genetic diversity?" In spite of her revulsion at Lok-Nih's proposal, Suh-Joh took a deep breath. This was new to her.

"Yes." Lok-Nih gestured toward the holographic terminal. "Read the files I posted—I know you have already taken at least one look. Did not war stop travel between the Hives? When the Chosen-Males were no longer free to travel, open access to the gene pool disappeared. That's why new Hive-Mothers are seized from outside of the Hive, to maintain genetic diversity."

"But that's the custom, the Way—"

"Yes, yes, I know, but it's just custom," Lok-Nih said. "It's a failure. Zak-Joh showed me through genetic analysis we are inbreeding ourselves to death. You're going to change that. It is time to go back to the old strategy. He believed the time for this is long overdue. You will be our tool."

"Me? No, no, not me, please."

"Yes, you."

"The other Hives will join together and destroy me." The vision of being ripened by her own mother made her want to withdraw within her shell. It was like being forced to perform an unspeakable act. She assumed the posture of abasement flat against the ground. "They'll kill me. I'll deserve to die."

"Bah. My Hive is the strongest on Hool. Believe me, its strength will shape the opinions of the other Hive-Mothers. You must seek out Chosen-Males from other Hives for breeding. It is the only way to arrest our genetic decline."

Lok-Nih took a deep breath. "Suh-Joh, my dear Suh-Joh, you're truly special. I shall ripen you. You will be the Hive-Mother that replaces me. You're the answer that Zak-Joh foresaw."

"No, no, no. You cannot." Suh-Joh's voice echoed throughout the great hall. "I won't be your experiment." As she tried to back away, Lok-Nih hooked her quills into Suh-Joh's flesh and pulled her back.

"Yes, you will," Lok-Nih's voice rang loud in the great hall. "You will be my Hive-daughter."

"Ah." Suh-Joh winced from the pain. "No, I won't, it's—"

"You will." Lok-Nih squeezed her.

A trace of Lok-Nih's venom penetrated her hide. Pain exploded through every nerve in Suh-Joh's body. "Spirit-of-the-Mother. Save me," she screamed. "I'm on fire."

Lok-Nih's beady eyes glittered brightly. "You're strong, my daughter, in the willpower you'll need to be a Hive-Mother. You shall do the things I was afraid to try."

"Please," Suh-Joh said. "Stop." Her vision shrank to a single center, focused on the white-hot, searing pain. Death would be a mercy. *Spirit-of-the-Mother, take me.*

Lok-Nih stared at her. "The Way." She nudged her quills deeper. "You will do it, won't you?"

"Yes." Suh-Joh moaned. "The Way." She held her breathing flaps closed until she panted. "I'll do it. Spirit-of-the-Mother, forgive me."

"Soon, my darling, the pain shall go." Lok-Nih's voice held gentleness not often heard. "I'll neutralize the toxin."

Suh-Joh gasped as a cooling wave swept over her, extinguishing the fiery pain. "Oh, Spirit-of-the-Mother." She sighed. "Thank you."

Lok-Nih took a deep breath. Her wrinkled and worn visage softened. "My daughter, my darling daughter." She raised her forelimb to stroke Suh-Joh tenderly. "Through you, Zak-Joh and I shall live forever." Her voice carried a note of affection. "Hold still, my darling, it is time for the gift of the maturation hormones."

Lok-Nih's eyes grew bright and her body began to shake. "Closer." She grabbed Suh-Joh and held her tightly.

Suh-Joh could feel Lok-Nih's flabby body press against her, the largest of her quills probing into a tender part of her anatomy.

"Yes." Lok-Nih breathed deeply. "It's near, now." She drove in the hormone-bearing quill.

Suh-Joh screamed as the hormones flooded her body.

Suh-Joh's world disappeared into a kaleidoscopic array of colors. A roaring sound overwhelmed her; every sense was amplified. Her entire body shuddered. Every tiny spine on her body came alive and erect.

She convulsed and ripped herself free from the flaccid grip of Lok-Nih's mating cloak. Slowly, the great hall came back into focus.

It looked altogether different. It was sharper, clearer, and everything had its place.

I, Suh-Joh, am now a Hive-Mother.

Her tiny quills, stiff and erect, were newly potent with deadly venom. Something had happened that made her feel strong, powerful. She breathed deeply and rippled her quills, forcing several to penetrate the flesh of her mother's skin between the plates on her neck.

Lok-Nih flinched. "That hurts." She gasped and sagged as though deflated. Her body softened with relaxation; it had the tranquil appearance she got after she'd mated long and hard. "Suh-Joh." She gasped. "Yes, my darling, you are so like him."

"Who?" Suh-Joh drew close to hear her faint voice.

"Zak-Joh," she spoke in soft voice that only Suh-Joh could hear. "I did the right thing. I brought you back. Your spirit will change Hool."

"Spirit-of-the Mother," Suh-Joh said. "She's dying. I've killed her." The enormity of what she had done, struck like a falling rock.

Lok-Nih looked old and smaller. Her mouth gaped open wide and her tongue protruded. She shook briefly, and air sighed out of her breathing flaps.

The twittering of the unripened female attendants in the alcoves of the great hall rose to a squeal.

Doubt and self-loathing filled Suh-Joh. Ignoring the attendants, she stared, afraid, into her mother's blank eyes. *Oh, Spirit-of-the-Mother, what have I done?*

Lok-Nih's body relaxed and out-gassed a sour smell of partially digested naad-luu insects, faint with spice.

Suh-Joh killed Lok-Nih's paat-kli with a quick poke of a quill. If she didn't, it would die from starvation because it would not rasp a single flake of skin from anyone else.

I killed my Hive-Mother. I must flee.

Suh-Joh glanced around, seeking a way out.

A column of Chosen-Male cohort leaders and priests entered the far end of the great hall.

Suh-Joh froze.

Somehow, she realized, the priests of the Spirit-of-the-Mother had been forewarned and brought Chosen-Male warriors. It will, she was sure, be only a moment before they kill me for the crimes of matricide and ripening with a relative.

The priests and warriors marched forward and silently formed a circle about Suh-Joh. Behind each priest stood a warrior.

CHAPTER FIVE

The priests and warriors dressed their ranks and became still, silent. In unison, they broke into a high-pitched chant:

... From Life to Death,
Death to Life,
As ever, the Cycle repeats.
Birth and Growth,
Night and Day,
Ripening and Death,
Dawn to Dusk,
As ever, the Cycle repeats.
From Mother to Daughter
From Life to Death
From Hive-Daughter to Mother,
From Death to Life,
As ever, the Cycle repeats,
It is the Way ...

The Chosen-Male cohort leaders chanted the Cycle of Life prayer in counterpoint to the priests.

Oftentimes Suh-Joh had listened to the priests in the deep caverns, chanting the Cycle of Life's many verses to reinforce their faith in the traditional ways. It was also the prayer used to comfort those who were about to be consumed by the insects.

Soon, she thought, *I shall die.* She rose to move away from Lok-Nih's body.

The Chosen-Male cohort leaders moved quickly, forming a line before her. The first in line stared briefly at the dead Hive-Mother, then flexed in ritual abasement.

"Blessed Hive-Mother," a voice spoke quietly. "You must acknowledge them. Prick them and imprint them with your hormones. They are yours."

"Mine?" Suh-Joh turned to the voice.

It was the scarred and worn visage of the senior priest. "Yes," he said. "They came to pay homage to you as their new Hive-Mother." Though stooped with age, he was still large.

"Me?" She glanced back and forth between the old priest and the cohort leaders. "Now?" She felt a wave of fear that threatened to bubble over.

"Yes," the senior priest said. "Zak-Joh foretold this to me. He said it was your destiny. And today, Lok-Nih confirmed it. It has come to pass. Now you must do your duty."

Suh-Joh hesitated. Things were moving too fast.

"If you don't, they will turn on you," the old priest said. "Then the insects will seem like a kindness."

Suh-Joh leaned forward and gently nicked the first cohort leader with one of her quills. The line moved forward as each Chosen-Male cohort leader abased himself to receive a touch from one of her quills.

"Now, blessed Hive-Mother," the senior priest said. "They are yours, in body and spirit." His breathing flaps stilled.

"In body?" Suh-Joh felt a strong urge to mate. It came from being in close proximity with the Chosen-Males. She could smell them.

"Yes, but you must not mate with any of these," the senior priest whispered. "They are your half-brothers. Inbreeding this close is too risky." His breathing flaps stilled momentarily.

More cohort leaders came out of the passageways, many of whom Suh-Joh had never before seen. It was like seeing a hive she never knew existed. There were far more Chosen-Males in the Hive's warrior corps than she had previously believed, many old and scarred from battles.

౭

After the last cohort leader gave his allegiance, the priests began to hum the refrain of the Cycle of Life Prayer. The oldest priests gathered up Lok-Nih's corpse and carried it aloft into the warrens. They beckoned to Suh-Joh to take her place directly behind Lok-Nih's body.

Suh-Joh followed. A mass of warriors fell into formations before and after her. As they marched through the tight passageways, from time to time their tough exoskeletons scraped and rattled against the rocky walls. Upward, through the tunnels, past the Hive's outer defenses, they marched to exit at the base of an orange sandstone cliff on the surface of Hool.

Shading her eyes against the brightness of the sun, Suh-Joh struggled up a path carved into the side of the steep cliff. She followed the priests who carried Lok-Nih up to the mesa overlooking the valley from where they had come.

The priests took the corpse to a scorched and blackened mound in the center of the mesa. Holding Lok-Nih's body up where all could see, they continued to hum the Cycle of Life prayer.

From below came a line of priests carrying bundles of quills that Lok-Nih had taken from the enemies she had defeated. The cohort leaders lined up, each placing a bundle of oil-bush branches on the mound. Long lines of warriors assembled behind their cohort leaders in formations among the spiny crimson xerophytic vegetation covering the plateau.

The Mother-of-the-Sky grew large and red as it sank toward the jagged snow-tipped mountains in the west. In the fading light, the lush maroon ribbon of food crops that followed the valley far below outlined its narrow waterway like a stream of blood.

The two Children-of-the-Sky emerged in the darkening heavens: One low and large in the east, the other gibbous and high above.

Fascinated and fearful, Suh-Joh watched, filled with uncertainty as the priests continued to hum the refrain. When the last cohort leader stacked the final faggot, the priests became quiet. Gently, almost reverently, the priests placed Lok-Nih on top of the byre along with bundles of quills.

The evening wind sighed distantly, and the air grew chill. The spicy scent of the bruised and broken oil-bush branches filled the air.

Suh-Joh approached Lok-Nih's body. A ripple of motion stirred the silent Chosen-Male warriors. She raised a forelimb.

The throng grew still. All eyes followed her.

"Hoo-Lii Lok-Nih, the Spirit-of-the-Mother calls you," Suh-Joh sang out the traditional farewell given to warriors who fell in battle. She knew it was rare for a new Hive-Mother to attend the cremation of the old; most cared little about those whom they replaced. But Suh-Joh had known and cared for Lok-Nih, her true mother.

Hesitantly at first, the cohort leaders responded, "Hoo-Lii. Hail Lok-Nih. The Spirit-of-the-Mother calls you."

Suh-Joh stepped back, wondering what came next. Again, silence settled over the dark mesa.

A Chosen-Male cohort leader advanced with a flaming torch raised on high. He paused before thrusting the burning branch deep into the stacked oil-bush branches. At first the flame flickered fitfully until the oil-bush branches ignited with an explosive crackle and began to burn with a greedy intensity. The black-tinged flames grew enormous, wildly imploring congress with a rising wind and a purple sky.

Light from the flames reflected off the nearby mourners' burnished hides as they backed away. The warriors took up the farewell chant, repeating it again and again until their collective voices echoed distantly off the far hills like the rarely heard sound of thunder.

"Hoo-Lii Lok-Nih. The Spirit-of-the-Mother calls you."

"Hoo-Lii Lok-Nih. The Spirit-of-the-Mother calls you."

Silence fell as the warriors ended their chant. Lok-Nih's rotund form slowly blackened and blistered in the rising flames. Her still-erect quills flickered one by one into a brief incandescent glory. As fire consumed her body, black greasy smoke roiled heavenward, carried away on a cool breeze to disappear into the star-studded night.

Suh-Joh stared away from the fire. *Lok-Nih, you chose me for this role,* she thought. *Why me?*

The senior priest made his way before the assembled warriors. He raised his forelimbs on high. The massed warriors grew still, unmoving, focused on the senior priest.

"Hail Suh-Joh, our blessed Hive-Mother." The senior priest's voice carried over the silent throng. He raised his forelimbs again.

"Hail Suh-Joh, our blessed Hive-Mother." The salute by the warriors echoed over the mesa, only to be repeated again, and again.

They're mine, Suh-Joh thought. *They're all mine.*

Her old ambition to be a Hive-Mother, quasi-dormant, burst forth with the ferocity of an oil-bush struck by lightning on a summer's day.

Lok-Nih, you made me a Hive-Mother, you gave it to me. She paused. *You loved Zak-Joh and you did it for him, too. Yes, you did say that I reminded you of him. It doesn't matter, I understand.*

Suh-Joh shivered as the heat from the funeral pyre's flames faded. *The Chosen-Male warriors have sworn their loyalty to me. Mine is their only Hive. When news of my succession reaches other Hives, there may be trouble. However, the strength and loyalty of the Chosen-Male warriors, no, my Chosen-Male warriors*, she thought, *should be enough to withstand any challenges and overcome any obstacles.*

"My warriors." Suh-Joh's voice stilled the assembled Chosen-Male warriors. "Fear not, for I will lead you to great victories."

"Hail Suh-Joh, our blessed Hive-Mother." The Chosen-Male warriors en masse raised their fore-digits as a sign of their support and willingness to fight.

"Hail Suh-Joh, our blessed Hive-Mother." Their voices swelled and echoed back from the hard rock surface of Hool.

Their voices stirred pride within Suh-Joh. *They are mine, mine completely*, she thought. *Yes, mother, you gave me my dream and the tools to fulfill it. Now, I must fulfill your dream too.*

CHAPTER SIX

CHUD-LOO

I, Kot-Nih, had to sift through the ruins on Chud-Loo to find out what happened to those unfortunates. As historian, I was blessed that many of its inhabitants had kept records of their activities. Between those items and the other physical clues, I believe we know what tragic events took place there. It was one of my more difficult tasks. I hope you will forgive me for taking some liberties and using my imagination to fill in some of the missing details....

Di-Nah could barely contain her excitement at being ripened and destined to be a Hive-Mother. She did resent being sent away from Af-Gih's Hive. The orbital space station was but one step to reach Kamah in the Sister binary star system where she would find her new hive. She had a passage on the spaceship "Young Mother," which would depart in ten sleep cycles.

Bored, she released a powerful whiff of desire-to-mate odor in the close confines of the waiting area. She was eager to become the center of attention of males and begin mating. However, the masking scent used to hide each individual Hive's odor wasn't strong enough to suppress her odor stimulus. Immediately, two newly ripened Chosen-Males from different Hives raised their spines and started to fight.

Di-Nah should have known better.

The sterile male warrior in charge of the orbital space station dealt harshly with troublemakers. He flooded the area with a soporific gas. He barred Di-Nah from traveling with any Chosen-Males and ordered her to leave on the next spaceship.

Di-Nah did not know the next ship would not jump through space-time to Kamah, but would go to Chud-Loo, the planet of exiles.

ॐ

Tuh-Kar adjusted his breathing pack and tightened the wire brace holding the transmitter's tower. The domed structure perched on the ridge of bleak gray rocks disappeared for an instant in a flurry of wind-blown snow. A tall tower of spindly metal struts at the base of the dome jutted into the sky. Its guy wires reached up from the rock-strewn mountainside and thrummed steadily in the rising wind. At top of the tower, the spidery dish of the ground-to-space transmitter for the orbital radio navigation pointed to the heavens.

Even in the valley below, the air was far thinner than the highest point on Hool. Low in the sky, a pale yellow star—the Daughter—peered through breaks in scudding clouds. At this altitude, ultraviolet radiation turned Tuh-Kar's hide black.

Tuh-Kar hadn't risen in the hierarchy of the Disobedient even though he'd been one of the first settlers on Chud-Loo. His tendency to speak out got him undesirable work assignments such as this. This gave him no opportunity to breed, unlike others in the hierarchy. Now he was alone with a freshly ripened female who, in spite of being ugly and thin to the point of emaciation, still aroused him.

ॐ

Why in the name of the Mother did I deserve to end up on this frozen hellhole as a worker? Di-Nah wondered. *I was supposed to be a Hive-Mother on Kamah, to have Chosen-Males at my beck and call.* She'd found Chud-Loo had too many females for her to be noticed and her desire-to-mate scent didn't work in these Mother-cursed winds.

As a new exile, Di-Nah realized the Disobedient hierarchy did not trust her. *To make matters worse, the cold killed my paat-kli and now my skin itches from lack of grooming. In the time I've been on Chud-Loo, I've had no chance to mate. I intend to change that and soon. The only male who talks to me is Tuh-Kar, the stupid fool who talks about everything but mating. He is almost impossible to manipulate. Almost.*

"And I thought Hool was dry and a difficult place to raise food. This is worse," Tuh-Kar said. "These mountains are filled with dangers that kill the unwary." He looked up.

Di-Nah started toward the domed shelter.

"Di-Nah, come here and help me." He tightened a guy wire.

"I'm freezing, Tuh-Kar. These heights scare me—"

"Don't think about it."

"It's cold and this breathing pack is uncomfortable. The wind and noise is so unlike home. I want to go inside—"

"First, please tighten the connector by your foot."

Numb from the cold, Di-Nah followed his direction. She wanted to get inside. She wanted to mate. As she bent to the task, she saw Tuh-Kar in silhouette. *He's aroused*, she realized. Task done, she moved next to him and stroked his skin. "Tuh-Kar, you have turned an attractive shade of black."

"Right," Tuh-Kar said. "We're free to burn ourselves black and work ourselves to death if we don't starve first."

"We have freedom to do those things only Hive-Mothers on Hool do." Di-Nah continued stroking him.

"What do you mean by that?"

"Mate." *Is he mentally deficient too?*

"When do we have time to mate? You tell me, Di-Nah, when do we have time?" He turned back to his work.

CHAPTER SEVEN

Tuh-Kar had not found the freedom on Chud-Loo to enjoy the pleasures he'd experienced on Hool in the Disobedient's movement. Constant work left him little energy and less time for sex with partially ripened females. Besides, even though there were as many females as males, they seemed to gravitate to the company of the male leaders of the Disobedient, Wod-Jur and his hierarchy.

I'm stuck on top of this mountain with an ugly female. He wanted a female with some bulk, one who would completely cover him, one with some size. He didn't want one who was a bag of bones, and Di-Nah was truly a bag of bones.

"Tuh-Kar, I know what I want and I want it now." Ever since assigned to work with Tuh-Kar, she knew she would mate with him, for her urge was strong. He was her only chance.

"Do you know what you want?" Tuh-Kar looked up from the adjuster at the base of the guy wire.

"Yes." She moved behind him. "I do." Di-Nah touched him in a way that gave him an unmistakable message. "We can go inside and be together." She touched him again.

Tuh-Kar looked up as though gauging the sincerity of her words. "Do you mean that?"

"Yes. I don't want to wait any longer. Let's go inside the shelter. No one else is here."

He glanced at the shelter. He hated working on the mountain. It had been a long time since he'd had the company of an unattached female. "Well, most of the guy wires are adjusted," he said. "It should be safe from the wind." Di-Nah's offer was the best he'd heard in a long time. It was the only offer. Her offer made him overlook her appearance.

Di-Nah didn't even glance at the tower. "Let's go. I need to get warm. There are more important things to do."

"Well, all right." He pointed to the shelter.

Di-Nah ran for the air lock.

Inside, Tuh-Kar peeled off his breathing pack and savored her scent, his arousal evident. It was warm in the metal dome. Its light was like that of a hive. Its walls muted the sound of the rising wind. There were even fabrics covering the metal floor and its denser air gave him energy.

Di-Nah coaxed him into the position of abasement favored by Hive-Mothers and quickly consummated their relationship. She imprinted him with her hormones and bonded him to her. *As she finished*, she sighed with satisfaction. *Finally*, she thought, *I'm going to be a mother, a real Hive-Mother.*

Tuh-Kar had already fallen asleep.

How typical of males, she thought.

I wonder, she thought. *How strongly he is bonded to me? Where can I get more Chosen-Males? And food? I need to bulk up. She knew she needed to increase her size to make her toxins deadly.*

Outside, the wind howled about the radio transmitter. A fierce gust of wind caught the dish and twisted it, stretching an over-taxed guy wire. The dish began to oscillate. Now, when it tracked the orbital radio navigation beacon at the boundary of the asteroid belt, the vibration caused an intermittent break in its signal.

꒰

Wod-Jur needed the transmitter operational. Two years ago, the deep space supply ship had hit a small rock on its final approach to Chud-Loo and been damaged, losing some of its precious supplies. As a result, they'd built the transmitter, which would function as a beacon for the arriving supply ships. The construction project taxed their resources even further. They desperately needed items that only came on the supply ship.

Wod-Jur often regretted making the decision to accept Zak-Joh's compromise for exile on Chud-Loo. He'd found the only resources it had in abundance were isolation and privation. He knew the past had no flexibility. Only the future could be shaped to one's desire with enough effort and willpower.

"When will the transmitter become operational?" Wod-Jur asked. "The supply ship will reach the asteroid belt in three planetary rotations. It must arrive safely."

"All components of the system have been tested and are functioning," the chief engineer said. "I'm waiting word the transmitter tower is secured. Then we can transmit the signal to the orbital beacon to provide a guide path for the spacecraft. I've also added the enhancement to the system you requested. Its radar beam is so powerful it will illuminate the uncharted asteroids. It'll be a supplement to the radar on the supply ship. It's many times more powerful than the ship's radar."

"When will the beacon start operating?"

"As soon as the tower is secured."

"When will that be?" Wod-Jur erected his breathing flaps and emitted the sour odor of disapproval.

"Tuh-Kar can answer that question. He's at the transmitter," the chief engineer said. "I'll contact him and find out."

"Good. Let me know when the beacon will be ready."

꒰

"Tuh-Kar, wake up, Tuh-Kar. Someone wants to talk to you on the communicator." Di-Nah poked a spine between two plates of Tuh-Kar's skin.

"What? Who is it?" Tuh-Kar had difficulty focusing his thoughts. He wanted to sleep.

Di-Nah poked the spine deeper and harder. "Wake up."

"Ouch." Tuh-Kar was now quite awake.

"The communicator, answer it, now." Di-Nah's voice was like a Hive-Mother giving a command.

Reflexively Tuh-Kar obeyed. "Hoo-Lii."

"Hoo-Lii. This is the chief engineer. Tuh-Kar, answer me."

"What do you want?" Tuh-Kar said in a voice filled with belligerence. Di-Nah's jab had hurt.

"Is the transmitter tower ready? We need to test the system as soon as possible. The supply ship will arrive soon. Wod-Jur is worried about it. You were supposed to have the tower finished several planetary revolutions ago. Have you been staring at the sunset again? I didn't send you up the mountain to gawk at the view."

"If you had contacted me earlier, you would have learned the tower was stabilized one sleep period ago," Tuh-Kar said. It was a lie, but he didn't want a reprimand, or worse work assignments in the future.

"I see. Can we test the system now?"

"Yes. It's ready now."

"Are you sure?" the chief engineer asked. "If it is, I'll inform Wod-Jur the navigation beacon can be turned on to guide in the supply ship. Check it again."

"Believe me, it is not safe to leave the shelter," Tuh-Kar said. "The wind has risen to the point it is dangerous to go outside."

"I see. Wait until the wind eases and then check it."

There was an element of the truth in Tuh-Kar's report, the wind was strong, but it was always strong on top of the mountain. He wanted the privacy of the shelter for a while longer, for as he spoke, Di-Nah was arousing him.

CHAPTER EIGHT

5,018 Year of the Mother.

It seemed to Wod-Jur that Chud-Loo's entire planetary system conspired against their very existence. A report from the geological survey showed meteorites and perhaps even small asteroids, impacted Chud-Loo regularly. The geologists found many craters existed under the surface of the ever-moving sand in the equatorial desert. And there were no higher life forms anywhere on the surface of the planet. The only vegetation present struggled for survival in sheltered valleys in the mountain ranges.

The Polar Regions had few craters, even taking the two high-latitude oceans into consideration. After the astronomers examined the shapes of the craters, they concluded most, if not all of the impacts, came from bodies originating in the asteroid belt of their system. The impacting bodies had come in on the plane of the planetary ecliptic, thus approaching the polar regions at a shallow angle. The astronomers believed the impact angle was sufficiently obtuse to induce an atmospheric skipping or deflection. They were not sure it was the only reason animal life thrived solely in the polar oceans.

Wod-Jur remembered the disaster of trying to harvest food from the polar oceans. Initially, the fishing vessel caught large amounts of nutrient-rich aquatic life. It was on the second food harvesting expedition, when the vessel was filled with catch, that clawed creatures came out of the ocean in vast numbers, crawling onto the vessel to feed upon the harvest. No one knew what these creatures were; the radio report said there were too many creatures and no way to stop them. They just kept coming and coming until the crew's weapons ran out of charge.

The crew reported the clawed creatures tore through the polymer structure of the vessel and broke into the cabin where they had sought refuge. The last radio message contained the sound of screams. The icy polar oceans remained a place of mystery and terror.

The astronomers had recently informed Wod-Jur a comet of an unknown size was on course toward Chud-Loo. There were no planetary defenses; all their resources had been dedicated to building infrastructure.

"Get the chief engineer," Wod-Jur said to the partially ripened female who was his attendant. "Bring him here."

"Immediately," she said and hurried out.

"You wanted me?" the chief engineer asked. He wiped his front appendages. He had been working on a heating system cobbled together from spare parts. It hadn't gone well and he was tired.

"Have you scanned the report by the geo-scientist on the frequency of asteroid impacts on Chud-Loo?"

The chief engineer's breathing flaps opened. He rarely had time to use the holographic data terminal. Much of his day was spent maintaining equipment necessary for their survival. As for reading, he had other ideas for his spare time. "No. Was I supposed to?"

Wod-Jur ignored his response. "It says asteroids frequently strike Chud-Loo. At one time, some even hit these mountains. It says this valley, in which we live, may have been formed by an asteroid impact. Should another strike here, we would be wiped out. Now a comet is heading toward us, on a collision course." Wod-Jur waved toward the data terminal as though inviting the chief engineer to scan for himself.

"Are you sure? How big is it?" That news got the chief engineer's attention. "When will it arrive?"

"Scan the report. It's all in there. What can we do about it? Can you build a planetary defense system?"

"Well, yes, I suppose so—"

"When can you have it operational?" Wod-Jur again waved toward the data terminal.

The chief engineer activated the terminal and started to scroll through the report. "Ah, now I see—"

"Pay attention. When can you have a defense system ready?"

The chief engineer looked up. "I thought you wanted me to read the report." His breathing flaps became still.

"Not now, later." Wod-Jur raised his voice to convey his anger. "Can you build a planetary defense system?"

"Maybe." The chief engineer stared at him for a moment. "I don't know. I can build anything within the realm of practical engineering. We do have a copy of such a system from the archives." He hesitated for a moment. "Yes, I think it's possible to build. It will take a lot of resources." His breathing flaps flared slightly.

"Do it."

"What resources and authority do I have?" the chief engineer said. "Who will obey my instructions without your blessing?"

"It has to be built. Since you need resources, I will approve the requisition. Just get it built as soon as possible." Wod-Jur said with anger. His breathing flaps opened wide.

"I will need to spend time with the archives to get details of the technology," said the chief engineer. "Without that, I'm in a dark tunnel. First, authorize supplies for the project."

"Fine. Just figure out how to provide a planetary defense. A comet is on its way. Now it is your responsibility to provide the defenses. Also, get that Mother-blessed navigational beacon operational, too." Wod-Jur had the faith of a fanatic that the resources would be found when he gave an order. If the chief engineer failed to find them, he knew it would be the chief engineer's spines that would be clipped.

CHAPTER NINE

5,018 Year of the Mother.

Suh-Joh was puzzled. Even though her senior priest whispered instructions and advised her as to her role of Hive-Mother, she didn't know how get the males to breed and keep her Hive strong.

Soon, she thought, *I must bring forth young.* Mating with her half-brothers was borderline incest with all the dangers of inbreeding. *I have done enough to earn the condemnation of the other Hives without doing that. I need young males from another Hive.* But no Hive-Mother would weaken her Hive willingly by giving up future warriors. Her Chosen-Male warriors had to breed periodically, otherwise they became prematurely sterile and useless for battle.

There has to be an answer; otherwise Lok-Nih and the Spirit-of-the-Mother, Suh-Joh thought, *would not have ripened me.* She remembered Lok-Nih's pride in the strength of her Hive and the disdain she'd held for the others. A burst of excitement ran through her. *I'll just take what I need, for my Hive and me.*

Suh-Joh thought about the raid conducted jointly by the warriors from the Ag-Gih and Jan-Dil Hives. *Those warriors were emaciated and weak*, she thought. *Why had they combined forces just for a raid? They must be so few it will be only a matter of time before a stronger Hive conquers them. Could that be my Hive? And why not?*

The raid on Jan-Dil's Hive was a complete surprise.

Columns of Suh-Joh's warriors descended upon the four entrances to Jan-Dil's Hive and swept-away its guards. Her invading force penetrated into the heart of the hive, surprising the unprepared warriors. The unripened ones, small and undernourished, gave way without resistance.

Suh-Joh knew she had won when the unripened ones, the May-be-Chosen and the Never-to-be-Chosen, signaled their willingness to serve her with the symbolic gifts of water. When examined, the food stores proved to be almost empty; the insect pits showed little movement and the granaries contained only dust. The Hive was on the brink of starvation. It was certainly on the road to death.

She took their food, knowing it was the last of their reserves, and made the ritual response; "Hoo-Lii. I will lead you, this I promise."

Even though Jan-Dil was Lok-Nih's daughter and her half sister, Suh-Joh killed her without a second thought. She ordered her warriors to neuter Jan-Dil's Chosen-Male warriors, pluck their spines and send them to work on the surface. The unripened ones, now prisoners, carried the dead and nearly dead back to her Hive where they became fodder for the food-insects. She was pleased the entire operation was completed before the Children-of-the-Sky rose twice.

Suh-Joh selected the healthiest of the May-be-Chosen females and removed their spines. She picked one, ripened it, and turned her over to a small group of older Chosen-Male warriors. As expected, the males mated with the newly ripened female. Since the female had no spines, she could not bond the males to her. That eliminated any threat of competition to Suh-Joh, which meant the newly ripened female would never be a Hive-Mother.

In one cycle of the Children-of-the-Sky, it became obvious the female was pregnant.

"It worked." Suh-Joh celebrated the news. She gave the order, "bring the rest of the females to me."

One by one, after removing their spines, she ripened the captured females. She explained their role was to be brood females for her Chosen-Male warriors. They would be able to mate and bear young, but they would never ripen any Chosen-Male and get the juvenile hormones needed for long life.

Suh-Joh took the best of the captured May-be-Chosen-Males, ripened, and mated with them until she was exhausted—it wasn't too soon as far as she was concerned. In the process, they bonded with her and became a part of her Chosen-Male warrior contingent. Her first gestation produced healthy offspring. The Hive celebrated the birth of healthy young. There would be more workers and warriors. Now, the Hive had a future.

One cycle of the Children-of-the-Sky later, Suh-Joh struck again; she attacked Ag-Gih's Hive. Once again, the unripened sued for peace with gifts of water, to which she responded with the ritual promise to lead them, thus sparing them from the insects. She took more May-be-Chosen for mating stock and servants. Other unripened ones and neutered Chosen-Male warriors became workers in the fields on the surface. The ones for which she had no use became fodder for the food-insects.

Suh-Joh's conquests increased the area under her control so much, so she controlled more fertile valleys than any other Hive-Mother. The ranks of her Chosen-Male warriors grew with new recruits. However, managing such a large area proved difficult. In desperation, she sought answers in the archives on how to achieve economies of scale. There, she found techniques and technologies used in the past to increase food production.

Little by little, she pushed her workers to implement these techniques, adjusting the Hive's work force in the fields, seeking out the best areas of the land recently brought under her control. At first it was difficult, but as the workers saw more could be produced with less effort, they became enthusiastic.

For several cycles of the Children-of-the-Sky, Suh-Joh focused on organizing her new resources to produce food efficiently. Even before the first harvest was completed, she knew her Hive would have a surplus of food and many young born from the brood females. As a result, the population of her Hive doubled in less than a season. Keeping track of the genetics was just another task that technology from the archives made easier. During this time, no Hive-Mother called upon her.

Due to the rich harvest, Suh-Joh increased her contribution to the Shrine of the Spirit-of-the-Mother. *My warriors are strong and well fed, and I've taken care of my tithing. Now,* she thought, *I'm ready to talk to the rest of the Hives about them accepting me as their equal.*

She sought counsel from her senior priest, on what might be done to join the Council of Hive-Mothers. During their discussions, he suggested the use of a religious practice could be turned to her cause to avoid war with the other Hives.

"Let there be a meeting of the Council of Hive-Mothers." It was the call sent out by the priests at the Shrine of the Spirit-of-the-Mother. "Let the meeting be held at the Shrine. Come in peace and piety to discuss the succession of Suh-Joh to Lok-Nih and her position of Hive-Mother." It was a call to the Hive-Mothers to acknowledge Suh-Joh as Hive-Mother.

Her senior priest used his contacts to urge a meeting. He assured the priests at the Shrine that Suh-Joh had no say in her selection as Hive-Mother and was a faithful follower to the Way-of-the-Mother.

That and a second generous contribution to the Shrine, resulted in a summons being issued for the Council Meeting. At the same time, Suh-Joh posted Lok-Nih's data file on the history of Hool where all could read it. It provided the rationale for Suh-Joh's ripening and elevation to Hive-Mother.

The news of the summons and the data file flashed around Hool almost instantly. *Who is this new Hive-Mother? What is she doing?* At the same time, those Hives adjacent to Suh-Joh spread the word of her conquests. Many signaled their intentions by questioning the need for the meeting. Dissent and distrust cast the meeting in doubt.

"There will be a meeting of the Council of the Hive-Mothers. It will start when the Little Child first appears in the night sky at the beginning of the next cycle of the Children-of-the-Sky." It was the message again sent out by the priest in charge of the Shrine of the Spirit-of-the-Mother. "It concerns the selection of a new Hive-Mother and the implications to the Way-of-the-Mother. Those who fail to attend will be judged lacking in piety." It was the closest thing to an order he could give.

Suh-Joh's old priest had whispered to her the priests at the Shrine-of-the-Mother had read and agreed with Lok-Nih's data file. She did not fear the meeting; for she knew the priests would not condemn her. However, she also knew the priests were not the ones with poisonous spines; those were the other Hive-Mothers.

CHAPTER TEN

"Sisters." Suh-Joh felt a pang of fear as she stared out at the arrayed rows of bulky and bloated Hive-Mothers, each draped across ancient resting rocks, polished from generations of use, each separated from the next by at least two body-lengths to prevent accidents from happening.

The Shrine lay in a steep-walled valley into which rivulets of crystal-clear water tinkled. The meeting area was in a bowl-like depression, lush with red vegetation. In the center, the ground underfoot had a thick mat of soft, almost springy ground cover as rich as any fine weaving. Insects twittered and sang among the carefully trimmed vegetation at the base of the cliffs. The entire Shrine was a monument to the Hool that existed prior to the great wars. The lush richness of that small valley inspired awe in all who came to visit.

"I stand before you," Suh-Joh said. "To seek your acceptance. I am but a child of Lok-Nih and Zak-Joh, thrust into the role of Hive-Mother as a tool of their desires. As you well remember, Zak-Joh spoke of the need for unity; first to combat the ways of the Disobedient and then as a means to save Hool. His vision of salvation did not come to fruition in his short but glorious lifetime. Little did I know he had chosen me to fulfill that role."

The Hive-Mothers' breathing flaps moved in unison to release a collective grunt. For a moment, aromas of anger, fear, and disbelief filled the air. Zak-Joh's role in beating back the movement of the Disobedient was history.

"His concern, no, his fear," Suh-Joh said before any could issue a call for action. "Was the Way-of-the-Mother and peace on Hool would disappear."

There was another sound. Some was agreement, perhaps even approval. More pleasant aromas mingled with the earlier emissions of suspicion and anger.

"It was his belief the way we chose to preserve genetic diversity increased conflict between the Hives. To test this belief, he and Lok-Nih have thrust me into this role. A role I did not take on willingly." She paused to rise to her full height on her hind limbs.

She gestured toward the assembled priests. "A role which I am willing to give up should it be a violation of the Way-of-the-Mother." She paused. "Yet recognize I carry a full complement of the genes of Zak-Joh, one of our greatest warriors in recent memory," she said. "This means I can and will fight to preserve both the Way-of-the-Mother and my Hive, once recognized as the legitimate heir."

The Shrine grew still. Even the insects seemed quiet. Perhaps they too, sensed the aromas of tension filling the air. Or perhaps it was because the Hive-Mothers were focused on Suh-Joh's words.

"I did not come to this place of peace to threaten war." Suh-Joh lowered herself. "I came in humility to be judged by those responsible for the purity of the Way-of-the-Mother, ready to accept whatever they decide."

A rustle of movement swept the Hive-Mothers as their heads swiveled collectively toward the priests. None wished to be first and none wished to speak words the priests would refute.

The priests remained still and quiet. None issued any aromas.

"It is my desire, no, my commitment to work with the Council of Hive-Mothers to strengthen the Way-of-the-Mother and spread its truth to those who do not know its purity and truth." She had deliberately made an oblique reference to the Disobedient. "To do that, I urge the Hive-Mothers, no, I beg them, to meet in council, at regular intervals, to resolve conflicts and find ways to promulgate the faith. As for my role in this experiment of Zak-Joh, I can only ask the guardians of the Way to examine the facts before they judge me." She turned toward the priests and slowly lowered herself into the position of complete abasement. "I will accede to their judgment."

Time ticked by. The vale remained silent.

She held the position.

A mournful wail of a solitary go-lik insect broke the silence.

The senior priest rattled his armored exoskeleton briefly. "Arise, it is time."

Suh-Joh rose onto her hind limbs with her mid-limbs clasped in earnest supplication and head held high. "May the Spirit-of-the-Mother preserve Hool, my Hive, and least of all, may she grant mercy to this unfortunate child."

A rustle of comments rolled across the Hive-Mothers, heads twisting every which way.

The senior priest of the Shrine rattled his exoskeleton plates against his resting-rock and raised himself up to his full height. He rattled again until the assemblage was silent.

"I have but few words, offered in humility." The senior priest bent low. "The faith of Zak-Joh is without question," the senior priest said. "The dedication of Lok-Nih to the Way-of-the-Mother was strong, unselfish, and will be long remembered. The history posted by Suh-Joh is accurate." He paused and straightened. "After much deliberation, the Shrine believes her selection as Hive-Mother does not violate the Way-of-the-Mother." His whispery words barely carried to the most distant Hive-Mother. The aroma of his approval was strong. "May the Spirit-of-the-Mother preserve us." He turned toward Suh-Joh. "You may leave us while the Council discusses your fate."

Suh-Joh bowed and retreated.

For several moments it was quiet. Conversation broke out among the Council. Strong voices rose to dominate the discussion. Powerful Hive-Mothers had interpreted her words as a sign of weakness. Others, neighbors to Suh-Joh, knew of her strength and understood her implied threat. Many secretly hoped for the restoration of peace between the Hives they enjoyed during the time of Zak-Joh. Constant preparation for attacks had for too long diverted resources needed to raise food. The constant struggle sapped the energy of the Hives, pushing them closer and closer to the edge. Suh-Joh's call for peace sent a secret ripple of hope throughout the Council.

As the Mother-of-the-Sky touched the purple mountains in the distance, the Council voted to admit Suh-Joh as a member. The senior priest of the Shrine sent word to Suh-Joh she now had a resting-rock among the Hive-Mothers.

When Suh-Joh heard the Hives had listened to the priests, her fear of being destroyed as an abomination was over. She knew she owed her life to the priests.

I am forever in their debt. I must obey them in all things, she vowed. *I must be a good child.*

CHAPTER ELEVEN

CHUD-LOO

5,028 Year of the Mother.

"Where is that worthless piece of naat-jii dung, Tuh-Kar?" the chief engineer asked. "The transmitter is malfunctioning and he's the only one who knows how to fix it." The orbital power satellite no longer transmitted power to the surface and the orbital navigation beacon flashed uncontrollably. He shivered, for the temperature had steadily dropped overnight. The emergency lighting had begun to dim. And Tuh-Kar didn't answer his summons on the communicator.

"I don't care that Tuh-Kar has disappeared. All I care about is getting the electrical power turned on," said Wod-Jur, the leader of the Disobedient. He gave off a threatening odor. "Why haven't you fixed the power shortage?"

"What do you think I've been trying to do? Teaching my paat-kli to fly?" The chief engineer was fed-up with Wod-Jur's stupid questions and peremptory commands.

For the eighth squared time, he wondered, *how did this idiot end up as leader?*

"If I need comedy, I'll use the holo-terminal. Explain why you cannot fix the orbital power station and restore power."

"There's nothing wrong with the orbital power station," the chief engineer said. "The navigation beacon is locked in a strobing mode and its energy demand leaves nothing for the power satellite to transmit. For some unknown reason, the ground-based transmitter is sending signals that triggers that mode."

The power shortage caused a shutdown in heating and other systems dependent upon electricity. That had gotten everyone's attention.

"That's too complicated for me to understand. Just fix it. I'm tired of the cold and all the complaints about power shortages. Get it fixed, and soon." Wod-Jur gestured dismissal.

"I cannot." The chief engineer emanated a hostile odor. "I've tried everything I know. The entire system checks-out properly. There's something wrong with the transmitter. We can shut down the navigation beacon, but that poses a danger to the supply ship. It needs to get through the asteroid belt. When the beacon strobes, it illuminates the asteroids."

"Why did you build it to use so much of the satellite's power output?" Wod-Jur's spines erected as though ready to do battle.

"Me? You don't remember? You said we need the strobe mode to illuminate the orbit of every asteroid and rock fragment for the supply ship, so it could see any danger, that's why. It was designed and built the way you ordered."

"That's all well and good, but we need power now. Get it, I don't care how you get it, just get it." Wod-Jur rose to his full height. He snorted fiercely and filled the air with an intimidating odor.

The chief engineer solved the power shortage by shutting down the navigation system. His solution worked until the supply ship arrived, and again there was a power outage.

A comet passed so close to Chud-Loo that reflections from the navigation beacon's radar revealed its composition to be mainly ice fragments. Even though it proved not to be a threat to the planet, it drew attention to the geoscientists' earlier report on asteroid strikes. That convinced the settlers in Freedom Valley a planetary defense system must be built.

The responsibility of constructing the system fell to the chief engineer who chose a laser system previously used but later banned by the priests. He placed three fusion pumped lasers in geosynchronous orbits above Chud-Loo. He calculated the lasers had enough power and range to change the course of an approaching asteroid. Since the lasers were so powerful, he knew safety demanded the lasers had to query every target multiple times before firing to prevent the accidental destruction of a spaceship. It was a complex and lengthy project.

Wod-Jur continued with his demand that the power lost from the orbital powersat be replaced immediately.

Immediately would take time and the chief engineer needed help now. "Tuh-Kar, please answer me. I need to know why the ground transmitter is behaving so erratically."

Even after many calls for Tuh-Kar's help, no one answered, and the radio navigation beacon continued to strobe.

No one knew it would eventually catch the attention of others, elsewhere.

Di-Nah continued to recruit both males and females to be members of her Hive. Her new servants carved out a home. It was a rudimentary Hive that was carefully concealed from the main Disobedient community in the Freedom Valley.

With followers to feed her, she became more powerful and her venom more deadly. Her discipline upon her followers was like other Hive-Mothers; she killed any who disobeyed her. When Tuh-Kar tried to answer the chief engineer's call for help, she killed him, too. Now that there were plenty of males available for mating, Tuh-Kar mattered little.

⌇

CHUD-LOO

5,029 Year of the Mother.

It was only after I, Kot-Nih the historian, led an investigative expedition to Chud-Loo with excavation equipment, we learned the Disobedient had broken into two factions. It was one of those things they concealed, even when the supply ship arrived. I suppose they feared Hool would cut them off if we knew about their internal dissent. Many of the records of this time were destroyed. Even today, other historians continue to dig in the wreckage of the failed colony on Chud-Loo, seeking to fill in the details of the Disobedient's civil war.

Apparently, it was at the ceremony for the start-up of the new ground-based power station when Wod-Jur offended his chief engineer with an intemperate remark about the length of time it took to build the fusion power station. Since the chief engineer had expected accolades for his effort, not a public chastisement, he walked out of the Disobedient's camp.

Through the years, the radio beacon continued to strobe. Sometimes, inexplicably, it would cease and then start again. During this time, the former chief engineer wandered at the fringes of the Disobedient society until Di-Nah recruited him. Apparently, he appreciated the order and discipline of her Hive, for once he joined them, he worked hard. Di-Nah's Hive grew until it finally attracted Wod-Jur's attention.

It was clear Di-Nah refused to acknowledge Wod-Jur's leadership and the philosophy of the Disobedient. After negotiations failed, war broke out between them. Wod-Jur knew how to motivate the Disobedient in the face of a threat and drove them to unceasing war against the Hive of Di-Nah in the struggle for supremacy. This war was different from the strife on Hool. The issue was not religion; it was survival. Whoever controlled the supplies brought by the spaceship had the power of life and death over all others. It was a bitter war, pitting brother against brother, and sister against sister.

Di-Nah moved her Hive out of Freedom Valley into an adjacent valley they named the "Nest." It was small and deep and protected by a narrow pass and sheer walls. About this time, the former chief engineer revealed his talents, for Di-Nah promoted him to a position of Chosen-Male cohort leader.

It wasn't until much later, that I, Kot-Nih, had traveled to the home planets of both of the Others—the Qu'uda and the humans—and searched through many records that I learned the following from the aliens....

CHAPTER TWELVE

STAR SYSTEM EPSILON ERIDIANI, THE QU'UDA PLANET

The Qu'uda were an old race, long-lived and patient. Their world consisted mainly of water with five small equatorial continents; each filled to capacity and short of living space. Its astronomers had examined the nearby star systems for habitable planets. They even sought planets that might be modified into livable locations. Though their deep-space observatory was old, its polar orbiting antenna array gathered faint interstellar signals and shunted them down to the ground-based data analysis system.

"Look, this signal cannot be natural. It's in a digital format and appears at regular intervals. It looks like it might have information content," said the technician on duty at the deep-space data analysis center.

"What do you think it means?" asked the resident astronomer. He represented the Community of Astronomers who reviewed all astronomical information before it was distributed.

"I don't know. The same sequence keeps repeating."

"How do you interpret it?" asked the astronomer.

"It seems artificial."

"That cannot be."

"Have you ever seen anything like that before?"

The astronomer's head crest flared. "Well, no, but—"

"There is only one explanation."

"Great Egg, it must come from another star system—"

"I've scanned this system on and off for years and I've checked the records. This is a new signal. It's both new and artificial."

The astronomer looked up. "But, but, that means—"

"There's nothing else that can explain the digital nature of the signal. It has to be artificial. Our work has finally hatched." The technician pointed to the graphical representation of the faint radio signal.

The astronomer stared at the peaks of the signal intensity. "Look, it has regular variations." He used his biocomputer's communication module to access the massive data files of the orbital observatory to get a summary of the data from the past several days. "See how the signal fades in and out in a sinusoidal fashion? That may mean it's on a revolving source, perhaps caused by planetary rotation." The signal stood out clearly like a brilliant gem of radio energy winking in the depths of interstellar space.

"Dare we tell the Prime Communicator of this before we are certain?" The astronomer knew the discovery of an alien life form would bring fame and move them closer toward the center.

Pi'Rup, the Prime Communicator at the center of the community, had thousands of biocomputers that kept him in contact with the members of their society through the universal comm-link. He was the disseminator of information.

"No, by Egg, we'd better start with the Community of Astronomers. Let's get their opinion and support before we present it to the entire community."

"Quick. The signal may disappear, and we would only have a recording." This was an opportunity to gain status. The technician needed a more central position to change gender, into the egg-bearing stage. He stared at the screen for a moment.

"Another intelligent species, and so close."

The timing could not have been better, coming when the Qu'uda had begun constructing a spacecraft with interstellar capabilities.

But aliens?

The community of Astronomers analyzed the signals intensively and discovered the digital signals showed traces of a square wave function. They considered this further evidence of its artificial character and presented their findings to the Prime Communicator.

A collective call arose to investigate. The spaceship, called the Star-Seeker, would seek out the cause of the strange signal pulsing among the stars. Changing the mission of the Star-Seeker would require alterations. The ship required more fuel.

Additional bulbous fuel tanks, along with a shuttle—the Bird-that-Soars, were strapped to the rear of the Star-Seeker. Though its appearance was ungainly, it was the culmination of their efforts and carried the hopes of their planet.

After several years, their engineers completed the Star-Seeker. The entire planet watched as it accelerated out of the system. Once free of gravitational perturbations, ChaKut DuJutu, astrogator and spokesperson for the crew, estimated the amount of relative star system drift during the voyage and fine-tuned their course. In the depths of space, nothing would affect the vessel during its long coasting phase.

The Star-Seeker reached its terminal velocity—almost one-fourth the speed of light—and the crew entered into the carefully monitored deep-sleep. They lowered their life functions, including their biocomputers, to the barest trace of activity. Now, it was just a matter of time.

The Star-Seeker coasted on; all activity shut down except for a minimal life support system. An ancient solid-state computer patiently watched over the ship, keeping its vigilant eye on the heavens, tracking their position.

Time went by. The computer measured the relative luminosity of their home sun and estimated the distance traveled. At the same time, it measured the distance to the star system they were approaching and decided when it was time to restart the Star-Seeker's engine.

The ship rotated and pointed its fusion drive towards its destination. A warming sequence in the fuel module started vaporizing deuterium ice into gas, which flowed into the fusion drive reactor along with the helium three. The reserve power system came to life and electricity flowed to the pulsating magnetic containment coils.

The mixture of deuterium and helium three, compressed into a standing shock wave, flowed into the reactor in harmonic pulses generated by the magnetic constrictions. An energetic laser flared and joined the beat of the system. The deuterium and helium three fused together amid the release of prodigious amounts of energy.

The drive lit. Its thrust slowed the Star-Seeker as it plummeted down into the star system where a powerful radio source still flashed its blatant signal.

The solid-state computer went about its tasks, monitoring the Star-Seeker's course toward the planet emitting the pulsating signal. At the same time, the computer slowly brought the ship back to life. The temperature in the living-quarters rose to a temperature more typical of their watery home world.

ChaKut DuJutu felt paralyzed. Even though the hibernation quarters rotated to maintain gravity, his muscles felt weak. The solid-state computer activated his biocomputer, which took over the rehabilitation of his atrophied muscles. It was painful, but the combination of stimulants, muscle relaxants, and pain deadeners, along with nerve excitation, got him moving.

The Star-Seeker continued to shed speed as it approached the inner cometary belt of the star system, having already lost most of its deep-space velocity. The solid-state computer continued to operate the ship, watching for stray comets and asteroids.

"Computer, scan and obtain the plane of the comets. Bring the Star-Seeker onto a parallel approach," ChaKut DuJutu said.

They would drop into the star system in such a fashion as to resemble a natural object. As the crew gained mobility, they gathered data on the system. The inner asteroid belt was densely populated and adjacent to the planet that was the source of the powerful radio signal.

There were other radio emissions—faint and indecipherable—the planet was definitely inhabited.

"Set the Star-Seeker on a course to take us by the planet and around its sun. Set the out course for the gas giant planet so we can gather fuel for our return," said ChaKut DuJutu.

"I must gather more information before I dare contact the inhabitants of the planet," MingLik TuKan said. He was their planetary analyst and had been trained by the Defenders. He also provided security for the ship.

"Prepare a message drone to send back to Qu'uda, but do not launch yet. Feed all of the sensors into the message pod's records. Set it to launch automatically should anything untoward happen."

"The Defenders would approve of your plan," MingLik said.

The Star-Seeker reduced power and moved into position for the fly-by course. Its speed had dropped to that of a comet on a rare trip to the inner orbit of the planetary system. The Star-Seeker descended, stern-first, multiple recorders storing every detail. The system had a vast number of asteroids.

MingLik and ChaKut studied the source of the radio signals from the planet. In addition, spectroscopy revealed its atmosphere was breathable. However, it seemed to have little life. The planet had a single continent spanning a portion of the equator like a belt fragment. It appeared to be very dry, in spite of the huge area of the polar oceans. It was very different from the watery world of Qu'uda. They puzzled and wondered whether they were mistaken in their earlier conclusion the radio signals were proof of intelligent life. They continued to drop sunward.

A new radio signal, a short chittering squeal, burst from the radio. After a brief pause, it repeated the sequence exactly. It came from the vicinity of the planet, perhaps from an orbiting satellite. Then the signal ceased. Time passed, more than enough time for the signal to transit. Again, the chittering squeal of pulses started, and this time, more powerful than before. The pauses between the sequences grew longer.

"Are they trying to signal us?" MingLik asked.

"Do you think they know we're a spaceship?" ChaKut DuJutu asked. "Maybe we should replay their signal."

"Perhaps." MingLik took his responsibilities seriously.

"The analysis shows binary data. Mathematically, it doesn't mean anything." He manipulated the data.

"What if the signal is a greeting? If we don't answer, they might think we're hostile?" MingLik asked.

"We cannot reveal ourselves prematurely. We will stay silent, for we look like a comet. It would take a very close examination to prove otherwise."

"How about releasing the message drone?" MingLik said. "Let it drift along behind us, at a distance, ready to return to Qu'uda?"

"Very well, I'll do that. If something should happen, it will inform the Defenders."

They filled the message drone's fuel tanks and updated its navigation module. The small fusion-powered vehicle had only one purpose: to accelerate to a tremendous speed on a course toward Qu'uda until its fuel was exhausted. When it reached the Qu'uda system, it would broadcast its message as it flew by on a never-ending voyage through the universe.

CHAPTER THIRTEEN

CHUD-LOO

5,097 Year of the Mother.

"Why do you bother me with astronomical data and other such nonsense? I'm fighting a war with that cursed Hive-Mother. I don't need stupid distractions." Wod-Jur's breathing flaps flared as he gave off the odor of anger. He had been doing a lot of that since losing a major battle with Di-Nah's Hive.

"A comet will cross our orbit; it may be on a collision course. I need your approval to arm the planet's defenses," the young female astronomer said. She had the planetary defense ground control assignment to watch the space around Chud-Loo. It was a lonely job and she was its sole operator.

"Will it divert resources from the war?"

"The planetary defense system doesn't need any additional resources. It is ready to be activated," the astronomer said. Wod-Jur should have known that.

"Well, arm the system and defend the planet. Do whatever is necessary. Don't bother me." Wod-Jur turned back to the battle hologram, ignoring the astronomer. The Hive-Mother had grown strong and had a strongly defended position. Many young Disobedient had died in an assault on her Nest.

No one had tested the planetary defense system. That made the astronomer nervous about arming and deploying such a powerful weapon.

What if I make a mistake? she thought. *What if I fail to use it soon enough to deflect the comet? What if Chud-Loo is raked by a storm of cometary fragments?* She hurried down the tunnels into the control center. Again, she was alone.

She activated the defense system and released a module from the orbital satellite, setting it on course toward the intruder. She transmitted another query to the approaching body on the remote chance it was an unannounced supply ship.

The image of the comet appeared on the holographic radar display. *It's odd*, she thought. *If it's not a ship, then it must be very old. Maybe it's a very small comet.*

Later, she made optical observations that confirmed that the comet had no streaming tail. It continued on the same heading—toward them. Several days passed and it steadily drew closer to Chud-Loo. Now she was sure she had to use the defenses. Carefully, she initiated the full activation sequence.

The fusion device separated from the laser with a tiny jet of gas, which drove it out to the full length of its tether. The assembly began spinning and unfolded a thin-film mirror, which expanded to its full diameter. A puff of gas gently accelerated the mirror's hub and pushed it away until its guy wires tugged it into shape, for perfect focus. The fusion laser lined up its aperture at the focal point. A laser confirmed its alignment.

The astronomer sounded a planet-wide alarm to warn both friend and foe of the coming pulse of electromagnetic radiation. She repeated the warning and started the countdown.

The laser activated its ultra-fast electronics and warmed its crystalline lensing system to optimum temperature. One by one, the safeguards on the fusion explosive dropped away until the system verified the laser's aim was clear of any planetary body. It was ready. The final alarm sounded.

She touched the control.

A chemical laser flared into savage brilliance, focused on a thin strand of tritium within the frozen mass of deuterium. The temperature and radiant flux soared. A fraction of a nanosecond later, a tiny point of dazzling violet light grew with frightening speed. A storm of photons expanded to meet the reflecting film, which bounced them into the hungry aperture of the laser before the aluminum film mirror vaporized. The laser greedily swallowed vast quantities of energy until its crystalline structure could no longer contain the flood. The energy overload cascaded into a gigantic pulse of single-frequency radiation.

The laser converted the energy from the fusion explosion into a pulse of coherent radiation that was short and stupendously powerful. Ultraviolet light of incredible intensity beamed undiminished through the clarity of empty space straight at the intruder approaching Chud-Loo.

CLAAAAANG!

The Star-Seeker rang like a bell and shook as though struck by a giant hammer. As the sound of the explosion faded, a high-pitched whistle started. It was air racing past torn metal into the hard emptiness of space.

The living quarters' rotation ceased with an abrupt jerk and the scream of tortured metal. Centripetal gravity vanished. Emergency alarms bleated warnings and faded as the air pressure dropped. Plastic rescue bubbles popped out of emergency lockers. Lights dimmed and failed.

ChaKut DuJutu crashed into a bulkhead.

A tough, elastomeric bubble popped out and enveloped him. A hurricane of escaping air dragged ChaKut along in the bubble. He tried to control the bubble's motion as it spun and bounced against unseen surfaces. As he tumbled pell-mell through the ship, he lost count of the times he slammed into unseen objects in the dark maelstrom.

Dim emergency lights flickered on, revealing a cavalcade of loose objects flowing toward the hole in the rear of the ship. An emergency seal slammed shut, closing off the damaged section. The howling wind faded, and the Star-Seeker became silent except for the faint whistle of tiny air leaks. All the familiar sounds of the life support system had ceased.

Battered from his helter-skelter ride through the ship, ChaKut could only float motionless in the air. The quiet scared him. "Is anyone there?" he said into his communications module.

"ChaKut."

He heard a strained whisper. "In the control room."

It was MingLik TuKan.

"MingLik, are you injured? Do you have an air supply?"

There was a moan. "I can't move."

"MingLik, do you have air?"

"Help me."

"MingLik, listen carefully. The Star-Seeker still leaks air. I must seal the leaks before I do anything else. Have you got enough air to last for a while?"

Silence.

"Answer me, for Egg's sake, answer me. Do you have air?"

"Yes ..."

"I'll be there as soon as I get the air leaks fixed, MingLik. I promise." He knew that MingLik's biocomputer would keep him alive, at least for a while. He kicked his feet and, inside his elastomeric bubble, he bounced from wall to wall. He made his way to the nearest lockers by the entrance to the air lock. Everywhere, broken equipment and supplies mingled with bent and torn fixtures.

At a bulging locker, he found a space suit. He dragged it into the plastic bubble through its entrance slit. He put the space suit on and checked the integrity of its seals before splitting the bubble open. He grabbed a tool kit and headed for the stern. Dead crewmembers were everywhere. Tallying the numbers, he realized three were still unaccounted for.

As he approached the heat-stained bulkhead door leading to the fusion drive section, sensors warned him of hard vacuum beyond. A high whistle came from the doorframe, which confirmed it still leaked air.

ChaKut applied foam-set from an emergency leak-seal canister to the doorframe. Slowly, the air pressure stabilized as one-fourth normal, sufficient to support life as long as no great exertion was required.

"I pray to the spirit of the great Egg this works," ChaKut said as he queried the Star-Seeker's computer system for a status report.

Every section had damage; the Star-Seeker was all but dead. Seven-eighths of the air supply was gone. No data were available on the drive system and the main fuel tanks. The fusion plant supplying internal power was shut down. There was still deuterium in the emergency fuel system.

I might be able to restart it, ChaKut realized.

He worked his way forward to the control room, sealing leaks as he came across them. At the end of the central corridor, he found a missing crewmember. Fluids leaked from all body openings. The crew had been trained for space service, but none could breathe hard vacuum.

The door to the control room was sealed tightly and instruments showed that inside, pressure was normal. ChaKut retreated to the section aft of the control room and closed its hatch, sealing it with foam. The air pressure began to rise. He went forward and opened the control room door.

MingLik was jammed under a control panel.

ChaKut carefully pried MingLik out and laid him on a clear section of the control room floor. He straightened a broken limb, wrapped it with plastic film, and covered it with foam-set. It was difficult, for both anger and sorrow tore at him.

ChaKut and MingLik were not only crewmates, but also co-parents. Previously they had mated and raised a young wriggler until he was ready to live with their families. Even before boarding the ship, they had shared living quarters.

A low groan broke the silence. Under a tangle of equipment was another crewmember, head up against the wall. His brain cavity was cracked—probably from impact. Even with the best of medical attention, the injury was fatal.

Consulting the astrogation computer, ChaKut saw the Star-Seeker's course had changed. They no longer headed toward the planet from where the radio signals originated; they were rising at an angle to the plane of the planetary ecliptic and tumbling slowly.

ChaKut queried the ship's computer to find the cause of the damage to the Star-Seeker. Playing back the monitoring record showed, just before the explosion, a brilliant violet flash had emerged from the bright fire of a fusion flame. It came from the direction of the planet.

So, the damage to the ship was no accident, ChaKut thought. *Only civilizations that fight wars use fusion pumped lasers.* He turned his attention back to MingLik and applied a stimulant. *Please, I cannot face this alone—that is the path to madness.*

MingLik groaned into wakefulness. "What happened?"

ChaKut dressed MingLik's injuries and offered words of comfort. "Let your biocomputer work on you a while. You do want to get home and see our little wriggler, don't you?" He moved MingLik into a comfortable position and left the control room.

CHAPTER FOURTEEN

ChaKut eventually explained their situation to MingLik. By then he had gathered up the bodies of the crew, freeze-dried them in hard vacuum, and placed them in storage. He had a fuzzy idea of saving them for a proper burial in a mud flat, somewhere on Qu'uda.

"ChaKut, is the Bird-that-Soars damaged?"

MingLik's question caught him by surprise.

They were on a new course to nowhere. Rescue was impossible and there was no way back. He hadn't considered using the planetary landing craft strapped onto the fuel tanks. After methodically rerouting messages through the Star-Seeker's damaged communications system, ChaKut had activated the external viewers. The tail and tip of one wing of the Bird-that-Soars had been sliced off—it would never again enter an atmosphere. They were trapped on the shattered hulk of the Star-Seeker as it fell ever deeper into the black emptiness of interstellar space.

ChaKut thought the Bird-that-Soars was useless, but when he queried its computer, he learned its fusion drive system was still functional. It also had a full tank of fuel.

"Wod-Jur, the planetary defense system deflected the comet," the young astronomer said. "It's been diverted into deep space. However, it remains in one piece. I had expected the laser to shatter it."

"Why?" Wod-Jur asked. "Is it important?" The battle hologram showed no improvement. Di-Nah's Hive was well dug-in and defended.

"The comet must be old. You see, it has no streaming tail, therefore it should be a fragile conglomeration of rocks."

"So?" *I need something to break the stalemate.*

"The laser should have shattered the comet."

Something that powerful could give me an edge. "Can you aim the laser at that cursed Hive-Mother's Nest?" Wod-Jur asked. *My forces needed something. Anything.*

"What? Even if I wanted to, the safety interlock system won't let me aim the laser at any planet-sized body."

"Could you override it?" He let a whiff of encouragement drift out.

"No. And if I could, I would not. You know what weapons of mass destruction did to Hool."

Wod-Jur emitted the sour odor of disapproval.

"We have nothing more to fear from the comet," the astronomer said. "It's moving away from the center of the system."

Why does she continue to blather on? Wod-Jur emitted the bitter odor of rejection.

The young astronomer could have explained the comet's course had taken it out of the beam of the navigation beacon, which was oriented toward the asteroid belt and the outer reaches of their system. The comet had disappeared from view. But Wod-Jur's displeasure dissuaded her from speaking further.

～

"So, no matter what we do, within eight to the third planetary revolutions, we die," ChaKut said.

MingLik did not bother confirming the laser beam had to have come from an advanced civilization. They both knew the technology required to build such a weapon was highly advanced.

"We must strike back at them, MingLik." ChaKut said.

It took several sleep periods before they completed their preparations. During this time, ChaKut and MingLik began to refer to themselves as the Dying Defenders. It was their last mission. They loaded their records into the message drone.

"The Bird-that-Soars' drive system is now operational. It's ready to start," said MingLik. The shuttlecraft was still attached to the Star-Seeker and its engines would provide thrust.

"Put the Bird-that-Soars under the control of the Star-Seeker's computer. It has the firing sequence."

"I worry we may not be doing the right thing."

"We've already decided on our course of action. Do you want the Star-Seeker to fall into the hands of these warlike aliens and have them learn Qu'uda's location?"

"No. I also don't want to die."

"These aliens sealed our fate when they fired the laser. We can die quickly while striking back. Or we can die slowly, the death of cowards. I'm surprised that you, as a Defender should flinch from striking a blow to protect our community."

"In all the time I've been a Defender, I've never struck a blow in anger, even though I've trained for it," MingLik said. "Now I'm going to die. I'm afraid."

"Remember your training, remember your oath. And, remember our beloved Qu'uda," ChaKut said. "And remember our wriggler. If we do not act, it could be in danger."

Controlled bursts of power from the Bird-that-Soars' fusion drive stopped the Star-Seeker's tumbling. Once stabilized, the Bird-that-Soars' engines ran for longer periods to change the Star-Seeker's velocity. They used the shuttle's engines to slow their flight into deep space and return to a course that would take them back into the system.

ChaKut monitored the planet closest to the source of the laser beam until he located a source of electromagnetic activity. *Ah*, he thought, *I've found you.* He fed the data into the Star-Seeker's computer. He made a course correction, refined it precisely; there was only one spot on this planet that mattered.

MingLik methodically reviewed the control program in the message drone and set up the parameters to trigger its departure from this system. He ran through the sequence several times until he knew it would function as intended.

The Star-Seeker steadily accelerated until it reached a velocity usually considered too high for interplanetary travel and then coasted toward the planet. ChaKut transferred the remaining deuterium into the Star-Seeker's fusion power plant and altered its controls. Now it would do something very different than its original design.

CHAPTER FIFTEEN

"Wod-Jur, Wod-Jur. The comet is coming back, only this time, it's headed straight at us. It's going to strike in less than one planetary rotation. I don't understand it. It's like it's aimed at us." The young astronomer reeked of fear.

"Don't be silly. How can it hit Chud-Loo?"

"It's worse than that, it's going to hit us, here, in Freedom Valley."

Wod-Jur opened his breathing flaps wide and snorted. "What? Are you sure?"

"Yes—"

"Use the planetary defense."

"There's not enough time to activate it."

"Then use its fusion device, do it. Don't argue."

"I'd have to override the safety interlocks."

"Do it. Get to work right now. Don't show your face again until you've destroyed the comet, understand?" Wod-Jur drew up to his full height, erected his spines, and exuded his most powerful odor.

The young astronomer flinched and fled to the planetary defense system's control room. She doubted she could activate the planetary defense system in time.

But she would try. Oh, she would try.

In desperation, she bypassed every system safety interlock to get to the control program. She worked non-stop through the night, descending ever deeper into the logic and instructions of the program that controlled the fusion device once launched.

On her instructions, the orbiting planetary defense system launched a fusion device at the rapidly approaching comet. *I did it*, she thought, *I got it activated in time.*

The device accelerated and headed towards the path of the approaching comet.

౨

"Look, there's a missile approaching. We'll be destroyed before we can strike back." MingLik pointed at the monitor.

"Let me see." ChaKut queried the long-distance radar. "We're moving faster than the missile, and it doesn't seem to have much acceleration. If we accelerate, I don't think it'll catch us."

"Then do it."

ChaKut input data into the astrogation computer, and then he initiated a short burn in the Bird-that-Soars drive, which also changed their course. He examined the data from the monitor. "It won't hit us." He increased the sensitivity of the detectors and scanned the missile again. "No."

"Are you sure? It looks very close."

"It'll come close, but we're moving much faster, we'll out-run it. See? Look at the projection in the view screen, this is where we are now. These are the positions when we reach the planet." ChaKut operated the astrogation computer. Glowing orange lines indicated the two spaceships' courses. It was clear the missile was changing course to follow the Star-Seeker towards the planet.

"Is the message drone safe?"

ChaKut operated the computer. The objects in the view screen shrank rapidly. He pointed to a tiny glowing sliver, far from the two ships that now looked close together at this scale. "Unless they can detect a very small object at a great distance, it should be quite safe," he said. "Is the message drone ready to leave?"

"Yes, it's continuing to record what is happening. When our tight-beam transmission ceases, it departs. It will accelerate above the planetary ecliptic before setting course to Qu'uda. That will make it impossible for them to locate our home. I've checked the program several times. It runs flawlessly. The message will tell our people about the attack on us and warn them of the dangerous civilization here."

"Well, MingLik, any last messages you want to send back? We've got only a small amount of time left," he asked with a fatalistic flick of his head crest.

MingLik shuddered. He knew what was coming. "Yes, let them see our efforts, our sacrifice. Let them see how we struck back after the vicious attack on the Star-Seeker. Let us download a recording of all our activities. Everything."

The young astronomer stared at the holographic projection. The latest course projection now showed the fusion device would not catch the comet. How could it change course and head toward ... No, that was impossible ... It was going to hit them, right here on Chud-Loo.

She slammed her fore digit down on the communications system override. "Wod-Jur, prepare for a comet impact," she screamed. Her words went into the open communications network and the entire planet heard her.

"You stupid piece of naat-jii dung; you'll cause a panic," Wod-Jur said.

She ignored him. "Hoo-Lii, attention. Warning. There is an imminent comet strike in the vicinity of the settlement. The impact will cause terrible damage."

She patched the image of the approaching comet into the communications network. Once she had completed that, she fled to the deepest tunnel in the control center of the planetary defenses. She managed to get the blast door closed.

The Star-Seeker flashed in and struck the radio transmitter on top of the mountain. The shock wave of the impact set off the trigger in the Star-Seeker's fuel tank, which ignited the deuterium into a fusion explosion.

The glowing fireball, propelled at the tremendous velocity of the Star-Seeker, bit deep into the crust of Chud-Loo. At first, it manifested itself as a violet-white column of incandescent light punching through the atmosphere, out into space, a violent pulse of broad-spectrum energy. Close behind, a column of fire vomited out of the mountain to grow into a giant mushroom cloud over Freedom Valley.

The column of light bathed Freedom Valley with fierce radiation, burning all life on the surface. The atmospheric shock wave hammered the surface structures, flattening them instantly. Ground shock rippled through the mountain range, collapsing buildings and surface instal- lations.

In the Nest, separated from Freedom Valley by high mountain ridges, most survived the initial strike. As the shock waves began to subside, something else streaked into the heart of the Nest and exploded with awful violence.

It was the planetary defense fusion device trying to catch up with the comet. Stripped of all safety interlocks, the device did not heed the warning that it was approaching a planetary body.

The fusion device detonated.

The small, deep valley called the Nest became a cauldron of sun- like temperatures. The rock of the valley's mountainous walls boiled before exploding through the thin atmosphere of Chud-Loo into outer space. It breached the crust of the planet and a new volcano sputtered into life, belching forth boiling magma, gases, and huge clouds of dust.

When the fusion device exploded, the message drone departed. With it went the record of the Star-Seeker, of how it was struck by a giant laser beam and its subsequent collision with the planet.

Many years later, the message drone reached the Qu'uda and told of its fate.

CHAPTER SIXTEEN

As I, Kot-Nih, mentioned earlier, I traveled to the home planets of both of the Others, both the Qu'uda and the humans, and searched many records. I learned there was an eyewitness to the Chud-Loo disaster—a message drone—that eventually reached the Qu'uda system. Its arrival caused a great stir....

The visual record of the attack on the Star-Seeker and the sight of the searing destruction on the alien planet rippled through Qu'uda's society. Planetary ecologists were sure the devastation had ended all civilization on the planet. Even though the Star-Seeker had been attacked without warning, the fact they had destroyed a civilization shocked the Qu'uda society.

They studied the records from the Star-Seeker to learn all they could about the ill-fated civilization, which they named Hoo-Lii from the sound made at the start of their recorded broadcasts. Scientists' analyses concluded that sound was a greeting used by those on the planet.

The Qu'uda engaged in a planet-wide debate on the morality of the crew's act, the crime of destroying a civilization. Yet, because the alien civilization had used a powerful weapon on the Star-Seeker, that posed a dilemma to their inward-looking ways. Perhaps there were other civilizations willing to use weapons of such horrifying power. The realization scared them, for they feared such weapons could be used on them. They quickly reached a consensus of the need to intensify their watch upon the heavens.

Meanwhile, the remnants of an ancient comet, worn-out by the ceaseless erosion from the solar wind of the Epsilon Eridani star, now myriad of tiny fragments, passed through the system. The storm of micrometeorites closed upon Qu'uda and shredded the receptors of the orbiting radio telescope facility.

With Qu'uda's ability to scan the heavens gone, blind to any signs of alien life, fear rippled through their world. This stimulated their scientists to action, for this was an opportunity to get a much larger array of receptors, one that would stretch wide in space with improved detection sensitivity. Interest in getting better deep-space data and worries about the aliens carried the day.

It took several years before their scientists and engineers completed a new radio telescope array. It was far larger, stretching across a measurable fraction of the distance between Qu'uda and its moon. Finishing its data processing and collection system took almost as much time as its construction. Once completed, the scientists wasted no time putting it to work.

To their astonishment, they almost immediately picked up a multitude of electromagnetic signals from a nearby system, including a video image of an alien. However, this image used analog radio signals of varying length—very different from Hoo-Lii signals. It was convincing evidence that there were other aliens and they were light years closer.

The Qu'uda held a planet-wide debate on what course of action to take. One faction that believed no alien civilization could be ignored—because it might have the capability of finding them—prevailed.

There was also the need for living space, and the presence of a civilization was a sure sign of a habitable planet. Yet, if the aliens were hostile, they were a potential danger to the community, and this could not be ignored.

This became the consensus on Qu'uda, which voted to send a community of investigators to this star system, which they called Kota, the home of the new aliens. The Qu'uda now had a goal, an objective, behind which they united to build a new interstellar craft.

This craft was different, for it was an immensely large, fusion-powered craft, which they made from an asteroid. They named it the Egg-that-Flies. It was powerful, armored and capable of withstanding the rigors of the long voyage; much bigger and stronger than the Star-Seeker. It carried a large crew and three fusion-powered shuttlecraft. After years of construction, the Egg-that-Flies finally departed, to head toward the Kota star system, the home of these new aliens.

War started on Earth for reasons that I, Kot-Nih, still find hard to understand. It was a bitter war that caused social and economic upheaval. A faction resorted to the use of nuclear weapons, destroying the leadership of many governmental units. Soon, all semblance of control crumbled; the nuclear weapon attack was the final blow to the stability of the countries of Earth.

In one country, the United States, the nuclear weapons decapitated its leadership. Riots started, and they spread rapidly as the hungry sought food. The internal security forces—called the police and the National Guard—with few exceptions, soon ceased to function. The riots caused widespread fires that destroyed much of what was left of the basic services in the cities. As the forces of law and order disappeared, strong and ruthless men and women took charge.

Once the Qu'uda ship, the Egg-that-Flies, reached the halfway point to Kota, it detected a series of powerful electromagnetic pulses similar to

those produced by fusion weapons. Soon after that, the electromagnetic emissions faded. Methodically, the Qu'uda checked their equipment; but it worked properly. They feared that something terrible had
happened to alien civilization they were about to visit.

CHAPTER SEVENTEEN

As the Egg-that-Flies dropped toward the center of the Kota system, it deployed a magnetic-sail as a supplemental braking system. After a close passage with the system's star, the Egg-that-Flies set course for the only place that could support life—the third planet. They approached from out of the sun to minimize chances of detection. Since the giant gas planet was on the far side of the system, they postponed the refueling until later.

Up close, the world was blue and white. It had more land than Qu'uda, with higher mountains and deeper oceans. Sensors revealed the atmosphere was breathable—the planet was habitable. The climate was drier and colder and more extreme than that of Qu'uda. Its gravity was seven-eighths as much, and its day was only five-eighths as long with a longer year.

Scouts in the Birds-that-Soars spotted bipedal life forms that seemed odd—even their gait was different. They were the same creatures seen in the transmissions received on Qu'uda—the aliens. It didn't take long to realize damage from a nuclear war was everywhere on the planet.

When it became time to refuel the Egg-that-Flies, the navigator, Cha KinLaat, set a course to pass close to the edge of the planet's atmosphere. As a scout craft crossed above the northern pole, a tiny point of light flashed. He examined the volume of space from where the light had originated and saw a long, ungainly satellite that appeared derelict.

$$\sim$$

However, a worn but still functioning rail gun platform left over from the pre-Collapse period remained in orbit. The heat from a rising Bird-that-Soars' engine had tickled its infrared sensors into life. The heat from the Egg-that-Flies' fusion drive exhaust attracted its attention.

The rail gun platform lined up on the mammoth infrared signal from the Egg-that-Flies. When aligned, its solid-state relays discharged a massive current flow into the electromagnetic coils of the rail gun. A depleted uranium slug, jacketed in a tough steel alloy, accelerated along one-hundred-fifty feet of rail to a velocity of twenty-five miles per second. The gyros, never designed to aim the rail gun, rotated the platform too far. The slug struck the Egg-that-Flies' thick iron-nickel hull with a flash of brilliant blue-white light.

$$\sim$$

The ship rang like a gong from the impact.

The defense system extended its sensors.

"Mata ChaLik," Cha KinLaat called over the comm-net. "The ship was struck by a fast-moving object."

"Damage report." Mata ChaLik BuMaru, spokesperson for the Defenders of Qu'uda asked. He was their military leader.

"None detected." Cha KinLaat continued the scan but saw nothing. The Egg-that-Flies accelerated closer to the turning point. As the fusion drive built power, the tail of rose-violet plasma grew and the ship approached escape velocity.

The platform's gyros reoriented the rail gun as its tattered solar cells recharged the capacitor banks. Its aim was on the source of the massive amount of heat.

It fired.

The slug's temperature—above that of the icy-cold of deep space—alerted the Egg-that-Flies' defense system. The object was moving fast and on a collision course—not natural, the defense system reasoned. It responded with a beam weapon.

It was too late.

The slug sliced through an outer cooling-coil on the ship's fusion drive. Silently, the polycarbon containment exfoliated in a cloud of glittering black flakes, driven helter-skelter by hydrogen jetting from the cut coil. The cooling system's pressure drop initiated an automatic shutdown. The flaring fusion drive winked out.

"Cha KinLaat." Mata ChaLik overrode the conversation on the comm-net. "Why did the drive shut down?"

"Loss of superconductor coolant pressure," Cha KinLaat said. "System status, pressure drop cause?" he asked.

"Gas leak, external line," the drive biocomputer answered.

The navigation biocomputer chirped for attention. "Yes?" Cha KinLaat said.

"Velocity too low and gas leak caused course change. Ship about to enter atmosphere."

The Egg-that-Flies could not land on a planet, for it was designed as a true deep space ship.

Cha KinLaat knew they needed a sustained burn. "System status, can fusion sequence be initiated?"

"Low coolant pressure mandates system lockout," the drive system biocomputer said. "Repairs required."

"What's going on?" Mata ChaLik asked. "Well?"

"The drive shut down. We may impact the atmosphere."

"May?" Mata ChaLik said. "Find out now."

"I'm doing that." Cha KinLaat calculated the new orbit. "It's going to ..." He rechecked the figures. The course is heading directly into the atmosphere. Fear gripped him like a predator—it was the end.

If the Egg-that-Flies crashed into the planet below, the explosive impact would be like that of a giant meteorite. It had been theorized the sun-like temperatures from a high-velocity impact could ignite deuterium in the fusion power supply reactor.

Oh, sacred Egg, thought Cha KinLaat. *Not only is it our end, but we may destroy all life on this planet.*

This is what happened to the Hoo-Lii planet—only this time, it would be an accident.

"Atmospheric impact imminent."

The image on the course computer showed the Egg-that-Flies sliding into the atmosphere, a cool, green object changing to flashing white.

Cha KinLaat imagined he felt the searing heat of impact dissolving him into his constituent atoms.

The ship started to vibrate. The roar turned into an insane shriek. The ship shuddered and rang like a giant cymbal. Gravity surged for an instant. Cha KinLaat slammed into a forward bulkhead. Pain exploded through his being. A red haze engulfed him.

CHAPTER EIGHTEEN

Cha KinLaat was surprised to be still alive.

The Egg-that-Flies pinged and crackled as it shed heat from its close encounter. The ship had skipped off the upper atmosphere to coast out into empty space.

Blood dripped from Cha KinLaat's face as he calculated the new course. It was a highly elliptical polar orbit. The apogee reached far into space with the perigee dipping back into the atmosphere.

"Mata ChaLik," he called into the comm-net.

"Yes?" His voice was faint and distant.

"We're in orbit around the planet."

"Then we're safe?" Mata ChaLik sounded relieved.

"No." Cha KinLaat hesitated. The image of the Egg-that-Flies being consumed in a fiery dive into the atmosphere again haunted him —that still lay ahead. He shivered.

"You have something else to tell me?"

"We will enter the atmosphere on the next perigee pass."

"What must we do?" Mata ChaLik demanded.

"We must boost the ship's orbit."

"Do it."

"Emergency options for drive start-up?" Cha KinLaat spoke to the drive biocomputer.

"Diversion of reserve fuel to increase cooling system capacity. Not known if coolant pressure can be raised to operate drive system. Leak cause and status unknown."

"Emergency override," Cha KinLaat said. "Blow down one-half of the reserve fuel through the cooling system."

"Initiated."

"Cooling system status?" Cha KinLaat asked.

"Pressure marginal and fluctuating, temperature stable."

It violates normal procedures, but I have no choice. We must have thrust, he thought. *This is a job for Bilik Pudjata, the builder of the drive system.* "Bilik, take control of the drive system. We must get it started."

Bilik realized something was very wrong, but knew the system and its computer. "Start drive sequence."

Deuterium and helium three entered the propulsion tube. Lasers flared like a sun and the fuel ignited. The fierce heat of the fusion reaction expanded the gas in the cooling system. Pressure rose in the damaged coil; it stretched and ruptured. Coolant spewed into space.

The superconductor coils overheated. Magnetic fields convulsed and collapsed violently. White-hot fusion plasma, pinched by the dying gasp of a powerful magnetic pulsation, cascaded into a fusion explosion. A ball of pure energy blossomed on the Egg-that-Flies' stern, slamming the ship forward.

Bilik collided with the rear bulkhead. There was no up or down. He spun freely in zero gravity and absolute darkness, lost somewhere in nowhere. Distantly, words echoed. Dizzy and sore, he focused on them.

"Bilik, answer me. What happened?"

The harsh tonalities of Mata ChaLik's voice were an anchor for Bilik. "The fusion drive ..." he said. He dug his claws into his sides. Their sharp bite and the new locus of pain helped him regain control. "I don't know." His head throbbed violently.

"We have no drive," Mata ChaLik's voice was lower in volume but even more difficult to ignore. "I have no data on my comm-net. What happened?"

Emergency lighting brightened to a dull orange. Status monitors flickered into life. The hull was intact. The life support systems still functioned. Warnings about the propulsion system flashed randomly.

Bilik activated the outside monitors. There was no sign of the propulsion system at the rear of the Egg-that-Flies. "I tried to start the drive system," he said.

"Explain what happened," Mata ChaLik said.

"The propulsion system ..." Cha KinLaat paused.

"Get on with it."

"Egg-that-Flies, do you hear me?" A voice came from the external communication system.

"Who is it?" Mata ChaLik's voice resonated with anger.

"This is Dekah NahBu, scout-pilot on the third Bird-that-Soars. The entire aft section of the Egg-that-Flies is gone. The drive system disappeared in an explosion."

"Bilik, what is our new orbit?"

"It looks stable, but for how long, I don't know."

"Then why don't you figure out how much time we do have?" Mata ChaLik said harshly. "And quickly."

ᘇ

Bilik found the explosion had raised their orbit. The computer warned the ship would still lose velocity on each perigee pass due to atmospheric friction. "First approximation shows the Egg-that-Flies has somewhere between 2,000 to 4,000 orbits before it dips into the atmosphere."

"Send me a precise estimate. And use a private channel next time." Mata ChaLik's voice was as cold as outer space. "Do you understand?"

"Yes, Mata ChaLik, leader of the Defenders of Qu'uda, I understand." The use of his formal title acknowledged the rebuke.

ᘇ

After Bilik inspected the stern of the ship, he saw the explosion had totally destroyed the drive system and had blown away the spare propulsion tube. In addition, one of the Birds-that-Soar had been vaporized and the other damaged beyond repair.

In normal operation, the chance of the main propulsion tube and the spare tube being damaged had been considered remote. The only remaining shuttle, piloted by Dekah NahBu, returned to land near the remnants of its hangar.

The thought depressed Bilik when the reality sank in the Egg-that-Flies needed a new propulsion tube to leave the orbit around the Earth. He knew it was impossible to cast a propulsion tube with the needed properties from pure iron in zero gravity, for that would result in a casting containing voids, which would be likely to fail prematurely. Without thrust, there was no gravity.

The crew on board the Egg-that-Flies could make the rest of the parts; replacement coils for the magnetic containment, the ion drive, and the tube's polycarbon lining. However, without the iron propulsion tube, they were stranded.

After Bilik informed Mata ChaLik of their situation, he chose Bilik to go to the surface of the Earth to make the repair parts because he was an alien specialist and drive system specialist.

The medical staff surgically modified him, fitting him with a skin-tight facemask designed to what they believed the Earth people looked like. After many difficulties, Bilik found a place among the Earth people where they had an iron caster.

The task was far, far more difficult than the Qu'uda originally envisioned. Earth's alien biosystem caused Bilik health and dietary problems. He had to fight for his life and mobilized an old electric steel furnace to make the huge parts needed to repair the damaged drive. In addition, he had to use a cannibalized fusion drive unit from the damaged Birds-that-Soar to run the generators to make electricity to power the iron melting furnace.

Unknowingly, Bilik provoked a civil war when he introduced new technology. When he called in the Qu'uda shuttlecraft to evacuate defenders from a besieged settlement, it confirmed the presence of advanced alien technology. The civil war worsened and precipitated a crisis among the humans. One faction sent an expedition to attack the main city of the Qu'uda agent's allies, which had the steel furnace where piece by piece, Bilik made a new propulsion tube.

CHAPTER NINETEEN

The Qu'uda ship's orbit decayed and delivery of the repair parts became critical. Frantic, its crew pressured Bilik to deliver the parts. Their relations deteriorated. When the shuttle came to pick up the last piece of the propulsion tube, it arrived in the middle of fierce battle. The shuttle retrieved the part, and while leaving, gunfire by humans damaged the shuttle. It managed to limp back to the orbiting ship with the vitally needed part.

Bilik was wounded in the battle. The Qu'uda abandoned him because he had become much too much like an alien to fit in anymore. The earthlings captured him and recognized he was not human. When he recovered consciousness, he learned his own species, the Qu'uda, had abandoned him. He was questioned and reluctantly agreed to cooperate with the humans. He no longer had a home with his fellow Qu'uda. Earth was now his home.

The Qu'uda departed in their repaired spacecraft. They promised to return and destroy all advanced technology, because they did not want the warlike humans entering space. First, they had to obtain fuel from the gas giant planet before they could start to rebuild their ship and make weapons.

I, Kot-Nih, found this to be a strange and disturbing series of events. Yet, it was only a prelude that set the stage for an even stranger encounter.

CHAPTER TWENTY

ASTEROID BELT, CHUD-LOO SYSTEM

5,100 Year of the Mother.

"Hoo-Lii, colony of the Disobedient, please answer," Vin-Boh called. He was the unripened male pilot-navigator on the spaceship Young Mother, which had just emerged from the gate in space-time that brought them from Hool. The Young Mother was a bloated cylinder, loaded with supplies and more prisoners destined for exile on Chud-Loo. The ship arrived in the outer reaches of the Daughter system and had to cross the asteroid belt to reach Chud-Loo. Even though the radio navigation beacon still worked, it no longer sent out strobing radar pulses that illuminated every asteroid.

There was no answer.

"Anyone on Chud-Loo, come in, please. Turn on the navigation strobe."

This was the first time Vin-Boh had approached Chud-Loo without radar guidance. His radar had less power and range, which forced the ship to travel at low speeds. Normally, the Disobedient on Chud-Loo answered the supply ship quickly, for their needs were never-ending and they always wanted to check the supply manifest.

Nothing.

Vin-Boh slowed the Young Mother further and activated the guidance system for the approach.

This, he thought, *will take days.* He wanted to get off the ship to break the monotony of space travel. The lack of response was odd; it was very unlike the exiles to be silent. Usually by now they were bickering over what supplies would go to which faction.

Vin-Boh found the trip through the asteroids stressful but uneventful. At low speed, the ship's radar provided sufficient warning as long as he was careful, and he was. Entering the orbit above Chud-Loo, the radio silence was absolute.

He was surprised to see clouds completely obscured the surface. No shuttlecraft rose from the surface. The planet was totally silent. No electromagnetic transmissions of any kind, none.

Something dreadful must have happened, Vin-Boh realized. For several orbits, he scanned the surface with high-resolution radar. He saw no signs of surface vehicles—no atmospheric craft flew anywhere. Were they hiding? Or what? He queried the planetary defense system and discovered it had been used—twice in close succession.

Vin-Boh felt an icy chill.

I must investigate. For if I bring back a ship full of prisoners on the basis of suspicion alone, I could join them and be sent into exile, too. This means I must go to the surface of Chud-Loo and find out what happened.

Vin-Boh had two to the fourth prisoners locked in the passenger area of the supply ship. The prisoners grew restless upon arrival, for the ship's quarters made the prisons of Hool seem luxurious. He informed the prisoners what he had observed including the fact the planetary defense system had been used.

Upon hearing the news, they became quiet.

In the Young Mother's small shuttle, Vin-Boh and Pun-Tih, his co-pilot, descended through the atmosphere of Chud-Loo. The atmospheric turbulence was more severe than he had ever previously experienced. Storms raced across the surface of the planet in a steady, never-ending procession. He descended under the heavy clouds to

Freedom Valley. Rain fell steadily. The planet was no longer dry and desert-like.

"By the Mother, where's the settlement? What's happened to it?" He stared at the empty valley. Mounds of rubble were the only sign of the buildings that previously dotted the valley floor. It had a scoured, desolate appearance. Muddy rivulets coursed down the sides of the valley.

"Is this the right place?" asked Pun-Tih.

"It should be." Vin-Boh stared at the navigation module.

"It can't be." Pun-Tih's breathing flaps dilated.

"Are these the right coordinates?"

"Yes. Do you have the proper reference points?"

"I thought so. Let's head to the desert and work our way into these mountains using a location description. Perhaps this navigation module is defective. Back to basics." Vin-Boh was as shaken as Pun-Tih.

There was no trace of the settlement.

They turned the shuttle about and headed out to the great desert. On the way, they had to avoid an actively erupting volcano, to which Pun-Tih could find no reference in their navigation module. They used the landmarks and carefully retraced their approach.

"This is it. This has to be the same place. This has to be Freedom Valley's location." Pun-Tih carefully examined the landscape below. "What's happened to it?" It was a huge depression filled with shattered and melted rocks. Traces of broken buildings abounded.

"I'm not landing the shuttle here. There's something wrong. Something terrible has happened. Look at these radiation readings," Vin-Boh said, pointing to a flashing yellow signal in the environmental monitoring holo.

"Let's get out of here, and quickly."

"Before we leave, I must make a record of what we've seen, including readings from our instruments. We'll take air samples for our scientists back on Hool." Vin-Boh knew it was the first thing he had to do.

Vin-Boh made an announcement to the crew and passengers; "Freedom Valley has been destroyed. We don't know how or why, but the radiation levels are similar to the restricted areas on the surface of Hool. Somebody, someone, or something." He paused to emphasize the word thing. "Used fusion explosives in that valley. I'm not a Chosen-Male warrior, nor do I have a Hive-Mother to die for."

Vin-Boh spoke for most of the crew. He was an unripened male and had been chosen for the position of pilot-navigator because unripened ones were submissive and avoided conflicts. They had a cautious nature and took the responsibility of bringing a spaceship back safely seriously.

Next, Vin-Boh realized. *We have to get water.* The ship's engines and passengers had consumed most of it. With the mountains radioactive and its water contaminated, that left only the polar ocean as a source.

Vin-Boh released several prisoners and took them with him to the surface to assist with loading water into the small shuttle. Once its tanks were filled, he left them on the surface while he hauled the water to the ship. When he returned, they were gone. The only trace of them was a few fragments of bone and fragments of exoskeleton. He hauled two more loads of water before a horde of multi-legged, hard shelled, clawed creatures emerged from the ocean, biting and snapping. The creatures caught a prisoner, who fell, screaming. He disappeared under a dark mass of creatures.

That delayed the creatures long enough for Vin-Boh to get the door closed before the creatures swarmed all over the shuttle. He fired up the shuttle's engines and took off. As the shuttle rose from the ground, he could see creatures clinging to the front observation port frame, prying and cutting with their pincers.

The last creature held on until halfway to orbit.

CHAPTER TWENTY-ONE

When Vin-Boh returned to Hool in the spaceship Young Mother with the account of the destruction of the colony Chud-Loo, he was surprised at the initial response of the Hive-Mother Nah-Kih, who said, "Too bad, it was a good place to get rid of troublemakers."

However, the news of the radiation and the implication of the type of weapons which had been used, silenced them. The priests at the Shrine-of-the-Mother knew what the high radiation levels could mean. The possibility fusion weapons had been used filled them with fear; no, it was not fear; it was horror.

The air samples that Vin-Boh brought soon confirmed fusion explosives had been used—weapons outlawed for generations. Before the Mother-of-the-Sky set, the priests at the Shrine-of-the-Mother sent out a call for the Council of Hive-Mothers to meet and hear the report of the conditions found on Chud-Loo.

It was harvesting season and the insects in the maroon vegetation surrounding the Shrine-of-the-Mother were in full chorus. The weather had been dry and the normal sound of the brooks tinkling down the valley's walls was absent. The dull red vegetative floor covering was dry and limp. Dust blown in from the great desert made a golden halo around the Mother-of-the-Sky.

After the priests finished offering prayers, the Hive-Mothers rattled their exoskeletons as they sought comfortable positions on their resting rocks. It was also their way of announcing the importance of the meeting.

Buk-Tar, the oldest Hive-Mother, extended her bloated body and rose on her hind limbs. "Call the witness who reported the evidence of an obscenity." She rotated her pointed head, seeking the presence of the crew of the ship, the Young Mother.

Vin-Boh and Pun-Tih moved before the assemblage and abased themselves. First they lowered their heads to the ground before the priests at the side and then to the Hive-Mothers. They remained in that position.

"Rise," Buk-Tar said. "Is it possible something else could have caused the radiation?" Her age gave her the privilege but not necessarily the wisdom to ask such questions.

"I don't know. At first, I thought we were in the wrong place, or, a defective navigation module had led us astray. So, we navigated by line of sight from the place where the mountains emerge from the desert. There is a valley opening in the cliffs that is a recognizable landmark. We went out over the desert and came back to the same place again." Vin-Boh hesitated.

"The high peak that over-looked Freedom Valley is gone, completely gone. The adjacent mountain ridge now has a volcano where there used to be a small valley. We know we had the right location for Freedom Valley. It was so horrible all we could do was flee."

"The scanners revealed no signs of movement anywhere else on the planet, is that right?" Buk-Tar asked.

"Not exactly. We only scanned the mountain range and the valleys. I don't think there's any other place on the planet where Hoo-Lii could live." Vin-Boh was conscious of the tightly focused stares of all the Hive-Mothers.

"Why not?" Buk-Tar asked, breathing flaps still.

"The desert produces sand and little else. The desert consumes anything that enters it. It is a place of death."

"I see." Buk-Tar raised one breathing flap, indicating skepticism.

"Well, that solves the problem of Wod-Jur and the Disobedient,"

Nah-Kih said. She was noted for her outspoken ways. "A fortunate accident on distant Chud-Loo."

Buk-Tar twitched her breathing flaps in disapproval. "What happened to the settlement of exiles?" she asked.

"A natural disaster, whatever. It solved the problem of the Disobedient. Good riddance." Nah-Kih raised her spines to emphasize the point.

"True," Buk-Tar said. "It was no great loss. The Spirit-of-the-Mother works in mysterious ways. Are there any more questions?" It was a ritual courtesy statement that normally signaled the end of a questioning session.

Several Hive-Mothers stirred as though to go.

"Yes." Suh-Joh rose on her hind limbs and glanced around.

The assembled Hive-Mothers took in a breath of surprise. They knew the eldest Hive-Mother did the questioning.

Suh-Joh's recent conquests had confirmed her military prowess. As for the hierarchy in the Council, that was another challenge.

"Vin-Boh," she said. She twitched her breathing flaps erect. Calling the pilot-navigator by name gave him status. "What do you think happened on Chud-Loo?"

"Blessed Hive-Mother Suh-Joh, it is not for me to offer opinions to this august council." Vin-Boh knew Hive-Mothers guarded their prerogative to issue opinions. They rewarded unripened males who spoke out of turn with a quick death.

"Consider yourself under my protection. I want to know what you believe happened to the colony of exiles on Chud-Loo."

"Honored Hive-Mothers, with your permission, I humbly offer you my interpretation of the data. Freedom Valley reminds me of some of the restricted areas that exist on Hool. You know, those areas destroyed by fusion weapons during the terrible wars in our past—"

Collectively, the Council of Hive-Mothers snorted, drawing in their breaths sharply. It was not what they wanted to hear.

Vin-Boh stood still, petrified, afraid to move, afraid to say more. Odors of anger filled the air.

"Are you sure?" Suh-Joh's erect breathing flaps focused intently upon him. She emitted no odor of anger.

"Yes, honored Hive-Mother. The evidence is strong. After thinking about it, the evidence is even more compelling." Vin-Boh carefully avoided the word opinion.

Suh-Joh's protection would mean little if he offended the Hive-Mother, unless he had constant protection in the form of a squad of Chosen-Male warriors.

"Fellow Hive-Mothers. It becomes the Council's concern when weapons of mass destruction are used, either by Hoo-Lii or against Hoo-Lii. We cannot allow that horror to visit upon us again. It is against the Way-of-the-Mother." Suh-Joh inserted a basic tenet of their religion into the discussion.

By their silence, the Hive-Mothers had acquiesced.

"What is to be done?" Buk-Tar asked. As the eldest Hive-Mother, her leadership had been challenged; she now asserted her authority.

"The Council must send an investigative team to find out what happened on Chud-Loo and make a formal report. Then the Council can determine if there have been any violations of the Way-of-the-Mother."

Again, Vin-Boh thought, *Suh-Joh invokes religion as a basis for her actions.*

Several conservative Hive-Mothers stirred, fanning their breathing flaps in approval. It was obvious they were coming to regard this young Hive-Mother in a different light. She struck a responsive chord, for few in the Council referred to the Way-of-the-Mother anymore. Some had been urging it was time to go back to their guiding principles.

"Who shall provide the means to send an investigative team all the way to Chud-Loo?" Buk-Tar had regained her composure.

"For the sake of the Way-of-the-Mother, the Hive of Suh-Joh will organize the expedition to Chud-Loo to seek the truth. We shall provide a ship and crew for the expedition. Upon its return, the crew will make a full report to the entire Council of Hive-Mothers," Suh-Joh said.

The Council burst into a twitter of discussion.

Vin-Boh listened as the Hive-Mother Nah-Kih expressed her opinion audibly to several of her immediate neighbors it was a good way to use up Suh-Joh's wealth and bring her down. No one had any questions for Suh-Joh; there was tacit agreement to proceed.

"Yes," Buk-Tar said. "That plan seems acceptable. Are there any objections?" Breathing flaps grew still. No one said anything.

Suh-Joh spoke up. "As members of this Council, I expect each of you to pay your proportionate share of the cost of the expedition."

A twitter of conversation burst anew.

Suh-Joh's voice cut through the high-pitched conversation. "It is your contribution to preserve the Way-of-the-Mother." She bowed in the direction of the priests. "It is the least we can do."

The gathering grew quiet.

Vin-Boh realized the Hive-Mothers had been given a chance to object, but they had frittered it away in speculative chatter about the imminent fall of Suh-Joh. Now they had to pay for the next expedition.

CHAPTER TWENTY-TWO

It pleased Vin-Boh to learn Suh-Joh had chosen him to be the pilot-navigator for the expedition to Chud-Loo. It made sense since he had been the pilot-navigator on the supply run to Chud-Loo. He was thankful a group of Suh-Joh's Chosen-Male warriors also accompanied him. The trip would give the offended Hive-Mothers time to cool off. At least, he hoped so.

It also pleased him to learn the spacecraft for this voyage would be the Good-Child, a newly constructed craft belonging to Suh-Joh. Its advanced faster-than-light (FTL) capability made it speedier than the Young Mother, which now would carry supplies to the planet Kamah. The Good-Child could carry as many as two times eight squared crew and passengers; for extended missions, its crew would be half that.

It did not please Vin-Boh to learn the Council of Hive-Mothers, having been maneuvered to pay for their share of the mission, insisted that their representative, Gat-Sun, be included as part of the crew. Gat-Sun was sure to have some Chosen-Male warriors as guards.

2

Except for the usual discomfort of the jump through space-time, Vin-

Boh found the trip uneventful. Passing through the portal in space-time, it was difficult to know how long the Good-Child was actually in the state of transfer on the gravity string.

Elapsed time from point of departure to destination meant a significant amount of time was lost somewhere in the nowhere that was the cusp of space-time. FTL transfer was at least eight cubed times faster-than-light speed, and on longer jumps, even faster.

After the disorientation eased, Vin-Boh set the Good-Child on course for the inner planets of the Daughter system.

When the Hoo-Lii first investigated the Daughter system, it seemed that Chud-Loo held much promise as a second home. Its star had many similar characteristics to their own Mother-of-the-Sky. The first expedition brought back images of a planet possessing an equatorial continent with extensive plains, plus two large polar oceans. Spectroscopic studies confirmed it had a breathable atmosphere.

A second, closer look showed the level areas were sand and rock, colored by a thin layer of lichen with a similar color as the vegetation on Hool. However, the lichen grew at an almost imperceptible rate and was inedible. The planet had little to offer settlers in the way of hospitality.

The Good-Child set its course high above the ecliptic plane to minimize travel through the asteroid belt. Even so, Vin-Boh found the approach to Chud-Loo was slow and tedious due to the need to avoid asteroids. Finally, it reached Chud-Loo.

From orbit, the planet gleamed a ghostly white under a blanket of clouds.

"Chud-Loo," Vin-Boh said. "It seems to have changed its appearance since our last visit. Earlier, clouds covered its entire surface; now there are some openings. When the Disobedient lived here, the great Sand Sea rarely had any clouds, particularly in the equatorial areas."

At the poles, ice glittered through cloud breaks with a cold intensity, revealing the polar oceans now had a significant portion covered with ice.

"Where was the settlement of the Disobedient?" Gat-Sun had never been to Chud-Loo.

"Look on the ground radar." Vin-Boh pointed to a small screen off to one side of the command room. "See this mountain range? Notice the deep valleys that lead up from the great Sand Sea? That points to Freedom Valley's location."

"Is that where we'll land?"

"Yes, this time tomorrow, we'll be in Freedom Valley, or what remains of it." Vin-Boh felt a spine of fear.

"Is it dangerous?" Gat-Sun asked.

"Only if you live there. Our suits will provide protection from the radiation. There will always be at least two Chosen-Male warriors keeping guard over you." Vin-Boh referred to the Chosen-Male warriors from Gat-Sun's own Hive that provided him protection.

Vin-Boh's Chosen-Male warrior escorts were to protect him from any assassins who may have been secretly inserted into the crew, rather than from the dangers of Chud-Loo. The presence of warriors from different Hives kept an edge of tension in the Good-Child—an unpleasant but necessary compromise.

Vin-Boh and the investigative team used the shuttle to reach the surface of the planet where, clad in protective clothing, they soon discovered remains of a burned Hoo-Lii. Excavating mounds, they found dried caricatures of Hoo-Lii, preserved by the sterile conditions and the frigid climate. They had died from a combination of heat, radiation, and physical injuries that could have come from a blast wave or a severe ground shock. As the evidence accumulated, it pointed more and more toward the use of a fusion weapon.

The planet is different than when we were here last, Van-Boh thought. *Even the volcano's activity has diminished.* It didn't take long for the investigators to discover evidence of a fusion device, for it had left its calling card in the lava. The rock from the new mountain was the most radioactive material on the planet.

The investigative team methodically combed the surface of Freedom Valley, discovering nothing different from their initial inspection until they came upon the remnants of the fusion power plant. In itself, the fusion power plant was barely recognizable—all of its deuterium was long gone. The fact the fusion power plant was still identifiable meant it could not have been the cause of the fusion explosion. Therefore, they concluded, the disaster was no accident.

Evidence from an extensive flyover survey indicated there had been two fusion explosions. One apparently took place on the high mountain where the ground transmitter had been; it was now occupied by a gaping crater. The other location was the new volcano which was in the valley called the Nest, the former home of a splinter faction of the Disobedient.

The memory of the planetary defense system, which still orbited the planet, confirmed it had been used twice. The first fusion device was used by the planetary defense system against a comet; the second had its safety interlock removed and had been used against a planetary-sized body.

"How can that be?" Gat-Sun asked. His breathing flaps flared, displaying his fear.

"It looks like one of the planetary defense system's fusion devices was used against Chud-Loo," Vin-Boh said.

"Is that possible? For what reason would they remove the safety interlock?" Gat-Sun asked.

Vin-Boh stared at the data. "I don't know."

"That must be the source of the fusion device. Did the Disobedient attack a rebellious faction among themselves?"

"It's possible. But two fusion explosions hit Chud-Loo. Where did the second one come from?"

"I don't know. It wasn't the power plant. The planetary defense system was used first against a comet, but there were two explosions." Gat-Sun stared at Vin-Boh. "That means there was a third fusion device. Where did it come from?" His breathing flaps flared, giving off the aroma of fear.

"Perhaps a Disobedient faction made a fusion device and used it against the main body of Disobedient who then retaliated with the planetary defenses."

Gat-Sun took a deep breath, flaring his breathing flaps. "If a splinter faction attacked first, there would be no ground control left to modify a fusion device in the planetary defense system."

"Maybe it happened in the reverse order."

"No, the shatter patterns show the first explosion was on the mountain. Both explosive devices must have arrived at high velocity to get such deep penetration into the crust."

"I don't know." Vin-Boh queried the computer.

A holo-terminal showed a projection of the path of the arriving missiles based upon analysis of the structure of the crater. The computer listed the estimated impact velocities.

"You're right, Gat-Sun. The speeds were greater than anything falling from orbit or ground-based ballistic missile. Both came in at velocities more typical of a space craft." His breathing flaps snapped shut.

"What are you thinking?"

"Is it possible the missiles came from some other source? Perhaps it wasn't squabbling Disobedient."

"What evidence do you have to support that idea?"

"Nothing direct, except their speed of arrival. Neither bomb came from a missile launched from the surface of Chud-Loo. That bothers me," Vin-Boh said.

He knew they would be asked many questions upon return. Mother-forbid should they overlook anything.

CHAPTER TWENTY-THREE

The unripened crewmembers collected the remnants of the bodies and covered them with rocks. The burial was a sign of respect by the unripened ones. Chosen-Male warriors stood by and watched, making no attempt to help.

Convinced they had searched the site completely, Vin-Boh prepared the Good-Child for departure. This time, he sought out a water source in the mountains, so that they would not have to face the ferocious clawed creatures of the polar oceans. With the change in climate, several small rivers now flowed out of the mountains into the sand sea desert.

The crew's final task was to dismantle the planetary defense system. They jettisoned the remaining stock of fusion devices into the system's sun. No one wanted to bring those horrors back to Hool or let anyone else get their mandibles on them. They preserved the memory of the planetary defense system within the computer as evidence.

HOOL

5,101 Year of the Mother

The cool season arrived. Low gray clouds scudded over the Shrine-of-the-Mother. The sound of water dripping from the crimson vegetation surrounding the vale had replaced the insects' symphony. The plate-covered hides of the Hive-Mothers glistened wetly. Some held their mouths open to the skies to catch the precious gift of water falling from the sky—a blessing from the Mother. Even the vegetation under-foot had more spring than usual. Yet the festive atmosphere usually accompanying the rain season was absent.

The Hive-Mothers had heard the account of the recently returned expedition from Chud-Loo. They had questions.

"So, fusion devices were used. We know the Disobedient had split into factions," Buk-Tar, the Eldest Hive-Mother said. "That is what you reported, as pilot-navigator of the supply ship to Chud-Loo."

"Yes, honored Hive-Mother," Vin-Boh said.

"The Disobedient corrupted the safety interlock on a fusion device from the planetary defense system, is that right?"

"Yes, honored Hive-Mother. The evidence points in that direction." Vin-Boh knew he had to avoid offering any opinions to this assembly of Hive-Mothers.

"It sounds like the Disobedient fell to quarreling and in their immorality, used banned obscene devices upon each other."

"Yes, honored Hive-Mother, but I'm not sure—"

"So, did the Disobedient kill each other?" Buk-Tar's breathing flaps flared and vented an odor of anger.

Vin-Boh hesitated before answering. "It is possible, Honored Hive-Mother. The evidence is very confusing."

"We should never have given them Chud-Loo. That planet should have gone to our offspring who would have made it thrive, and grow rich like Kamah. Those dirty Disobedient have destroyed a world. Let it be a lesson to us."

"Oh, most fecund Hive-Mother, another truth may exist." Gat-Sun abased himself, fearful at upsetting the eldest Hive-Mother's conclusion. He used a most flattering title for it was obvious this could be dangerous territory.

"What evidence gives you that conclusion, little unripened one?" The eldest Hive-Mother's high-pitched twitter contained a cold edge. The aroma of her anger was strong.

"What puzzles us is we don't know how the Disobedient could get both devices moving at such a high velocity. The depth of the craters suggests off-planet missiles. What was the source of the second fusion device? Did they make it? We do not know how. We confess we do not have the answers." Gat-Sun made the formal ritual gesture of abasement.

Vin-Boh matched him, head pressed tightly against the ground.

It was clear the eldest Hive-Mother's anger was growing.

An exoskeleton rattled on a resting-rock. It was Nah-Kih, a young Hive-Mother rising to her hind limbs. "So, Suh-Joh, your expedition cost us dearly in resources and gives no definitive answer. It is yet another affront to the Council of Hive-Mothers. What have you got to say about that?" Her words dripped scorn.

The Council grew quiet. Spines rippled. A squall of rain drifted between the valley's high walls.

Vin-Boh held his breath. The air was filled with the aroma of conflict.

Suh-Joh rose to her hind limbs and flexed with the motion of abasement toward the priests arraigned alongside the vale. She turned to the witnesses crouched close to the ground. "Tell me, Vin-Boh, have you synthesized any ideas you have not yet shared with this Council?" She forced herself to give no sign of having heard Nah-Kih's comment.

Suh-Joh tallied her Chosen-Male warrior cohorts. *I have more than enough to take out Nah-Kih's Hive*, she thought. *Getting there may be difficult; several strong Hives lie on the tunnel to Nah-Kih's home. I must think about this more, later.*

"Honored Hive-Mother, Suh-Joh. Forgive us for not returning with a complete answer. Even though Gat-Sun and I come from different Hives, we have shared our ideas and information. We find that working together is productive. It is difficult to believe this destruction was caused by internal dissent alone." Vin-Boh hesitated.

"We fear that another entity, an outsider, was responsible for throwing the fusion devices at Chud-Loo. What is peculiar, is the great velocity with which they arrived. And the accuracy of the aim was impressive." Vin-Boh pressed himself flat against the ground in the ultimate posture of submission and vulnerability.

"What are you implying?" Suh-Joh realized this little unripened one had a keen mind.

"We offer the possibility that the devices could have come from the Others."

It was a term out of their legends referring to a possible race of beings from elsewhere. No one but the very young believed it. "If not them, perhaps a group of Hoo-Lii who wanted Chud-Loo destroyed—"

The Council of Hive-Mothers hissed collectively. All breathing flaps froze in the exhaled position. His implication a Hive-Mother had made an obscene fusion device was, well, more than enough cause for war.

"Be careful what you say, little unripened one." Buk-Tar flexed her spines and erected her breathing flaps. The rank odor of anger filled the air. "Your words will have consequences."

"Do you have someone in mind?" Nah-Kih asked. "Someone present, perhaps." She swiveled her head toward Suh-Joh.

"Honored Hive-Mothers, please, I beg your indulgence. I accuse no one. You charged us to find out what happened. We are disturbed by what we saw. The Hoo-Lii on Chud-Loo died a horrible death from fusion weapons. It was a sacrilege, an affront to the Way-of-the-Mother, an act of vileness." Vin-Boh flexed quickly in the direction of the priests. "The evidence points away from the Disobedient on Chud-Loo. They did not have the means to accelerate a missile to the speed of that which impacted their settlement. Please, understand I am not offering opinion, only facts. I did say it could be Others."

No one spoke as the Hive-Mothers moved nervously, rattling their exoskeletons on resting rocks. Breathing flaps snorted.

Suh-Joh watched Vin-Boh out of the corner of her eye. *I am the only barrier between him and the anger of the Hive-Mothers.*

Vin-Boh pressed his head tighter against the ground.

Suh-Joh knew the reference to Others was speculation there might be alien civilizations. Over the years, theologians had debated a reference to Others in an ancient version of the Way-of-the-Mother. Eventually, the priests concluded this reference to aliens was merely a tale. For if they existed, where were they? That left Vin-Boh's findings pointing in only one direction—at a Hive-Mother.

The only individuals with access to the technology and resources to make fusion devices were Hive-Mothers; all of whom were present. Access to the FTL spacecraft capable of making the trip to Chud-Loo was limited to the Hive-Mothers. All of the spacecraft were busy on scheduled flights. There was no other spacecraft.

The members of the Council of Hive-Mothers glanced nervously at one another.

Who would dare risk the wrath of the entire planet and be cast from the fold of the Way-of-the-Mother by using such an obscenity, a horror from out of the past? Who had the ambition and ruthlessness to bring forth technology that had destroyed one paradise? A collective shiver ran through the Shrine.

Heads swiveled toward Suh-Joh and Nah-Kih.

"Vin-Boh, Gat-Sun, place your records before the Council," Suh-Joh spoke up into the silence.

Clouds thickened, and the Shrine grew dim. "It is my proposal, that before this day is over, each Hive-Mother shall appoint a scholar to review the data. The scholars shall work together and speak to no one while seeking an answer. In the time it takes for the two Children-of-the-Sky to complete a cycle, we shall reconvene and hear their findings. I request, in the name of the Council of Hive-Mothers, the scholars be given the freedom to access all Hives and all records in their quest for the truth. Do all agree?"

No one said anything, still shocked by the events. It was clear a deadly spine hung poised over the Council. If any Hive-Mother refused that request, they would be suspect. And if they were found responsi-

ble, the Hives would unite to fall upon the pervert who used obscenities; that was the Way.

No one raise a single spine of objection.

"May the Spirit-of-the-Mother guide us," Suh-Joh said into the
tense silence. She was the first to rise and leave.

The conservative Hive-Mothers silently assented to her request by
a trace of a motion of abasement in their assent. They had acknowledged her leadership.

Buk-Tar glowered in anger and emitted a sour odor of displeasure.
In effect, Suh-Joh had acted as leader of the Council of Hive-Mothers,
and she wasn't the oldest by far.

CHAPTER TWENTY-FOUR

"Mobilize my warriors." Suh-Joh felt her spines rise with her anger. "Bring the cohort leaders here. I need to make an example of a Hive-Mother." She loped forward using both her hind- and mid-limbs into the great hall.

The familiar brown floor coverings with their crossed quill motif softened both light and sound reflected from the yellow sandstone walls. In a curtain-draped alcove, Suh-Joh used a holo-viewer to seek out a section of ancient history about the times of the great wars. She remembered reading of the tactics employed then. She was so engrossed in what she found she did not notice the cadence of marching feet nearby.

"Oh, blessed Hive-Mother Suh-Joh, the Chosen-Male warrior-cohort-leaders beg permission to enter your presence," an attendant said, voice barely a squeak.

"Enter." Suh-Joh gestured to the warriors to seat themselves before her. Attendants scurried in carrying braised daah-lii and toasted seeds as snacks for the warriors. Light from overhead shafts reflected off their dark, brown armored hides. They grew still, quiet.

"My brave warriors, the Hive-Mother Nah-Kih does not fear you. She also implies I may have violated the Way-of-the-Mother. She feels no need to treat neither me, nor my Hive with respect. It is time to teach her a lesson."

"Blessed Hive-Mother Suh-Joh, my warriors would be happy to visit Nah-Kih's hive and kill many of them." It was Son-Nih, a scarred Chosen-Male warrior who often provided counsel. He looked as though he had enough experience to retire. "However, every tunnel on the way to the Hive of Nah-Kih passes through other Hives. Shall we conquer them, too?"

"Good question, my faithful warrior. No, we shall not conquer anyone else. I have a good reason to punish Nah-Kih. The Hive-Mothers at the Council smelled her contempt for my Hive." Suh-Joh paused. "I cannot let that pass. Do we have any recent images of the surface entrance to the Hive of Nah-Kih?"

"Yes, blessed Hive-Mother Suh-Joh," a warrior who specialized in gathering information on other hives spoke up. "The surface route to her Hive is dangerous, for it leads through forbidden zones. If the radiation level does not kill us, then it will weaken us and render us unfit for mating."

"Yes, my trusty warrior, you're right—if we were to march all the way on the surface. That I do not intend. I have an idea."

Suh-Joh spelled out her plan for the assault on the hive of Nah-Kih. As she spoke, the cohort leaders warmed to her plan and offered suggestions. She encouraged her cohort leaders to speak up, for she knew they could make the difference between success and failure.

"Is it allowed by the Way-of-the-Mother?" An old warrior asked, emitting a whiff of concern. His experience and conservatism frequently served as a counterbalance to the enthusiasm of the younger warriors.

"A good comment, my valiant warrior," Suh-Joh said. "I understand your concern. I cannot afford to turn the Council of Hive-Mothers against me, at least, not yet. Is this using a weapon of mass destruction? No. Will we not fight in the traditional fashion? As always. Will we not take the same risk of dying as our opponents? Yes. Is that not the warrior creed as called for in the Way-of-the-Mother?"

The old warrior agreed. "True, it is the Way."

The warrior-cohort-leaders signaled their agreement.

"Oh, blessed Hive-Mother Suh-Joh, lead us to victory." The cohort leaders gave a salute normally given to one of their own in recognition of their skills in warfare.

"Yes, my valiant warriors, to victory." Suh-Joh joined their salute.

The air filled with the odor of battle lust. The cohort leaders knew they would soon meet the warriors of Nah-Kih.

"What? How in the Name of the Mother did the warriors of Suh-Joh breach the main surface entrance to my Hive? Why were you not warned? This is treachery. My Hive-neighbors are in alliance with that abomination, Suh-Joh," Nah-Kih yelled into the communication terminal. Already her warriors had sustained heavy losses without slowing the flood of Suh-Joh's force into her Hive. The noise of fighting drew closer.

The retreat of Nah-Kih's warriors soon became a rout. The unripened ones, the May-be-Chosen, and the Never-to-be-Chosen signaled their willingness to surrender by abasing themselves and offering gifts of water.

Suh-Joh accepted the gifts and made the ritual response, "Hoo-Lii, I will lead you, this I promise."

She entered Nah-Kih's main hall. It had orange patterns inlaid on both the floor and the walls, extolling the valor of its Hive-Mother. At the far end, deep red tapestries covered the wall, before which lay an ornately carved resting mound. "Nah-Kih, it's over."

Nah-Kih rose from the mound and flared her quills. "Hoo-Lii. Never." She flexed her spines as though in preparation for combat.

Suh-Joh's Chosen-Male warriors surrounded her but remained out of range of her deadly spines.

"Finally, Nah-Kih, we meet face-to-face. Now you cannot hide behind the Council of Hive-Mothers or the Hives of your neighbors. Do you still wish to offer insults to me?" Suh-Joh moved within the circle of her warriors around Nah-Kih.

The circle of Chosen-Male warriors expanded.

"Hoo-Lii. You are an abomination. Mother-ripened scum, you're a perversion, an insult to the Way-of-the-Mother. You used weapons prohibited by the Way to invade my Hive. Even if you kill me, the Council of Hive-Mothers will avenge my death." Nah-Kih sprang toward Suh-Joh and slashed out with her spines.

Suh-Joh dodged the spines, turning on her hind limbs. "No one is safe if they insult me and think they can hide behind their neighbors. I came in the shuttle of the Good-Child. I do not trample upon those who respect me."

"You used technology from the time of the wars. That's forbidden. You're an abomination. You'll surely die, one way or the other." Nah-Kih's breathing flaps flailed wildly.

"That remains to be seen. The use of aircraft and spacecraft are forbidden in the warrior creed in the Way-of-the-Mother. But I do not use them as weapons, only for transportation." Suh-Joh's breathing flaps flared. "Your warriors fought well, but they are out-numbered, unprepared, and weak from lack of nourishment. You are unfit to be a Hive-Mother. You have a choice, either ripen one of my daughters or I'll ripen one of yours. Either way, you're going to die, and it will be today."

"Hoo-Lii. Never," Nah-Kih screeched and leaped forward.

Suh-Joh avoided her out-thrust spines. She closed on Nah-Kih and slashed at her with a spine.

Nah-Kih dropped back and spun, flaring her klut-shi at Suh-Joh. Nah-Kih stumbled and failed to see Suh-Joh's killing spine reach out. It struck Nah-Kih between two plates of her armored skin.

Nah-Kih screamed as Suh-Joh's deadly toxins flooded her system. Nah-Kih collapsed and died.

"Feed her to the digesters. Bring me the best of the unripened ones." She turned to a warrior. "Get the surgeon."

Suh-Joh's warriors spread throughout the Hive and brought the unripened ones to her.

Suh-Joh took the best of the unripened May-be-Chosen-males and females as prizes and sent them to her Hive under escort.

She selected one unripened female and beckoned her surgeon. "Cover the tips of this May-be-Chosen female's spines. I do not want to die on them, even by accident. Remember, little one," she said to the nervous unripened female. "That I chose you. I bear you no malice and ask only respect. I shall send you unripened ones from my hive to replace those I've taken. Remember, our paths shall cross again." Suh-Joh inserted her spines into the young female and ripened her. As she left, she was amazed at the speed of the changes that took place in the young Hive-Mother.

CHAPTER TWENTY-FIVE

The Mother-of-the-Sky had barely risen. The Shrine-of-the-Mother was cool. Mist clung to the valley's walls. Dew glittered on the red vegetation in dawn's first light.

"Honored Hive-Mother, we have completed our analysis of the data gathered by Vin-Boh and Gat-Sun on Chud-Loo. We find no disagreement with their analysis. We also cannot explain what happened there. We believe two missiles struck the settlement on Chud-Loo, both of which were moving well in excess of planetary escape velocities." The spokesperson for the scholars paused in his report presentation to the Council of Hive-Mothers.

A twitter of conversation broke out. "Continue." Buk-Tar, spoke quickly in her role of the eldest Hive-Mother.

"Thank you, honored Hive-Mother. We also checked the location of every spacecraft capable of lifting from the surface of Hool and Kamah, even those that were not capable of making the trip to Chud-Loo. Every spacecraft has been accounted for during the time span leading up to the time the missiles hit Chud-Loo. The evidence shows no Hoo-Lii spacecraft were involved in that disaster," the spokesperson said. "We inspected the records of every spacecraft and Hive-Mother.

None contained anything that would suggest involvement in this event."

A hiss echoed off the walls of the shrine. The aroma of relief wafted through the Council.

The spokesperson paused to see if any Hive-Mother wanted to comment. He peered around.

No one spoke.

"We cannot account for one of the fusion explosions. It is possible one came from the fusion device, which had its safety interlocks removed. However, one of the fusion explosives, the first one, contained material not found in the devices used in the planetary defense system. In fact, the materials are not from any system used by Hoo-Lii." The spokesperson referred to his data tablet.

"This weapon contained isotopic ratios not found on Chud-Loo, Hool, or even Kamah. It also appears to have more heavy elements, so it may have come from a star system that is older than the ones we inhabit. This information and the fact we do not know where that explosive came from, raise the possibility of Others—"

The Council collectively squeaked with surprise.

Suh-Joh knew the scholars were noted for being cautious, even conservative in their analysis and research. They had come to the same conclusion as the two original investigators. *So*, she thought. *There may be alien Others out there.*

CHAPTER TWENTY-SIX

THE HIVE OF SUH-JOH

5,102 Year of the Mother.

Suh-Joh rose from her resting-rock, her armored exoskeleton rasping rhythmically on the polished granite. She stepped into an oval of afternoon sunlight illuminating the floor of the great hall. It was warm, almost like the heat of summer. The hall was quiet; the naat-jii had ceased their busy scurrying.

"Attendant," she called, her voice echoing off a wall.

"Yes, oh blessed Hive-Mother?" An attendant emerged from a brown curtained alcove, advancing and dropping into the position of abasement. "What is your wish?"

"Bring Son-Nih." She needed advice from her trusted warrior. She had an idea. It was time to act.

"You called, blessed Hive-Mother?" Son-Nih lowered his scarred and worn aspect into the position of abasement.

"Son-Nih, I need you to leave your warrior-cohort—"

"Oh, blessed Hive-Mother, have I offended you?" Son-Nih pressed his head tightly against the floor and flexed. The armored plates of the exoskeleton pulled apart to reveal vulnerable connective tissue. It was complete submission.

Suh-Joh reached out and touched him gently. "Rise, Son-Nih, rise. You've served me valiantly and well. Unbidden, you've spoken truths I needed to hear, sage words. I value you. I don't want you to die in battle before your time. I have other plans for you. I want you to be my counselor."

"Blessed Hive-Mother, I am but a Chosen-Male warrior, unschooled in the ways of scholars. That is all I know and that's how I serve you." He remained rigidly flexed toward the floor. The odor of his fear hung heavily in the air.

"Yes, you've done that well, and more." Suh-Joh reached out and touched him gently. "I need the benefit of your experience and wisdom. I want you to continue telling me what I need to hear. Let me share my concerns with you. I worry the Council of Hive-Mothers chose to ignore the findings of the scholars."

Beckoning him closer, she pointed to the brown floor covering decorated with the crossed quills of her hive before her. "Sit." She extended her forelimb, indicating the place she wanted him to sit. It was at her side.

Son-Nih moved uneasily. "Oh?" He settled his four hind limbs on the floor covering, moving slowly as though tired.

"I need you to play the role of a retired Chosen-Male, a priest, harmless and free to travel. While doing this, I want you to recruit as many scholars as you can, those disaffected because the Council ignored their report."

"Blessed Hive-Mother Suh-Joh, I have to be sterile to do that." Son-Nih's breathing flaps closed in concern.

Suh-Joh's breathing flaps opened slowly in a gesture that signified approval. "Do you wish to live longer?"

"Of course."

His carapace carried many scars. It was obvious time had caught up with him.

"Would you like to feel young again?"

"Of course. Who wouldn't?"

"That's what you'll get in return for sterility."

"But—" His breathing flaps flared open.

"When did you last mate and produce an offspring?"

"It has been some time—"

"Sterility does not mean you will not still be able to enjoy the pleasure of a brood female, there are hormones for that. I need you free to travel without danger that a Chosen-Male warrior from another Hive might kill you. I need you, as I need those scholars. For you to do that, you must have the odor of a sterile male. Do you understand?"

"Yes, oh blessed Hive-Mother." Son-Nih's breathing flaps flared slightly and emitted the sour odor of fear, defeat.

"Good. Come, let's see if we can get a brood female to coax one last offspring from your valiant warrior's body before I induce sterility." Suh-Joh emitted an odor of encouragement. "And to help you do that, I'll ripen one just for you."

༄

"So, you had difficulty recruiting scholars?" Suh-Joh asked. The great hall was empty except for her and Son-Nih. Spotlights illuminated the battle trophies on the glistening sandstone walls. The curtained alcoves showed no sign of life. The normal backdrop of chittering servants and the buzz of insects was absent. All attendants had been cleared from the hall. Suh-Joh had tightened security.

"Yes, blessed Hive-Mother," Son-Nih said. "Only two."

Her breathing flaps drooped. "Well, I suppose two scholars are better than none."

"The scholars are afraid to show any signs of disloyalty to their own Hives. They thought I was testing their faith and loyalty. These two scholars are convinced the Others exist. They expressed more fear of the Others than their own Hive-Mothers."

His breathing flaps flared in anger. "Perhaps they need a touch of the pricker of pain to refresh their loyalty—"

"You're thinking like a warrior, Son-Nih. I value scholars far more for their ability to delve into the ancient archives of technology and history than to question their loyalty. Send them to me, now. I want to hear their opinions."

Son-Nih left the hall. Moments later, he returned with a contingent of warriors clustered about two unripened females. Both lowered themselves as they approached Suh-Joh. They were the scholars.

One was Sad-Loh, the former scholar of Buk-Tar who led the Hive-Mothers on the Council. Suh-Joh had learned Buk-Tar's assassins were looking for Sad-Loh. Her defection had raised the level of hostility between the eldest Hive-Mother and Suh-Joh; it was another insult, even though unintended.

The other scholar, Lil-Tih, had belonged to the late Nah-Kih. She had expressed a wish for intellectual freedom and her Hive allowed her to leave because it was Suh-Joh who needed a scholar. They remembered Suh-Joh had spared them when she came and killed Nah-Kih.

Son-Nih directed the Chosen-Male warriors to stations at the entrance to the great hall. There would be no interruptions. The two scholars took the position of abasement and remained still and quiet, heads tight against the cold stone floor.

"Welcome, Sad-Loh and Lil-Tih," Suh-Joh said. "You are now under my protection." She gestured for them to rise and pointed to the floor covering with a gesture for them to sit.

"Thank you, oh blessed Hive-Mother. You do us great honor by wanting the knowledge of these humble scholars."

"Tell me, Sad-Loh, what do you really think happened on Chud-Loo?" Suh-Joh asked.

"Oh, blessed Hive-Mother—"

"Sad-Loh, Lil-Tih, and you too, Son-Nih, forgo the honorific during these private discussions. Think of me as a fellow scholar. Talk to me like you would a fellow investigator. Even though I've studied, I confess a weakness in history. Technology draws my attention more strongly. I digress, please, continue." Suh-Joh's breathing flaps closed slowly.

"Oh blessed—" Sad-Loh began.

"Like a fellow scholar, remember?" Suh-Joh made a gesture of friendship and emitted a sweet fragrance, one of comfort.

Nervous, Sad-Loh began. "What happened on Chud-Loo will never really be known unless a witness comes forth. We can deduce what happened from the physical clues left behind and the memory of the planetary defense system...."

Sad-Loh methodically reviewed the evidence, pointing out the items that could not be explained by factional violence and expounded upon the physical data. From time to time, Lil-Tih added a point, but it was obvious that Sad-Loh was the spokesperson for the two scholars.

"So, you see, it was impossible for one or both factions of the Disobedient to destroy each other so completely in this fashion," Sad-Loh said. "Remember, the planetary defense used one fusion device against the comet to deflect it away from Chud-Loo."

"I, too, am convinced Others were responsible," Lil-Tih said. "The evidence is impossible to ignore."

"There's not much new in what you have told us." Suh-Joh stirred, as though restless. "I don't see any overwhelming evidence Others were responsible. Your isotopic data could, as skeptics have pointed out, be due to a meteorite from interstellar space. So, tell me, why are you so convinced that Others were responsible?" She exhibited a trace of impatience and disappointment. "Am I missing some of the evidence?"

Sad-Loh abased again and squeaked, "Perhaps, oh blessed—"

"Please."

"It was the images in the memory of the planetary defense system. Most of the scholars chose to ignore them, convinced that it was used to protect Chud-Loo. Look at this, when we enhanced the targeting and ranging laser reflection, we created a hologram of the comet." She touched a control. An image grew in the air. "Which isn't a comet—"

"Why didn't you show this to the Council?"

"It took a long time to get this enhancement. You see, the other scholars, the skeptical ones, said it was possible for a natural asteroid to have this shape." Sad-Loh touched the controls. The image expanded to a blurred section at one end of the comet. It had a dark, almost circular area.

"What is that?" Suh-Joh asked.

"I'm not sure. I believe it could be some kind of drive, fusion, perhaps. See, this is where the plasma would discharge. It has all the necessary components, even though the arrangement is unusual." Sad-Loh pointed to a bulbous shadow. "This section here, could be living quarters. Do you see this?" She pointed to a fuzzy outline on the side of the comet.

"What is it?"

"Perhaps it is an antenna. It could be a lot of things. Something like this is never seen on an asteroid. They never have structures growing out of them. That's what convinced me. Those feeble-minded, so-called scholars refused to believe that anything was there except noise in the signal."

"Do you have other images?"

"No. The planetary defense system depended upon the radar reflections from the strobing radio navigation beacon for primary acquisition. It only needed one laser ranging reflection to confirm the validity of its aim. That is all there was in its memory."

"From where did this comet come?"

"I extrapolated its course backward as well as I could. It came from deep space. Its course was similar to many comets, except it came in above the plane of the planetary ecliptic."

Suh-Joh carefully scratched herself with a long, sharp spine as she sat unbreathing. Her paat-kli moved to the scratched area.

Son-Nih stirred, clicking his exoskeleton with worry. "If there was one Other out there, could there be more?"

"I just don't know. Possibly. The universe is endless."

Suh-Joh looked up. "Son-Nih, what worries you?"

"Remember, they used a fusion device on Chud-Loo, a weapon of mass destruction on a helpless planet." He paused and gently emitted a whiff of the sour odor of fear before adding, "If they did this once, might they not do it again?"

No one spoke.

Suh-Joh looked from one to the other. Even the idea such a weapon might be used made them afraid. They recalled the horror stories told to them while young, part of their conditioning against using nuclear weapons. No wonder the Council wanted to seize upon an easy solution; they did not want to face the possibility of this nightmare coming to life. It was far easier to believe the Disobedient had wiped themselves out in a fit of madness.

"You may be right. What can we do about it?"

"We can tell the Council—"

"That bunch of inbred females won't face reality. It would distract them from thinking about their next mating cycle," Suh-Joh said. She softened her voice and added, "I'll do what is necessary. There must be some way to find from where the Others came. Scholars, your assignment is to search the archives to find the technology needed to seek out the home of the Others. Remember, the fate of Hool and the Way-of-the-Mother may be in your hands."

Suh-Joh hoped the answer was ready at mandible and would only require the right input to the holo-terminal to find it. She realized it was probably a tedious search with little chance of success. *That is why I recruited these scholars.*

Both scholars abased themselves and responded, "Oh blessed Hive-Mother, we hear and obey you."

Suh-Joh waved their dismissal. "Report back in one cycle of the Children-of-the-Sky. If you need to travel, see Son-Nih so he may arrange the proper protection."

She moved to the resting-rock and draped her four rear limbs over it. She used a long spine to scratch between the armored plates of the skin on her neck where the paat-kli had neglected a few flakes of skin. She was thinking.

Son-Nih started to say, "Oh blessed Hive-Mother—"

"Son-Nih, forgo the honorific when we are alone, please. You wanted to say ..." She paused to emit a soft fragrance, one of acceptance.

"Suh-Joh." Son-Nih hesitated, savoring the ability to squeak out her name in a higher pitch of informality.

"Yes, my dear Son-Nih."

"Using the complex technologies of the past will require many resources. From what area shall we take them?"

"My dear Son-Nih, have you forgotten I now control four Hives directly? That there are at least four more Hives whose fear I can smell from great distance? Every Hive-Mother within my sphere of influence will help us, willingly or not."

"The Council may not look kindly upon the use of more ancient technology."

"I will keep my ears and breathing flaps open. We may have to move quickly if there's any indication of action."

"I'll make sure our Chosen-Male warrior cohorts show their presence in the main connecting tunnels."

"Yes and demonstrate their ability to arrive quickly using the shuttle from the Good-Child. We don't want anyone to forget distance no longer buys safety from my spines." Suh-Joh squeaked amusement.

Son-Nih joined her.

CHAPTER TWENTY-SEVEN

THE HIVE OF SUH-JOH

5,103 Year of the Mother.

"So, Sad-Loh, my scholar, what have you discovered in the archives of our blessed foremothers?"

The day's sunlight had not reached the light shafts leaving the great hall dim. Along the walls, the ancient trophies were but shadowy outlines.

Sad-Loh got down on her forelimbs, preparing for the position of abasement. "Oh blessed—"

"Please, no honorific."

"Yes, I forget. Where to begin?" Sad-Loh squatted on the floor and rocked back onto her hind limbs. She raised her head. "The problem of detecting signs of civilization across interstellar distances is a stiff spine to bend. Since the Others demonstrated a willingness to use fusion explosives in the past, they may use them again and that can be detected. At least, in theory. Let me explain how we could use that ..." She finished explaining what she had learned.

"So, do it." Suh-Joh rippled her spines in a gesture of authority.

"It is not easy. A network of detectors scanning large distances of deep space need to be located far from Hool, away from any area of activity to reduce interference with the faint trace of the electromagnetic pulse associated with a fusion explosion. It must be on the outer fringe of our system."

"Son-Nih, work with scholars, find out what is needed and then do it." Suh-Joh's breathing flaps flared.

"The cost? Don't you want to know what it will cost?" Son-Nih's breathing flaps flared.

"We'll pay it anyway, won't we?"

"You are committed to finding the Others with no care about its cost?"

"If there is anything which can destroy our planet, then we must pay whatever is necessary to prevent it."

Son-Nih made a gesture of abasement as acknowledgment.

Suh-Joh indicated both acceptance and approval.

The records of the project to build the deep-space detection system are very complete. I, Kot-Nih, enjoyed learning how it was done. The scholars, Sad-Lo and Lil-Tih, trained technicians and put them to work learning the long-forgotten technologies of deep space construction. Sad-Lo and Lil-Tih used information from the archives to build the tetrahedral-shaped detection system, which they located at the outer edge of the Hool system. When the scholars found it necessary to provide metals and minerals that were difficult to find on the long-exploited surface of Hool, they sought them in the asteroid belt.

Over time, Suh-Joh's Hive developed an extensive mining operation in the asteroid belt, which supplied Hool with materials that once had been scarce and costly. Suh-Joh's space activities stimulated more interest in space transportation. As a result, demand for her off-planet resources grew.

The resources produced from the space activities of Suh-Joh impressed even those who ran the orbital station above Hool.

Everyone thought the only new source of resources was on the distant planet Kamah, under the double sun of the Daughter system. Suh-Joh proved otherwise.

Nevertheless, Suh-Joh's industry and wealth aroused jealousy. The Council of Hive-Mothers secretly called a meeting to discuss her growing power.

On the first day, they reviewed Suh-Joh's use of high technology equipment and computers. At the start of the meeting on the second day, Buk-Tar asserted her position as Eldest Hive-Mother and led the discussion on what should be done about Suh-Joh.

"That abomination Suh-Joh now uses the ancient forbidden technologies. Does that not mean she has stepped beyond the Way-of-the-Mother?" Buk-Tar asked.

The more conservative Hive-Mothers raised their breathing flaps, twitching them in disapproval. They held Suh-Joh in reluctant respect for her support of the Way-of-the-Mother. In addition, many used the resources she supplied and had also taken the first steps to expand their business interests into space. Those who had profited from dealing with Suh-Joh had already informed her of this meeting.

"Eldest and most honored Hive-Mother, we do not believe she has stepped beyond the Way. And she gives often to the Shrine-of-the-Mother," a conservative Hive-Mother said.

"Does she not use the technologies from the past?"

"She has made no secret of what she is doing or why. She uses it because she does not agree with the findings of this Council. She is determined to seek out the Others."

"Is that not an affront to this Council?"

"She is doing so at her own expense."

"Bah. She has the brains of a naat-jii. Let her waste her own resources chasing ghosts among the stars. She has ignored our findings. That demonstrates she is not fit for the Council. So, let us take up the issue of her right to sit among us."

"Eldest and most honored Hive-Mother. That can only be done in an open Council meeting. This is not such."

There was a faction of the Hive-Mothers who feared what Suh-Joh might do should they ban her from the Council. If this came to pass, she could hold them responsible, which might lead to civil war. In addition, those who profited in dealing with her, held her in respect. They too, did not want war, for that would disrupt their business activities.

"Leave then, if you wish to lick her feet like the paat-kli feasting on your dead skin," Buk-Tar said.

The Council went silent.

It was at that moment Suh-Joh appeared. "Hoo-Lii." She inflected her greeting with an element of challenge. "Buk-Tar. You have dishonored this Council. You have violated the rules you have sworn to uphold. You are no longer fit to lead the Council or even your own Hive. Once again, you must step aside."

"Hoo-Lii. Never."

"May the Spirit-of-the-Mother bless your offspring. Your actions are heresy against the Way-of-the-Mother. I choose to enforce the Way." Suh-Joh rose up on her two rear hind limbs.

"You abomination, you user of obscenities, I'll never step aside for you." Buk-Tar rose up and rippled her spines.

"You are wrong on those accusations, like much of what you do. You do not step aside for me. You will step aside because you no longer honor the Way-of-the-Mother. By the time the two Children-of-the-Sky set today, you will ripen a daughter, or I will ripen one for you." Suh-Joh emitted an odor containing an element of challenge. She raised her spines into a halo of challenge.

"You cannot—" Buk-Tar's voice rose to a snarl.

"I can, and you will. At this moment, my Chosen-Male warriors occupy your hive. Your unripened ones have already made the gift of water to me. You no longer have a Hive; it is now under my control. You have your choice; die either at the spines of your chosen successor, or on the open surface of Hool. You no longer have a Hive, nor a place on this council."

Collectively the Council of Hive-Mothers hissed.

Buk-Tar leaned back and called out in a voice high-pitched and shrieking, "Destroy her. She's an abomination. She cannot do this, it's against the Way-of-the-Mother." Her breathing flaps flared wide open.

"Again, you are wrong. The Way-of-the-Mother provides for the survival of the fittest in a world free from weapons of mass destruction. It does not exist to preserve those who would hide behind the Council when she is no longer fit to lead. The Council exists to solve problems without violence and act as an agent to protect the Way-of-the-Mother. I only tried to find the source of those weapons. The users of those obscenities must be rooted out and destroyed."

"Lies, lies, and more damned lies. You are seeking vile secrets of the past to conquer and rule Hool in your foul image."

"Your mouth is filled with untruths. Your aroma has the taste much like that of naat-jii dung." Suh-Joh's breathing flaps closed tightly as though near a bad odor. "Every bit of information I've obtained from the ancient archives is on the holo-terminals. Use it and judge. This Council meeting is over." She glanced around the meeting area.

The Hive-Mothers collectively made the faintest hint of the gesture of abasement usually reserved only for the Eldest Hive-Mother. This time it was directed toward Suh-Joh. They had acknowledged her power and ability to lead the Council.

"Hoo-Lii," Buk-Tar screamed in the fashion of a traditional challenge. "You cannot. I'll strike you down." She heaved her bulk and rose to her two hind limbs.

"Try." Suh-Joh stood fully erect on hind limbs as though in the position for personal combat. She rippled her spines. The quills on the fringe of her mating-flap erected. She moved, with the quickness only seen in young Chosen-Male warriors, to the position halfway between them. "Do not try me, for you will force me to violate the peaceful nature of the Shrine-of-the-Mother." Her spines rose, and her breathing flaps pulsated rapidly. She lowered her head as though preparing to enter combat.

Buk-Tar flinched and retreated.

"You live until the two Children-of-the-Sky set in the west." Suh-Joh slowly looked around the Council at each member, one by one. There were no challenges. She left as abruptly as she had arrived.

CHAPTER TWENTY-EIGHT

5,110 year of the Mother.

"So, the deep-space monitoring system comes online today?" Suh-Joh looked out over the large cavern from a high ledge that contained the warrens of the engineers and administrators.

Harsh light cast stark shadows on the rough-hewn rock walls and the cavern's flat, polished floor. Nearby, at one side, sat the exploratory ship, the Good-Child, which was undergoing a re-fit. Two new shuttles —small and fragile—clung to the side of the Good-Child like tiny offspring. It looked small in the giant cavern, now empty of the heavy lift shuttles used in the burgeoning space freight business.

Over the years, Suh-Joh's hive had built several massive space freighters at her manufacturing facility in the asteroid belt. In the process, she had branched out into other areas of construction, increasing her resources. Her hive now dominated interstellar transport. She remembered her debt to the priests at the Shrine-of-the-Mother and tithed an ever-increasing amount of food and resources each year.

"Yes, oh blessed Hive-Mother Suh-Joh." The engineer's body quivered. He was an unripened male who had become a specialist in spacecraft construction. "All of the receptors are now in orbit around Hekta."

Hekta was the most distant planet of their system, a ball of frozen gases, which had absolutely no life upon it. "They are ready for use." The engineer had supervised the construction of the receptors in this cavern, which had been lifted to orbit and then transferred to the distant space station.

Suh-Joh sought regular updates on the status of the project and had little patience for the normal delays of large construction projects. "So, tell me again what additional information can be gathered from this technological marvel that you have constructed." She emitted an odor that only the most powerful dared use.

"Oh blessed Hive-Mother, it is not for me to describe the capabilities of the system. I am but an engineer who assembled this creation under the direction of Sad-Loh and Lil-Tih. Much of this is beyond my comprehension." He rippled his breathing flaps in the direction of Sad-Loh who stood quietly to one side. "I am a builder, one who turns the dreams of scholars into reality."

Suh-Joh turned toward Sad-Loh. "Well, my little scholar, what have you created? Tell me, what can it do?" She spoke gently and emitted a fragrance of comfort.

Sad-Loh flexed in abasement to Suh-Joh. Even though she had explained the system to her before, Suh-Joh never tired of hearing about its development. "Oh, blessed Hive-Mother, the Ear-to-the-Universe is a simple collection of listening devices. It looks for the signature of a fusion explosion. At the same time, we may be able use it to find those strange portals that allow us to jump through openings in space-time faster than the speed of light.

"In the past, we knew only of two points, which were found by accident and after much tedious calculation and searching. Theory says the Ear-to-the-Universe will hear echoes from undiscovered transfer points when the fabric of space-time flexes as a ship jumps through."

"Have you found more of these strange points?"

"Not yet. If Others come, we will know their entry gates."

Suh-Joh's spines rose for just a moment. She wafted the odor of approval. "I see, my little scholar. Yes, we do indeed need to know that.

I look forward to a report each day on what you learn from listening to the universe."

"Oh blessed Hive-Mother, please be aware we may listen to empty space for a long, long time before we hear anything that speaks to us."

"Yes, my little one, of that I am aware."

Thirty years passed before the Ear-to-the-Universe picked up a faint signal that might have come from fusion explosions. The source was far from Hool and in a direction away from any of the worlds they visited. The scholars were uncertain as to their origin. Their distance made them appear to pose no danger to Hool; at least that was the opinion of the Council of Hive-Mothers.

These infrequent pulses continued for a twenty-year period and then ceased. Over time, the faint pulses provided a direction, but not an exact distance to their source.

"Sooner or later, the Others will reveal themselves." When Suh-Joh spoke those words, little did she realize how much time would pass before anything more was heard.

Bit by bit, Suh-Joh went from eagerly awaiting each day's report to a brief review of the annual summary. During this time, the astronomers made other discoveries of distant quasars, pulsars, and gamma ray bursters, adding to their knowledge and wonder of the universe.

The exploratory ship, the Good-Child, ventured forth and confirmed several new transfer points revealed by the Ear-to-the-Universe. None of the voyages encountered civilizations or heard any of the electromagnetic radiation from an inner planet. No system possessed planets offering any hope of conditions suitable for colonization.

Eventually, the Ear-to-the-Universe found a transfer point adjacent to a triple-sun system. Even though it had no habitable planets, it was near the system from where the faint electromagnetic pulse had originated. In the 5,200th year of the Mother, Suh-Joh ordered the installation of a monitoring station at the outer limits of the triple-sun system to watch the nearby system. The monitoring station focused on the system in which the astronomers believed the Others lived.

$$\sim$$

Lest you think that Suh-Joh enjoyed uninterrupted success in her activities on Hool during this time, let me, Kot-Nih, share with you a closely guarded secret. As you know, Suh-Joh had scholars continually searching through the ancient archives, seeking knowledge to prepare for the eventual meeting with the Others. It was during these searches that one of her scholars discovered something of immense value....

$$\sim$$

"Oh, blessed Hive-Mother, I seek a meeting with you at your earliest convenience," Lil-Tih requested over a communication link. Since the topic was not mentioned, it was clear she had found something important, too important to discuss via insecure means of communication.

"I shall send a shuttle for you," Suh-Joh said. "Go to the landing area immediately."

Before the Mother-of-the-Sky settled below the mountains, Lil-Tih appeared before Suh-Joh. She abased herself. "Oh blessed Hive-Mother—"

"Please, forgo the honorific. The hall is sealed." Suh-Joh waved her forelimb. The hall, light reflecting brightly off the yellow sandstone walls, was empty. No attendants, no Chosen-Male warriors. "Tell me what you have found."

"It is a technology for making hormones. The hormones of life, juvenile hormones."

"Are you sure?" Suh-Joh realized it was a secret desired by every Hive-Mother—and the Disobedient. In fact, she realized, it was technology that could completely revolutionize their society. "Does anyone else know about this?"

"Mother-forbid." Lil-Tih abased herself again. "I removed the record from the archives and replaced it with one that discusses the research and enumerates its failures." She raised her head to glance at Suh-Joh. "I hope you forgive me for this deception."

"I think I understand." Suh-Joh stared at her scholar. "Can you set up a facility to make these hormones?"

Lil-Tih rose as though proud of what she had found. "Of course. It is a biological process. The equipment required to purify the hormones are enzyme-keyed membranes." It was known technology.

"Work with Son-Nih." Suh-Joh hesitated. "I will have him provide you a safe place to work, in an area where none but my most trusted Chosen-Male warriors go. Make those hormones and I will give you your wish."

"My wish?" Lil-Tih rose higher. "What is it I wish?"

"You have always wanted to be ripened, to be a Hive-Mother," Suh-Joh said. "I will do that for you, even if I have to spill blood to get a hive for you."

CHAPTER TWENTY-NINE

When I, Kot-Nih, first read of this, I envied Lil-Tih. But later, I felt sorry for her. Apparently, it took many tries before Lil-Tih and Son-Nih produced a synthetic version of the hormone that warded off aging. It took time to prove it worked. Son-Nih was among the first to receive it, soon followed by Suh-Joh and her two scholars.

It wasn't long before the results of these activities caught the attention of the old priest who had been Suh-Joh's first advisor. Perhaps it was Son-Nih's new lease on life—maybe jealousy; perhaps the old priest believed his ultimate loyalty lay with the priests at the Shrine-of-the-Mother. Whatever the reason, he passed word on about the strange rejuvenations to the priests at the Shrine-of-the-Mother.

"You are summoned to a council of inquiry by the priests at the Shrine-of-the-Mother," the messenger said. "You are to bring your counselor, Son-Nih, along with your scholars, Lil-Tih and Sad-Loh."

"What is this about?" Suh-Joh asked. She rose from her resting-rock to her full height. "Why am I summoned?"

"I am but a messenger. I do not know." The wizened priest lacked one limb and had scars from the battles of his youth as a Chosen-Male warrior. He bore no signs of being a cohort leader, nor having any great intelligence. He flexed stiffly with just a hint of abasement before leaving.

In preparation, Suh-Joh alerted the cohort leaders of her Chosen-Male warriors to prepare shuttles for travel should there be trouble. That done, she went to the Shrine-of-the-Mother.

"Hoo-Lii." Suh-Joh abased herself before the semi-circle of priests gathered in the alcove that lay off the valley and was used for the Council of Hive-Mothers' meeting. "I am here, to submit myself to your summons and answer your questions." Dense clouds filled the sky, making the interior of the alcove dim and shadowy.

"There are things out of the past which we welcome." An old stooped priest at the center of a line of priests waved a mandible. It was the head priest. "And there are those which we do not. Our concern is to protect the Way-of-the-Mother. Anything which would change the Way and destabilize our society, is forbidden."

At the word forbidden, Suh-Joh felt a cold spine of fear touch her. That word was always associated with the opprobrium of obscene and perverse, which in many cases had led to someone's death.

"I understand. As a humble follower of the Way-of-the-Mother, I seek your guidance in these matters." *What*, she thought, *is this about?*

"We see that your counselor and scholars appear to have a benefit reserved solely for Hive-Mothers. They seem younger than when they were here last. What is the reason for this?"

Spirit-of-the-Mother preserve me, they know, Suh-Joh thought. *Do I tell them the truth? Or do I attempt to deceive them? Truth, for it does not spin an entangling web.*

"Most honored guardians of the Way." Suh-Joh flexed again in abasement. "I have found a way to make the juvenile hormone which confers the gift of life upon myself and my trusted assistants. It came from something we found in the archives beneath the Shrine-of-the-Mother." She held her position.

"This we already know," the head priest said. "We also know the record was replaced with something other than the original, by her. It was one of our most closely guarded secrets." He pointed to Lil-Tih. "Why is that?"

Suh-Joh hesitated. The truth, even if it seems like cowardice. "The information was found by my scholar, Lil-Tih, who has served me faithfully and well. If the information was replaced, I accept responsibility for that."

"I see. Yet you were never seen in the archives from whence this information came. Nor were your tracks found in the computers. Nor was your aroma detected near the records."

The head priest swiveled his head to look at his fellow priests. "The Way-of-the-Mother cannot survive if all have access to the gift of life. The unchosen will want to live and refuse to serve. Warriors would resent dying in battle for those who will live on. It would again bring the scourge of Disobedience. That, we know, would be destructive to our society. We cannot allow this to happen."

"The Hive-Mothers garner the juvenile hormone—"

"That is different." The head priest rose on his hind limbs. "If I knew I could live forever, why would I risk my life in battle?" His scars testified to his experience.

"I understand." Suh-Joh felt the icy spine of fear dig ever deeper and sensed the worst was yet to come. "I accept your guidance." *Mercy is all I can ask. If they condemn me as one who uses forbidden technology, I am dead. My bloodline will be gone and my Hive reduced to bare rock.*

"What is your wish? What must I do to preserve the Way-of-the-Mother?" Suh-Joh asked.

The head priest moved uneasily on his resting-rock and leaned his head toward Suh-Joh. "I am disappointed you should stray and become as a Disobedient. You have supported the Shrine-of-the-Mother for many years, and yet, you do this." He rattled his skeleton. "Death or exile is the penalty for disobedience."

The cold spine of fear changed into a giant mandible gnawing at the center of her being.

The room grew still, no one moved.

"Until now, there have been few who have followed the Way with your devotion." His breathing flaps opened as though sniffing out a new course. "Since you did not seek to profit from this technology." He uttered the word as though speaking a profanity. "Nor caused any other to stray away from the Way, death may be too severe a penalty."

Suh-Joh allowed herself to exhale.

"Exile." The old priest paused. "It would be a suitable sentence." He hesitated and sighed. "We had thought of Chud-Loo, but it has become a frozen wasteland and exile there is the same as a death sentence." He moved as though seeking a more comfortable position. "The Hives on Kamah have bred without restraint and filled all habitable areas. They war among themselves and refuse to accept more exiles, especially Hive-Mothers.

"I believe." The head priest hesitated. "We must find another path, one that will bring you back to the Way."

"Honored guardian, guide me, please." Suh-Joh crouched lower to the ground and flexed every vulnerable connection wide open between the armored plates of her exoskeleton to show her willingness to accept punishment.

"First, you must destroy the means of making the synthetic gift of life." The head priest rose onto his two hind limbs and swiveled toward the silent Lil-Tih. "Including the one who found the path to the knowledge of how it is made."

Lil-Tih collapsed to the ground, breathing flaps wide open. "No, no, I beg you. I have hurt no one. I have only brought life to those who would do more for Hool than any other."

"This is the one?" asked the head priest.

"This is Lil-Tih, my good and valued scholar who has done much to help me defend the Way-of-the-Mother. Please, I beg you, spare her." Suh-Joh's words squeaked out at their highest pitch.

"She does not see the death and destruction that will come if others learn there is the gift of life on demand. All will seek it; many would die to get it. It will pervert those who follow the Way. It would bring back times like our darkest days." The head priest exhaled heavily. "It would corrupt us, even me, and those who sit here at the Shrine." He settled heavily onto his resting stone. "Therefore, Suh-Joh, you must kill her." His voice carried finality.

"Me?" Suh-Joh raised her head.

"Now." Every spine on the old priest's body was erect.

"Spirit-of-the-Mother, forgive me, for I have sinned." Suh-Joh leapt onto Lil-Tih and deployed her klut-shi. "Lil-Tih," she whispered, "I am truly sorry." Her rage rose, angered at the demand placed upon her and her venom boiled forth.

She killed Lil-Tih as quickly as she knew how. *I have sinned*, she thought. *And now I have murdered a dear and loyal servant. I am unworthy.*

"That is but the first step," the head priest said. "You must leave Hool." He settled low on his resting-rock. "You must seek out another world upon which to live."

"Most honored guardian, I beg you," Suh-Joh said. "We have searched far and wide. Even with our Ear-to-the-Universe, the transfer points to star systems are difficult to find. In those visited, none possess planets which are habitable."

"That is your problem. Find one. You have the normal lifetime of an unchosen one to remove yourself. If you are not gone by then, you must ripen your successor. In addition, you are forbidden to ripen any more of your hive."

Fear and hope filled Suh-Joh.

"Leave now," the head priest said. "Return in one cycle of the Children-of-the-Sky, and report what you done to remove the threat to the Way." The head priest rose stiffly and shuffled into a narrow passage in the rock. The other priests, followed, humming the refrain from the prayer "Cycle of Life."

CHAPTER THIRTY

It is not known what Suh-Joh resolved; however, I, Kot-Nih, believe she must have kept some of the gift of life and used it to prolong the lives of Sad-Loh, her other scholar, and Son-Nih, her counselor. They slipped from sight, yet the records later revealed they continued to advise Suh-Joh. It was easy for her to hide them; she had vast underground holdings and space construction facilities in the asteroid belt. Apparently, that is what she did.

The other clue is that Suh-Joh aged far less than the other Hive-Mothers. Perhaps it was genetics, or it was her regime of moderate consumption. Perhaps she secretly ripened large numbers of males. Or ...

However, when Suh-Joh returned to the priestly council of inquiry at the Shrine-of-the-Mother, she brought records of the destruction of the facility where they had made the gift of life. In addition, the priests demanded she ripen Hive-Mothers for two of the four hives under her control and give one-half of her resources to the Shrine-of-the-Mother. They also forbade her to station any of her shuttlecraft on the surface of Hool. It was clear the priests wanted to reduce Suh-Joh's power.

The priests required she appear before them every year for continuing inquiry into her activities and to remind her of the time remaining until she departed Hool. It seemed that not only did they mistrust her, but also they resented the fact there was a gift of life. For it had tempted them, too.

CHAPTER THIRTY-ONE

In 5,227th year of the Mother, Sad-Loh the scholar scurried quickly into Suh-Joh's great hall, puffing and panting through her breathing flaps. "Blessed Hive-Mother Suh-Joh."

As Suh-Joh rose, the plates of her exoskeleton rattled against her resting-rock. Light from the overhead shafts filled the great hall with the orange glow of dawn. "Yes?"

"The Ear-of-the-Universe has detected a series of signals. Many." The scholar exhaled vigorously. "They may be electromagnetic pulses from fusion explosions."

Suh-Joh rose to her full height on her rear limbs. Her spines erected, and her breathing flaps flared. "Many?"

"Well, yes." Sad-Loh's voice conveyed doubt.

"Are you sure?" Suh-Joh's tone was hard.

"Yes, well, no, what I mean is ..." Aromas of uncertainty and fear surrounded Sad-Loh.

Suh-Joh beckoned to Sad-Loh. "Come closer and tell me just what you do mean." She sank down on her resting-rock and flattened her spines. A soft fragrance wafted from her.

Sad-Loh crept forward and looked up. "The signals were very faint and in close sequence. They have all the characteristics of a series of fusion explosions."

"A series?" Suh-Joh's' breathing flaps stilled.

"Yes." The scholar's voice quavered with uncertainty.

"Are you sure?" Suh-Joh's voice was low, gentle.

"Yes," Sad-Loh said. "You see, I have never before recorded a fusion explosion." She hesitated. "We only know what the signal is like from data in the archives from fifty generations ago. These signals have an uncanny similarity to those recordings." She rose on her hind limbs and spread her fore limbs widely. "I believe they are the same."

Suh-Joh exhaled, loud and with force. "Where did they come from? How far is that from here?"

"I need to double check the data, but I believe they came from the Lin-Fed system. That's the bright single star just beyond the triple-star system." Sad-Loh brought her forelimbs together in a gesture of supplication.

"We have a monitoring system near that star."

"Yes, it was installed after the first pulses were generated," Sad-Loh said. "Due to the signal travel time they took to reach us, here on Hool, we missed them. Lin-Fed is almost twice the distance as to Chud-Loo. It is about the distance light travels in thirty-two years. These pulses revealed to the Ear-to-the-Universe there is also a transfer point within the Lin-Fed system."

"What would we need to get there?"

She gestured toward the image on the wall of Suh-Joh's ship, the Good-Child. "That could make the trip."

"I see." Suh-Joh looked up, toward the light shaft. She turned her gaze toward the scholar. "What do you think happened?"

"I'm not sure, because the number of fusion explosions puzzles me. That many fusion explosions would devastate a world of the size of Hool." Sad-Loh quivered. "That planet must have civilized life, if it was the source of the fusion explosions. Either there was war between factions ..." She looked down and shivered. "Or, they were attacked from the outside."

"Their use is an obscenity. Either way, we know there are Others out there." Suh-Joh's spines rose momentarily. "Prepare a formal report with your observations and interpretations for me to take to the Council of Hive-Mothers. They must know about this, even those who doubt the existence of Others."

Suh-Joh betrayed her nervousness by tickling her paat-kli, encouraging it to rasp more vigorously on her skin. Now more than ever, she knew the Others were out there, somewhere.

"Keep looking for the Others. We cannot assume they've destroyed themselves."

Sad-Loh made the silent gesture of assent and left.

At first, the Council of Hive-Mothers was skeptical. They adjourned so their own scholars could review the data. When they reconvened, they were much subdued. At that time, the Council voted to support the search for the Others to expand the deep-space network of detectors.

Suh-Joh's engineers increased the Ear-to-the-Universe's sensitivity to look for more distant transfer points by installing more sensitive receptors. It was a long-planned change because they'd wanted the capability to hear the radiation created by hydrogen fusion drives, which would provide an early warning system to detect the ships of the Others.

After much debate, the Council authorized construction of a planetary defense system based upon fusion pumped lasers, much like the system on the ill-fated Chud-Loo. Once again, fusion weapons came into existence on Hool; this time guarded by a consortium of Chosen-Male warriors from each Hive. The Council took on the collective burden of supporting the detection system.

Suh-Joh's engineers rebuilt the spaceship Good-Child to make it more suitable for exploration of a potentially hostile system, including a powerful weapon whose design came from the archives beneath the Shrine-of-the-Mother. Suh-Joh did not inform the Council of Hive-Mothers the Good-Child was also now a craft capable of battle. She was determined the fate of Chud-Loo would not befall Hool, nor to the Good-Child. The engineers modified the ship so that it could carry a large amount of fuel and supplies, thus greatly extending its range.

CHAPTER THIRTY-TWO

"Where are they?" Suh-Joh asked.

Three years had passed since the Ear-to-the-Universe had heard the drum-roll of electromagnetic pulses, but it had heard no more. There were no sounds of approaching fusion drives, no unknown radio transmissions. Nothing.

"Perhaps they killed themselves," Son-Nih said. "Maybe there are no more planets for them to destroy."

"Please, don't say that." Suh-Joh's spines flared out and she emitted an aroma some might think was fear. "They could find us, here on Hool. We must find them before they find us. Where are they?"

"Patience, my dear Suh-Joh, patience." Son-Nih had accumulated many years and still remained as counselor. "Meantime, we make progress on the Mother's Servant." He referred to the secret project of building a gigantic interstellar transport ship that would become their new hive and refuge.

Suh-Joh emitted a sweet fragrance, one of comfort and acceptance, for she continued to value the sharpness of his mental faculties and his sage counsel. "Sometimes I find it difficult to be patient."

"It is almost as though they don't exist anymore," he said. "Perhaps we worry for nothing."

"I believe the data. The Others exist." Suh-Joh rippled her spines. She turned to Sad-Loh the scholar. "Have we done enough to protect Hool?" she asked with a fierce twitter. "Those obscenities the Others used on Chud-Loo are an affront to the Way-of-the-Mother. That cannot be allowed to happen here."

"We have taken every precaution possible."

"Perhaps. What about our history? Is there anything in it that might guide us and protect us from such a foe?"

"I have searched the archives. There is only speculation Others may have visited in the dim past." Sad-Loh paused. "Yet, we know portals to distant stars exist. Who built them?"

"That does not worry me. Those obscenities do."

"The weapon systems developed in the time of the wars are frightening. It is no surprise the Way-of-the-Mother forbids them. Those weapons would be useful if the Others attack us, but they are of no use in finding them."

"Are there any additional ways to find the Others?"

Sad-Loh made a faint gesture of abasement as she spoke, "I know of none."

Suh-Joh settled onto her resting-rock and closed her eyes.

Sad-Loh rose and left.

Suh-Joh flexed toward the senior priest of the Shrine-of-the-Mother. The summons had been terse, with no explanation.

"There are rumors that your counselor, Son-Nih, lives still." The old priest flared his breathing flaps and raised his spines.

Behind him was a row of priests lining the cavern with military precision. They too, had raised their spines. A beam of sunlight from the Vale of the Shrine-of-the-Mother barely penetrated the rocky alcove. The lichens on the floor were damp and cool. The place felt like death.

This news angers them, thought Suh-Joh. *I will not give them Son-Nih. I gave them Lil-Tih and that grieves me still.* The burden of guilt still lay heavy upon her. "Honored Keepers of the Shrine, I know not from where you gained this fabrication, this tale." She flexed in abasement. "I can assure you that Son-Nih's funeral pyre has been lit. He is no longer among us."

It was true, in a way. For flames had consumed an old warrior, one who had served me well, one whose spines bore the same markings as those of Son-Nih.

She had made sure that Son-Nih was safe, hidden among the asteroids, where he readied the craft that would take her to the stars.

"Then, why do we hear in the words you utter, phrases often used by Son-Nih?" The old priest inhaled deeply as though trying to detect a faint smell, one that might lead to prey.

"I remember his words," Suh-Joh said. "As one who served me well, and I savor his memory. I wish I were to smell his presence again." She flattened her spines. "As all good warriors should be remembered."

In unison, the row of priests against the wall flexed slightly at the acknowledgment of their prior profession. Every priest was a former warrior, many of whom had fought valiantly for Hive-Mothers who had forgotten them.

"Yet," the old priest said. "I still detect his smell when you make your presence known to us."

"True." Suh-Joh extended her forelimb. "I wear a bracelet woven from the quills plucked from Son-Nih. See?" She held her breath, trusting her explanation would work.

The old priest breathed deeply as he stared at her. "Perhaps that is it." He rose onto his hind limbs. "There is the matter of your departure. Soon, it will be time to ripen another Hive-Mother." He referred to the last of Suh-Joh's conquests and the priests' determination to remove her presence from all hives other than her own.

Suh-Joh flexed deeply. "It is the will of the Spirit-of-the-Mother." *First they grow fat on my tithing. Now they want to drive me out and then render me down so they may lard their hides.* She forced her anger below the surface as quickly as it rose. *They want no war over my possessions when I go. They wish only the best for Hool.* "What more do you desire from me?" she asked.

"Go, make your preparations to leave. Either go into exile, or die on the spines of the Hive-Mothers. You have but eight cycles of the Mother-of-the-Sky left."

Suh-Joh flexed low and departed the cavern. *I must honor the Way-of-the-Mother*, she thought. *Even as I deceive its guardians. The completion of my ship, The Mother's Servant, will be close to my time.* Most of the output of the expanded asteroid mining operation had gone into its construction.

Every shuttle that rises from my hive carries more workers and warriors. My hive is almost empty, and the priests of the Shrine-of-the-Mother know it not. Fortunately, the other Hive-Mothers still fear me, for if I need to defend my hive today, I lack the warriors to even delay them.

CHAPTER THIRTY-THREE

Later, I, Kot-Nih, learned during this time Suh-Joh had been deploying her off-planet resources for years to construct a large spaceship, which she called The Mother's Servant. The existence of this giant craft was only discovered after it departed the Hool system, but that comes later. It was many times larger than any previously constructed space-craft, many times larger even than the biggest freighter.

I found out it carried some eight to the fourth Chosen-Male warriors plus crew. It is apparent she trained her warriors in the art of warfare in space long before the ship departed.

Apparently, Suh-Joh built this craft to take her into exile. It also held a large amount of food, equipment, and armaments. It was a formidable vessel, capable of serving as both an interstellar ship and upon arriving at its destination, an orbital station to protect any settle-ment they placed on the surface of the planet below. However, the Council of Hive-Mothers knew nothing of its existence. But I'm getting ahead of myself in this narration about our encounter with the Others.

5,235 Year of the Mother

"Oh blessed Hive-Mother. The exploratory ship has returned with a recording of a fusion explosion," Sad-Loh the scholar twittered.

"Where?" Suh-Joh asked. Her spines erected momentarily, showing the impact of Sad-Loh's words.

"The Lin-Fed star system. It came from the monitoring station in the triple-star system adjacent to the Lin-Fed system."

"After so long. How could anyone survive the previous torment? Was there just one or more explosions this time?"

"Just one, and very small. The monitoring station's ear-to-the-universe clearly picked it out from the background noise. We also heard something else. It sounded similar to the electromagnetic noise made by a fusion drive—a long and sustained signal. It would have to be an immensely large drive for us to hear it at a distance between stars. But the noise of the fusion explosion was unmistakable." The scholar quivered with excitement.

So, Suh-Joh thought. *The Others still exist.*

CHAPTER THIRTY-FOUR

HOOL

5,236 Year of the Mother.

Suh-Joh called a meeting of the Council of Hive-Mothers to reveal her findings. Prior to the meeting, the head priest of the Shrine-of-the-Mother summoned Suh-Joh. "Your time to depart grows near," he said. "Have you chosen a successor?"

"I still hope to find a new world upon which to start a new settlement dedicated to the Way-of-the-Mother," Suh-Joh said. The high pitch of her response did not reflect her inner fear. *So many barren systems, so much empty space. Can I find a new home in time?* She made the gesture of abasement. "As the Spirit-of-the-Mother wills."

"You have a meeting," the head priest said. He flicked a forelimb in the direction of the vale of Shrine-of-the-Mother. "It is time. Go."

As Suh-Joh entered the vale, the late afternoon sun, low and orange, glinted off the armored exoskeletons of the assembled Hive-Mothers.

It was warm in the lush red vale. The click-drone of the purple maa-lii insects was a counterpoint to the hum of the go-liks busy in the background. Their sounds mingled with the almost musical tinkle of water running down the glade's rocky walls. If it had not been for the purpose of the meeting, she would have found it restful.

Truly, thought Suh-Joh. *If this is what Hool was like before the wars, then it was a paradise.* She turned her eyes to the many Hive-Mothers gathered before her, settling into positions of comfort on the widely-spaced resting rocks. How long shall I be able to see this sacred place?

"Hoo-Lii. The report describing the events that took place on Lin-Fed has been on your holo-terminals for one cycle of the Children-of-the-Sky. It was your duty to read and understand it." Suh-Joh glanced over the assembled Hive-Mothers.

The tension of seeing so many eyes watch her with varying degrees of hostility drove away thoughts of finding a new world. Her attention snapped back to the present, to the onerous subject of the Others and the dangers of dealing with this council.

"We must decide what to do about the Others, those alien creatures who use the fusion weapons. We cannot sit and wait, here on Hool, as trusting as a paat-kli on its owner's hide, hoping nothing will happen. We must go forth and learn more about the creatures who use such vile weapons—"

Collectively, the assembled Hive-Mothers exhaled. Odors of fear and anger filled the air. Her call to action was a call to risk exposing themselves to the danger of the Others. No one had ever before asked them to get in harm's way. As the aroma of anger faded, the sour smell of fear still lingered. The Hive-Mothers shifted uneasily, their exoskeletons clicking on their resting rocks.

"Yes, we face danger. Yet we must go outside our system; no longer can we wait until the Others come to us. If they discover Hool, our precious home, then all is lost." Suh-Joh paused and swiveled her head as she took in the assembled Hive-Mothers. *Once they followed me when I was the most powerful of Hive-Mothers. Now I must beg them to protect the Way-of-the-Mother.*

"The spaceship, the Good-Child, has been rebuilt. It now carries technical features we discovered while searching the ancient archives. The crew is trained and ready to go. We shall send the Good-Child to the place of the Others to find out what manner of creatures exist there."

The Council of Hive-Mothers stirred uneasily.

Were they afraid of taking this step to expose themselves to the Others? Suh-Joh wondered.

"Hive-Mother Suh-Joh, do you think it wise to send the Good-Child into the den of the Others? Will that not awaken them to our presence? Would that not imperil Hool and our way of life even more?" Mog-Lih was a young and restive Hive-Mother who had not witnessed Suh-Joh's treatment of Buk-Tar.

Suh-Joh briefly opened her breathing flaps and delicately sniffed to see if the air carried any odor of challenge. There was none. Her concern was genuine.

"Hive-Mother Mog-Lih." Suh-Joh spoke softly and respectfully. *I see no reason to antagonize this young Hive-Mother*, she thought. *I need to build an atmosphere of conciliation within the Council to face the real challenge.* "You ask a good question. It is the same one that once worried me. Now I offer this as a solution: The Good-Child can never return to Hool if in the hands of the Others. If the crew is taken, the ship will destroy itself. It is something we learned how to do from writings in the archives."

The Hive-Mothers breathed a sound of agreement.

"Because of the danger, I armed the Good-Child with a weapon out of the past—"

"Sssss." The Hive-Mothers unanimously responded with an expression of disapproval.

Mog-Lih rose onto two of her hind limbs. "That's against the Way." She emitted a trace of the odor of challenge.

"No," Suh-Joh said. "You are mistaken. The Way-of-the-Mother prohibits weapons of mass destruction on Hool. The Good-Child can never again land on Hool—"

"So the priests have ruled, Hive-Mother Suh-Joh," Mog-Lih said. "What will prevent the weapons on the Good-Child from being used from orbit upon those who displease you?"

Suh-Joh turned toward the Shrine and flexed into the position of abasement. "I swear by the Way-of-the-Mother the weapons on the

Good-Child will never be used against Hool or anyone who lives here. Those weapons exist solely to protect the ship against the Others."

"That is a most solemn oath. How can you assure us your crew will follow your oath and pledge?" Mog-Lih's voice carried the low tones of skepticism.

"Your concern is valid." Suh-Joh paused for a moment as though gathering her thoughts. "Let the crew of the Good-Child come from many Hives. That way it carries no secrets and can never be turned against any one Hive on Hool." She paused again. "Remember, this investigation is being done for the benefit of Hool and the entire Council of Hive-Mothers." She again turned in the direction of the Shrine, raised her head, and rippled her spines for emphasis. "May the Spirit-of-the-Mother guide me and show me the Way."

Heads twisted back and forth; no one spoke.

One by one, the Hive-Mothers made the faintest hint of the gesture of abasement, the traditional sign of agreement given to the Eldest Hive-Mother on the Council. It was grudging acceptance to Suh-Joh's plan. Perhaps they took her demonstration of piety at face value; perhaps they saw no better way, maybe they had faith in their Chosen-Male warriors. After acknowledging her decision, the glade grew still once again.

"How do you propose to select the crew that will ensure the safety of Hool?" Mog-Lih rotated her head to look at the rest of the Hive-Mothers. Waving flaps indicated that they agreed with her question. "Tell us."

"Hoo-Lii, as you wish." Suh-Joh surveyed the Council; now she felt more were with her than against her. "By the time the Children-of-the-Sky next appears, each of you must submit one Chosen-Male warrior and one scholar as candidates for inclusion in the crew of the Good-Child. Let no one doubt my commitment to the Way-of-the-Mother." She paused a moment and flattened her spines fully. "The Spirit-of-the-Mother is sacred," she said, her voice squeaking at its highest pitch.

"The Spirit-of-the-Mother is sacred," came the response from the assembled Hive-Mothers. They too, flattened their spines in the traditional gesture of peace and non-aggression.

For an instant, the feeling of harmony and trust swept through the

Council of Hive-Mothers. The fear of the terrible danger of the technologies out of the past, now installed on the Good-Child, still hung over them.

However, the knowledge the Others had used the most obscene of the forbidden weapons on Chud-Loo—even if its inhabitants were exiles—was more frightening than a heavily armed spaceship. Even if the majority of the Hive-Mothers did not believe Suh-Joh's oath, they would trust their own warriors to protect them. It did not matter what each Hive-Mother chose to believe, it was now the path they had chosen to preserve the fragile peace on Hool.

CHAPTER THIRTY-FIVE

The selection of the crew took longer than Suh-Joh anticipated. Some of the candidates did not have the right skills to crew the Good-Child. Some of the Hive-Mothers used the selection procedure as an opportunity to bully further concessions from Suh-Joh. They forced her to cede disputed territory to them in the name of harmony. After much haggling, the current crew leader of the Good-Child, Not-Joh, was again chosen to lead the expedition due to her experience and record of reliable performance.

Suh-Joh added a priest to the crew. It was her counselor, Son-Nih in his new disguise.

Suh-Joh confided in Not-Joh about her plan for Son-Nih and gave her a secret mission, "You must find me a habitable world, and soon. If the world of the Others is suitable for habitation, I want you to take over the ship and keep that knowledge from the Hive-Mothers."

"I understand," said Not-Joh. "Does Son-Nih?"

"Absolutely." Suh-Joh emitted a strong aroma of command.

Once the Good-Child returns, thought Suh-Joh. I will choose a course of action at that time. I have many resources in space and the finest Chosen-Male warriors on Hool. I do not want to die, but I will not violate the Way-of-the-Mother.

Worried the electromagnetic signature of the Good-Child's fusion drive might reveal itself during interplanetary travel, Suh-Joh's scientist equipped it with multiple ion drives. The ship now looked like a long-stemmed flower—one that had barely opened—with each ion drive unit resembling a petal.

Prior to departure, the crewmembers presented themselves to the Council of Hive-Mothers for questions about the mission. Suh-Joh knew that many of the Hive-Mothers still did not trust her. Why should they? Deceit and treachery were time-honored traditions they proudly followed. The Way-of-the-Mother was the only glue that kept the Hoo-Lii society together.

"So, you will depart for the system of the Others via a transfer point deep in space. How do you know this transfer point will take you where you want to go?" Mog-Lih had become a spokesperson for the growing group of Hive-Mothers opposed to Suh-Joh. It was apparent she had ambitions to lead the Council. She was also technologically illiterate.

"Honored Hive-Mother Mog-Lih, the Good-Child has made many jumps through the transfer point to both Chud-Loo and Kamah. Therefore, we know this gate works," Not-Joh said. She was an unripened female and the ship's pilot-navigator. "It resonates at our destination."

"I asked you about the transfer points."

"We found the new transfer points the same way as the old ones. An exploratory scout craft traveled to the triple-star system adjacent to Lin-Fed and detected its location. There were no problems. We have no reason to expect anything different, as long as the Spirit-of-the-Mother guides us." The pilot-navigator flexed slightly in the gesture of abasement.

"So you will go to this unknown star system by jumping through an untested transfer point to meet with these unknown Others?" Mog-Lih twittered in a low and unfriendly tone. "This is your basis for telling me you know what you are doing?"

"Honored Hive-Mother, it is near a tested transfer point. The fabric of space-time in this area appears similar to other areas." The pilot-navigator hesitated. "You are right, we have not used this point before."

"Why haven't you tested this transfer point?"

"We chose not to send a message announcing our presence."

Mog-Lih appeared to think about the answer before speaking again. "What will you do once there?"

"The scholars estimate the transfer point is adjacent to the Fed-Lin's cometary belt, well above the plane of the planetary ecliptic," the pilot-navigator said. Her voice was muffled while she was in the position of abasement. "Once through the transfer point, we will approach the planet of the Others using the ion drive."

Mog-Lih appeared puzzled by the answer. "How far is it, little unripened one? And how long will that take?"

"It will take almost as long as it takes Hool to make a half an orbit around the Mother—less than half a year."

"Why so long?"

"We must approach the Others slowly, quietly, so they do not detect our presence. Like a hunter catching a daa-lii. Rest assured the Good-Child will never return if taken by the Others. Still, we wish to return with the knowledge of what they are," the pilot-navigator said.

This Hive-Mother is a fool, she thought. *What's the point in going if we bring nothing back?* Belatedly, she made the gesture of abasement. "That is the wish of the Council."

"Careful, little unripened one, you will not make the voyage if you do not show me the proper respect." Mog-Lih's voice pitched low and dangerous.

"Hive-Mother Mog-Lih," Suh-Joh said. "Many of the answers to your questions are in the report on your holo-viewer. Allow me to have my scholars show your scholars where these answers are in the report. Perhaps they will provide you with more details." She softened her remark with a gesture of peace and a whiff of an odor of agreement.

Mog-Lih's breathing flaps briefly twitched as she sniffed the air. "I see your point. Let us move to more important items. Little unripened one, what will you do once you arrive within the planetary system of the Others?"

"Honored Hive-Mother Mog-Lih, we shall survey the system, plot the orbits of the planetary bodies, and look for the home of the Others. Once we find it, we shall approach and gather as much information about them as possible. How many, how they live, and what kind of technology they use." The pilot-navigator flexed into a position of abasement again.

"That course of action makes sense. I will review the report and reserve my right to call you before the Council again for further questions," Mog-Lih said. Her voice rang loud in the silent vale.

"The Good-Child departs when the two Children-of-the-Sky next rise. There will not be time for another meeting of the Council of Hive-Mothers to discuss the voyage of the Good-Child." Suh-Joh flexed her breathing flaps and emitted a faint whiff of agreement. "Please, you agreed this would be your chance to question the crew. Ask what you will."

"Who shall represent the Council on the Good-Child?" Mog-Lih asked. She briefly raised her spines before flattening them.

"Oh most blessed Hive-Mother Mog-Lih, it is I, Har-Lih. I have represented the Council on many occasions previously. In your collective wisdom, you have seen fit to appoint me to this position. If there is any concern you wish me to investigate, I will. As a representative of your Honors, I have free access to the entire Good-Child. I will protect your interests." As the tiny unripened female spoke, she abased herself with the practice that came from long service to the Council.

"How will you be able to do that?"

"Honored Hive-Mothers, it is my duty. I will follow it and obey the Way-of-the-Mother. You have assigned two Chosen-Male warriors to protect and assist me. That is sufficient on the Good-Child, for most of the crew are unripened ones. I am your instrument, your will and your eyes. As the Spirit-of-the-Mother guides me, I shall protect your interests on this voyage."

The Hive-Mothers stirred in response to Har-Lih's words.

"Yes, I remember your prior service. Are there others who wish to question this servant of the Council?"

The Council remained silent.

Suh-Joh sensed traces of a fragrance of comfort. It was time to end the meeting. She gave a signal.

A chant broke the silence. It was the sterile Chosen-Male priests singing a prayer used to bless the crops. The chant was an old and well-recognized wish for a fruitful outcome of their endeavor. The priests marched before the Council of Hive-Mothers and formed a line where they finished the prayer chant.

A priest stepped forward, abased himself, and prayed: "May the Good-Child be like a seed cast upon fertile ground with water. May it sprout and grow, to bring forth riches and fruit. For it is a start of a new path, for the Way-of-the-Mother shall grow and spread throughout the Universe. May this Council share in the riches and fruit of their efforts, may the Spirit-of-the-Mother nurture you."

The priest waved his forelimb and opened a mandible. A cloud of immature daa-lii insects rose into the sky. The red fluttering creatures, a staple in their diet, were a symbol of food, harvest, and prosperity. It was an ancient and rarely invoked blessing.

The more conservative Hive-Mothers flattened their spines, making a brief gesture of abasement. They closed their eyes and breathing flaps in peaceful submission. They squeaked out a collective response and emitted a pungent fragrance of nostalgia.

"... May the Spirit-of-the-Mother nurture us,

May the Way-of-the-Mother prevail and guide us,

For the Word of the Way has been spoken."

Thus the meeting of the Council of Hive-Mothers ended on a serious and solemn note, reaffirming the Way-of-the-Mother.

Suh-Joh, like all Hive-Mothers, feared the unknown and the Others. Her plea to the Spirit-of-the-Mother to make the voyage of the Good-Child successful was sincere. For that brief moment, the Hive-Mothers were at peace with one another.

CHAPTER THIRTY-SIX

5,237 year of the Mother

"May the Way-of-the-Mother prevail and guide us ..." The priest's prayer for a safe voyage echoed through the Good-Child as it neared the transfer point through space-time. The ship's power generator hummed more loudly as its output rose to a maximum. The whole ship vibrated as the resonator created the force field that unlocked the gate between the stars.

Ping.

A solitary note rang through the craft. Lights dimmed. The power generator groaned under the demand. The cubical gate of the transfer point appeared, and the Good-Child entered into a place that was neither space nor time but a strange collapsed combination of the two. The ship's computer system shut down as the ship slid across a cusp of space along a gravity string, the nowhere between here and there.

A kaleidoscopic flash of color announced the re-melding of the fabric of space-time as the ship eased back into normal space amid a totally different sea of stars.

They had arrived in the Lin-Fed system, the home of the Others.

The strangeness of the jump across space-time disoriented the ship's crew. Even experienced travelers hated the feeling induced by the transfer point. Many of those making their first jump through space-time voided their bowels. The sharp, sour smells of fear and loathing mingled with the pungent aromas of fresh fecal pellets. The air circulation system clanked as it brought additional filters online. Slowly, awareness and concentration returned.

"Spirit-of-the-Mother, please tell us we arrived safely," Not-Joh called out. As her nausea and disorientation eased, her concentration returned. The aromas of arrival began to fade.

She touched the controls to reset the computer. The control room was dark except for the computer's flashing warnings of shut down. As it ran through its check out sequence, Not-Joh did mental exercises to force her thinking into focus. One by one, the floating shapes in holographic image of the ship returned to the comforting red of normal operation.

"Normal operation sequence initiated," the ship's computer announced. "System on standby."

Not-Joh initiated a series of validity checks to reassure herself this technology from the past had again survived the jump. She released her breath when she saw it had.

"Status of main power generator?"

"Operating at one-eighth capacity," the computer said in an impersonal yet quite familiar voice.

"Condition of ion drive?"

"Capable of sustained acceleration at normal output."

"Navigation system status?"

"Confirming location. Ship is on a course at right angles to the planetary orbits and above the ecliptic of the Lin-Fed system. Velocity within acceptable range. Show precise orientation?"

Not-Joh waved a mid-limb. "Show orientation."

A holographic image of the Good-Child shrank to display its navigation vectors. The jump had put them further inside the system than she had expected, but they were above its plane. There were no cometary or asteroid bodies nearby.

They were safe.

"Activate the ion drive. Low output." Not-Joh gave further instructions to the computer.

The Good-Child began to move.

"Bring course parallel to the plane of the planetary ecliptic. Set a course for the center of the Lin-Fed system. Low energy course change, increase velocity." Not-Joh scanned the immediate region of space, seeking cometary bodies to learn their orbits around the sun. Acceleration built to one gravity and stabilized.

Not-Joh gave the computer instructions, "Begin passive scanning of the system to locate the planetary bodies." She knew it would only be a matter of time before the computer built up an inventory of planets. It reported the existence of eight planets, which she was sure, accounted for most of the system's total mass. In several days the sensors had identified those asteroids in the belt that lay ahead of their course. The system spotted asteroids down to the size that0 would be a threat to their ship. The ship's beam weapons would deal with those of a smaller size.

꩜

The Good-Child entered the asteroid belt, which marked the region of the system between the gas giant planets and the inner planets where Not-Joh expected to find the home of the Others, when the computer sounded an alarm.

"Look, Har-Lih, there." Not-Joh pointed at the holo-image.

There was a faint spot of light to which the computer had plotted a faint green line. It was adjacent to one of the gas giant planets whose orbit they'd already crossed during their drop toward the inner planets.

"What is it?" She started to read the symbols associated with the point of light.

"It's radiation from a fusion reaction."

"Is it one of those obscene weapons?"

"No. It's an operating fusion reactor. Probably, a fusion drive," Not-Joh said. "I think we've found the Others."

"But that planet is a gas giant. Surely it's not their home?" Har-Lih adjusted the sensors. "It has random and broad-spectrum electromagnetic emissions. Its planetary conditions are inhospitable."

"Even its satellite moons are far too cold for life to evolve. What they are doing there? Should we watch them?"

"Yes, but quietly," Har-Lih said.

"Computer, cut the ion drive to zero output, reduce all electromagnetic and radiative emissions. Silent running condition, warn the crew." The Good-Child became dark. It was rigged to look and act like an ancient, dead comet hurtling inward from the outer reaches of the planetary system to orbit the system's star. The battle station warning system sounded an alert throughout the ship, an automatic response to their stealth mode. As systems shut down, the instruments reported the shutdown had minimized the ship's electronic signature.

"Continue scanning the rest of the system. Concentrate on the inner planets, locate the home of the Others." Not-Joh wanted the crew to continue looking for those who had used fusion explosives.

The ship's powerful instruments focused on the source of emissions and used repetitive scanning and signal averaging techniques to concentrate the signals and build up an image of their source. The image in the holo steadily grew more substantial.

"Well, it looks more like an asteroid," said Har-Lih.

"Look. See at its far end, do you see the glow? It's a source of infrared emissions. That's never seen on an asteroid. It must be the fusion drive or the reactor's heat exchanger."

"If you say so. I'm not as experienced as you in examining these types of images. How big is it?"

"I don't know yet. Computer, superimpose a scale," said Not-Joh. As soon as she spoke, a scale appeared below the image in the holo-viewer. Numbers crawled along the scale. "Sacred Mother, it is big."

"Are you sure that is the source of the emissions? It is many times larger than the Good-Child. It looks more like a large asteroid," Har-Lih said. "Maybe it's a ship that has landed on an asteroid."

Not-Joh touched a control. The holo-image grew larger. There was no sign of a separate ship moving within the vicinity of it. "I think the size of their ship tells us a lot about their technology. That ship must require a lot of fuel." She stared hard at the image.

Why, she thought, would they make it so Mother-sacred large? What are they carrying? Is it a freighter or a battleship? She slumped into the hunched-over body crouch typical of one deep in concentrated thought.

"What is it?" Har-Lih asked.

"Perhaps it is a mining ship," Not-Joh said. "Gathering fuel to power their society." She paused. "A ship that size would carry an enormous amount of fuel and their society would generate a signal that would be obvious. Computer, scan inner planets for radiation emissions."

Four data tables appeared as an overlay on the holo-image. All the numbers were in normal red. The showed no sign of a civilization using vast amounts of fusion power.

"Then why do they have such a huge ship?" She touched a control and the data tables disappeared.

"Maybe they gather fuel for their fusion bombs—" Har-Lih began.

"No." Not-Joh snapped. "Why build a ship that could bring material for enough bombs to destroy their world a thousand times over ..." She straightened up. "It is not for bombs; it's a fuel tank on the ship. That must be it," she said. "They don't know about transfer points. They have to drive across the distance between the stars. They don't know how to open the cusp of space along a gravity string. They are less advanced than us. In fact ... Computer, does that ship have radiation screens?"

"No screens detected. Ship is emitting many different types of radiation, typical of low efficiency energy conversion."

"It is likely they cannot see us, except perhaps in the visible wavelengths." Not-Joh continued to adjust the sensors.

"Why do you say that?"

"Their own radiation aura is so powerful it should mask our emissions, even those from the ion drive. Let us set a course directly toward the center of the Lin-Fed system." Not-Joh twitched his breathing flaps. She was nervous, even afraid. These were the Others. They used fusion explosives and that made them dangerous.

Where in the name of the Mother, Not-Joh thought, *do they come from?* Even after extensive scanning, the system had not revealed its secret. The scanners had not detected the typical electromagnetic radiation that came from busy planets.

Where is the home of the Others?

CHAPTER THIRTY-SEVEN

Ping!

The computer issued a warning signal. "Electromagnetic emissions detected. Appear to be non-random."

"From where?" Not-Joh asked.

"From this planet," the computer said. A brilliant blue and white planet appeared on the holo-image. A message scrolled across that identified it as the third planet from the star with the cryptic notation. A brilliant blue and white planet appeared on the holo-image.

"What kind of signal?" Not-Joh asked.

The computer immediately responded: "The electromagnetic emissions appear to be in a simple analog format and quite weak."

"Compare them to those coming from the ship orbiting the gas giant?" Not-Joh asked.

"They do not have the same characteristics."

"Tell me what is known about this planet."

"Water covers the majority of the planet's surface. High oxygen content, high probability of organic life developing, capable of supporting large numbers of life forms—"

"Compare it with Kamah," Har-Lih said. This planet was beginning to sound like something of value.

"The Lin-Fed star has a similar luminosity as the 'A' star of the Sister system." The computer referred to the brighter of the two stars. The Hoo-Lii colonists occupied the planet that orbited the lower luminosity star, since Hool, their home planet, had a similar star of low luminosity. "The planet orbits further out, has more water than Kamah and is slightly larger in size, with a greater concentration of oxygen, thus implying a more biomass—"

"Is it suitable for Hoo-Lii life?" Har-Lih said.

"Data insufficient for definitive answer. High probability the planet could support Hoo-Lii life forms."

Har-Lih and Not-Joh both hissed with excitement. They had found a habitable world, which could potentially be a treasure.

"Change course. Set it for this planet. Minimum acceleration for course change," Not-Joh said.

"Do not let the Others detect our flight to this planet," said Har-Lih.

"Oh, yes. I'll be careful."

"We must find out if the third planet is suitable." Not-Joh recalled Suh-Joh's secret orders.

If it were a habitable planet, she would send the message as soon as they exited the transfer point on their return. Suh-Joh had to know about this planet.

The Good-Child turned and headed toward the spot in space where they would meet the third planet.

"Look, the asteroid ship is diving into the upper atmosphere of the gas giant planet. Surely it's not capable of entering its gravity well?" Har-Lih pointed to the faint image of the spaceship orbiting the planet. It was the first change in the orbit of the Others' asteroid-like spaceship in some time. The computer projected the trajectory of the spaceship: It was diving through the atmosphere.

Not-Joh realized how little Har-Lih must understand about spacecraft to think that. "The Others must be mining hydrogen for fuel.

They are only skimming through the upper reaches from the planet's atmosphere."

"Does that mean they are about to depart?"

"I don't know. We must keep a watch on them. Let me know if they depart from orbit," Not-Joh said to the computer.

Data flowed in from the ship's observation equipment focused on both the planet and the Others orbiting about the gas giant planet. The more data Not-Joh saw, the more certain she became the Blue Gem had a benign environment. It was unlike any planet, because of its huge seas and evidence of massive amounts of biomass. The level of excitement in the Good-Child rose. She knew the crew had expectations for advances in status for the discovery of such a treasure.

"The Others are departing from the gas giant planet."

"Are you sure?" Not-Joh asked.

"Yes. An increase in their velocity and their course is now beyond the moons of the gas giant."

"I see. Project their course using available data."

The computer created a holo-image of the gas giant and projected a course, along with an indication of the degree of uncertainty. The acceleration vector of the Others' ship showed the course wrapped around the gas giant.

"Why are they doing that, Not-Joh?"

"I'm not sure. Perhaps they want to set a course with a high initial velocity and not use their fusion drive. Computer, will the Others' ship course take it to the third planet?"

The holo-image changed, showing the projected course going around the gas giant and extending like an arrow. The holo-image superimposed the cool, blue-white image of the third planet on the course, with the symbol for destination underneath.

"Confirmed," said the mechanical, not quite real voice of the computer, breaking the silence of the control room.

Not-Joh looked at the image with alarm. "Computer, is the Others' ship pursuing us? Is it on an interception course?"

"Negative. The probability the course of the Others' ship will intercept the third planet is high. Its course will not converge with the

Good-Child. If the Others' ship intends to orbit about the third planet, significant changes in velocity are needed. Insufficient data to estimate orbit."

Not-Joh felt a sense of foreboding. Would the crew of the Good-Child meet the Others at the third planet?

CHAPTER THIRTY-EIGHT

"Look at these data." Not-Joh rippled her breathing flaps.

The Good-Child's control center was quiet and the status icons on the walls glowed red, indicating all was well. The holographic projection, suspended before the pilot and navigator's resting pads, contained a blue and white streaked globe—it was the third planet of the Lin-Fed system, which they called the Blue-Gem. Below the white streaks of weather systems were the vague outlines of the planet's landmasses.

"Closer," she said.

The image zoomed in. Observation statistics in red scrolled down as a faint but distinctly visible overlay. An orange dotted thread, looping in a circular formation around the planet and its satellite moon, projected the Good-Child's course.

Not-Joh touched a control.

The white overlay disappeared to reveal the land below.

Har-Lih stared at the image. "Water covers more than two-thirds of the surface. Vegetation grows everywhere."

Not-Joh touched a control and the white clouds reappeared. "Life thrives here." She emitted the odor of excitement tinged with a trace of joy. "Watch this," she said. "Accelerate time sequence." The planet in the holo-image rotated. "Notice the movement of the clouds. They carry water deep into the center of its land masses."

"What makes the clouds move so far inland?"

"With all that water, there must be strong storms." Not-Joh touched a control and an orange line snaked out to the top of the global projection. "The polar regions have huge amounts of water trapped as ice."

"Is this planet like Hool, only with more water?"

"No, there are other significant differences. Those clouds mean the atmosphere has a greater density than Hool, since a denser atmosphere carries more water."

Har-Lih examined the control panel before looking up. "Are there any more electromagnetic emissions from the Blue-Gem?"

"Yes, but we haven't made sense out of them. Either they're cleverly encoded analog signals, or they're from a truly primitive civilization."

"Why do you believe that?" Har-Lih's breathing flaps oscillated in an uncertain fashion.

Not-Joh's short spines ruffled, showing her frustration. "I'm not sure. If this is the Others' planet, then where are the Others' spaceships? If they have fusion drive, even those as primitive as the one on the asteroid spaceship, then they should be mining the asteroids. However, their asteroid belt shows no signs of any activity. When we passed through, there wasn't the faintest trace of a signal."

"I hadn't thought of that. What does it mean to you?"

"The Others do not belong here."

"You think the Others may have come from elsewhere?"

"Yes." Not-Joh was emphatic. "I'm almost certain."

"Why? What are your reasons?"

"The size of the ship, the one resembling an asteroid. The only reason to build it so large, other than for interstellar travel, would be for space warfare. Since there are no other ships of the same size, that makes it unlikely. The amount of fuel it carries is far greater than any fusion-powered craft requires for interplanetary travel. Therefore, I must conclude it is a visitor to this system."

The holo-image changed to show the asteroid spaceship. The navigation vectors indicated it was on a course toward the third planet. The data overlay gave a projected time of arrival. It also displayed the assumptions it used, which included an efficient velocity reduction flight plan similar to that used by the Good-Child.

"Will the Others arrive before us?" The sour odor of fear vented forth from Har-Lih.

"No. There's only a small difference in our relative velocities but we started ahead of them. We should arrive first, even if we use a low-energy deceleration program."

"Will they see us?"

"I hope not." Not-Joh pointed to the image of its moon. "We will keep this between them and us whenever possible as they draw near."

"How will you know where they are if you cannot see them?"

Not-Joh nodded. "As we pass this moon, we shall drop space-watch sensors on its surface. They will be our eyes."

Har-Lih turned toward the holographic projection. "What else have you learned about the Blue-Gem? Can we live there?"

"I don't know. It's larger than Hool, has more gravity, denser atmosphere, and more illumination. And it has only one moon, though larger than those about Hool." Not-Joh paused. There were many unanswered questions.

"What about plant life?"

"It grows everywhere, not just in the valleys but on the plains and mountains. This sun is hotter and brighter. The plants must have evolved for these conditions." Not-Joh looked up. "And they're not like ours. They're green, for Mother's sake."

"Red, green, what's the difference? Anything else?"

"Its radiation may be hazardous." Not-Joh breathed deeply.

"It cannot be any worse than the toxic materials left over from the war that destroyed the surface of Hool."

"No, I meant the radiation from its star."

Har-Lih scrolled the scanner over the surface of the planet at the limit of its visibility. "So much water, so much life."

"We shall reach the third planet eight sleep periods before the Others arrive. That gives us time to study the planet before we go into hiding." Not-Joh spoke with a confidence she did not possess. "I think we should practice with our weapons," she said. "We may need them."

"Weapons training?" said Har-Lih. "Are not the warriors already trained?" Her breathing flaps flared.

"Yes, they are. They must become familiar with the weapon installed during the rebuild of the Good-Child. It is a very large spine. We may have to use it to ward off the Others." Not-Joh spoke softly.

"What kind of weapon is that?"

"The name means nothing to me but it projects beams of energy great distances, particularly in the vacuum of space."

"An energy weapon? We cannot use energy weapons. They are forbidden by the Way-of-the-Mother."

"You didn't listen to what Suh-Joh said. She pointed out the Way-of-the-Mother forbids energy weapons on Hool and nowhere else. We can use these weapons to protect Hool and the Way-of-the-Mother from the Others. Besides, they're not as destructive as those obscene fusion explosives used by the Others."

"I fear this voyage is becoming more dangerous."

"You are right, but you knew that when you accepted the position as representative of the Hive-Mothers on the Good-Child. I pray for its safe return to Hool," Not-Joh said. A maggot of fear began to gnaw at her guts.

"I pray we do not slip from the path, which leads the Way-of-the-Mother to become corrupted by contact with the Others."

CHAPTER THIRTY-NINE

Not-Joh found Son-Nih in his tiny cubicle adjacent to the ship's shrine to the Spirit-of-the-Mother. He was stooped with age, conveying the humility of a warrior now turned toward peace. "Honored counselor," she said.

"Do not use that title while on this ship," Son-Nih said. "Remember, I am the ship's priest." He moved to the entrance and sealed it tightly.

"Forgive me," she said. "I meant only respect."

"Understood. We must not give ourselves away." He emitted an odor of conciliation and comfort. "What brings you to me?" He clambered back onto his resting mound.

"The Blue-Gem is aptly named," Not-Joh said. "It is rich in water and biomass. Our initial observations suggest it is habitable. It has much land, covered with biomass. That means it may be suitable—"

"Say no more," Son-Nih said quickly. "This is great news, news that our ..." he hesitated and looked around as if someone might be near. "Our Hive-Mother will find comforting."

"It too, was my thought."

Son-Nih moved on his resting mound. His armored plates rasping against the hollow metal dome that was a poor substitute for a rock. "You will, of course, continue with your observations?"

"Of course," she said. "What must we do with this information? With whom do we share it?"

"Ah, now I understand the reason for your visit." Son-Nih drew his head closer to Not-Joh. "Listen," he said. "Let me make the plans on how to deal with this. I have no intention of letting what we've found here get back to those who do not appreciate its true value." He raised his head. "It would be futile to try to limit the spread of that knowledge within the ship. So, we must prevent it from leaving the ship."

"You will let me know when you will make your move?"

Son-Nih hesitated. "No, it is you who must choose the moment. I cannot show too much curiosity in the operations of the ship or the course of its action."

"I don't know when to choose that moment—"

"Listen." Son-Nih flexed even closer. "We need all of the crew—even those Chosen-Male warriors who stand in our way—while we are close to this planet. What," he asked, "if we have to fight our way out?" He referred to the warriors on the ship who came from different Hives to ensure the ship would not act against the will of the Hives in common. "We would need them, every one. So, it must be when we are on our way back, when we no longer need them, when they could prevent us from doing our duty for Suh-Joh and our Hive."

Not-Joh made a trace of the flexion of abasement to indicate acceptance and understanding. "So, I should call you at that time?" Her spines quivered with excitement.

"Yes, and be prepared to act so this ship can be purified from those not of our Hive. Seek out a way this old warrior can handle all those young Chosen-Male warriors."

"Yes," she said slowly. "I know how to do that."

Son-Nih rose and opened the door to his cubicle and gestured that she should leave. "Bless you, my child," he said loudly. "May the Spirit-of-the-Mother guide you. May the tunnel before you be wide and straight."

"Thank you, priest, for your guidance. This unworthy child shall strive ever harder to follow the Way-of-the-Mother."

"Mother, that energy weapon was awful. How could anyone spend their creative energies designing and building such a horror?" Har-Lih had just observed the discharge of the Good-Child's weapon as they had passed the fourth planet, which had provided a screen to hide the violent radiation from their weapon. Soon, they would reach the Blue-Gem.

"It does have a lot of power. However, the most powerful weapon of the Good-Child requires activation of the ion drive."

"Why is that?" Har-Lih reached out for the question like a wild naat-jii in the desert seeking a morsel of food.

"It uses ionized gases from the propulsion jet and makes them into a coherent radiation beam. Its power exceeds all of the rest of our weapons combined, many times over."

"Isn't it difficult to aim?"

"It is just for defense. If we are discovered and pursued, then it is lit up and used on those who chase us."

"Ah, I see," Har-Lih said. "Now I understand its value."

"Unfortunately, it cannot be tested without lighting up space with a beacon that half of the planetary system would see." Not-Joh emitted a faint odor of irritation.

"When do we start to decelerate? Surely we're getting close to that point soon," said Har-Lih.

"Yes, and I'm concerned about approaching this planet too closely. I still fear the Others may already be there and could detect our ion drive."

"Won't the Others' ship behind us discover our presence when we use the ion drive?"

"No. The ion drive will point at the Blue-Gem. That's why I fear we may announce our arrival to the Others who are there."

"Ah, I see." Even though they had worked together on two voyages, Har-Lih still did not understand all the technical details of space travel. She also avoided every opportunity to study and learn more about them. Her concerns tended to focus on the political loyalties of the crew, and she sought favor among those close the Hive-Mothers.

"Once we start deceleration, that will mask the electromagnetic signals from the Blue-Gem." Not-Joh felt uneasy about not knowing what they faced on the planet ahead. She derived comfort from knowing the Others' spacecraft was equally blind, whether or not they used fusion or ion drive.

"That's better, isn't it?"

"Only if there are no Others on the Blue-Gem. I still do not know what those analog radio signals mean."

"Perhaps we should fly by the Blue-Gem without slowing down or starting our ion drive. You know, just observe and record," Har-Lih said in response to Not-Joh's fear.

"We must learn all we can about the Others. It is our duty," said Not-Joh.

Yes, she thought, *but you don't know the true value of the Blue-Gem. If it is suitable for settlement, it may be the planet of refuge for my Hive-Mother, Suh-Joh. If that happens, I will surely be ripened.* Not-Joh paused to stare at the image of the Mother on the ship's bulkhead. *I've always wanted to be ripened,* she thought. *And be a Hive-Mother.*

"True," said Har-Lih. Her voice was low with reluctance.

"If we come back with incomplete information, other things may happen to us." The lesson of the incomplete first survey of Chud-Loo was the classic lecture given to pilots training for exploratory work. The pilots who discovered Chud-Loo never piloted a spacecraft again.

"When shall we start the ion engine?"

"After the next sleep period. Keep the Others' asteroid ship under observation at all times. We want no surprises."

Not-Joh began the preparations for the deceleration phase, which included testing the ship's ion engines. Briefly, she operated the controls to simulate a full range of its power parameters. Nervous, she ordered the replacement of several components she suspected of marginal performance. When she could find no other item that needed attention, she knew they were ready.

"Start the ion drive. Minimum power until all systems are active." It weighed heavily on Not-Joh. If anything went wrong, there would be no help here. She waited patiently while the computer examined the data from the ion drive units. Finally, the system reached operating equilibrium.

"All operating parameters are within normal ranges," the computer reported.

Not-Joh flexed in the symbolic gesture of abasement to signify she accepted whatever fate the Spirit-of-the-Mother chose for her. They began to slow into an orbit around the third planet, the Blue-Gem, even as the Others grew closer.

Not-Joh drew a deep breath. "Use a low-energy deceleration program," she said.

It would conserve fuel and present the lowest possible energy profile. Though they might give up some of their lead to the Others by approaching slowly this way, their deceleration would be difficult to see from the distance of either the asteroid ship or the Blue-Gem.

Not-Joh did not want to be seen by the Others.

CHAPTER FORTY

It was only after I, Kot-Nih, visited the Blue-Gem in the Lin-Fed system—known as "Earth" by its native peoples—I learned the details of what happened during that fateful meeting. At that time, the Earth peoples had a concerted effort underway to prepare for visitors from outer space.

However, their preparations were not for we Hoo-Lii, but for different alien visitors—those whom we knew as the "Others" who called themselves the Qu'uda. Those preparations were the result of the Earth natives meeting the Qu'uda years before the Good-Child arrived. It was the time when the Qu'uda came from the Epsilon Eridani system in their interstellar craft, which they called the Egg-that-Flies.

As the Egg-that-Flies orbited the planet, a weapon from the time prior to the collapse of human civilization fired upon the ship and destroyed its fusion drive. A Qu'uda agent, Bilik Pudjata, descended to the surface of the planet and spent several years making a new propulsion tube to repair their ship.

I learned the Qu'uda had many opportunities to observe the natives during this time. They experienced violence first-hand when their last remaining shuttle, the Bird-that-Soars, was crippled by human guns. Without a means to return to the surface of the planet, they abandoned their agent Bilik and the females guarding a clutch of eggs and departed Earth.

The Defender of the Qu'uda expedition, Mata ChaLik BuMaru, vowed to prevent the warlike natives of Earth from keeping any Qu'uda technology that might lead to space travel. It was, they believed, their duty to prevent this. The Qu'uda began to build a new craft to return and remove all traces of technology.

The humans took in the abandoned Qu'uda agent and the females guarding the eggs and made them welcome. It was this way they learned of the threat from the Qu'uda in space. In the intervening years, the humans assimilated the alien technology and built defenses against the return of the Qu'uda.

During this time, the humans, or more particularly, a human faction known as the Clan, expanded and incorporated areas they called Ohio and Indiana and Pennsylvania into one territory. They established a university where both human and alien worked to disseminate Qu'uda technology. Once they mastered the construction of aneutronic fusion drive systems, they rehabilitated previously abandoned atmospheric fliers—aircraft—and fitted them with fusion-powered engines.

From the human records, I found the Clan established contact with military survivors at a US Navy base in Washington. This group used a powerful fusion drive unit to lift two modified submarine hulls —boats that swim under water—into orbit. They connected these hulls together and made them into a permanent space station in preparation for the Qu'uda's return.

ᘓ

As time went by, the humans set up a system to watch for the approach of spacecraft. This space observatory used a telescope on the space station and relayed its images to the university to look for spacecraft. The clarity of the images and the number of points of light from the space telescope caused difficulties for their astronomers to identify objects approaching the planet.

I examined the records and learned they used computers to sort out objects approaching their planet from more distant objects. Apparently, the data processing took place in a university in the heart of the Clan—a place called Berea, in Ohio. Once they established a computer operated optical comparator, their task was simplified. Soon, they discovered many previously unidentified asteroids, none of which were heading toward Earth. Every day, the space telescope transmitted a set of images to the university's astronomy department. Slowly, they built a set of electronic files on all the objects in the solar system. Even some of the distant bodies in the Kuiper and Oort belts became apparent as a fuzzy haze. The volume of data grew so they dedicated more resources to the area of astronomy—especially as the time drew near for the expected return of the Qu'uda.

The time came and went, but no spaceship appeared. This caused the astronomers to wonder if they had failed in their task to provide early warning. They even speculated the Qu'uda had left the system, rendering all their efforts for naught.

One of the Qu'uda abandoned on Earth pointed out the eggs— unborn offspring in fragile shell cases—had been left on the planet. That was a compelling reason for their return. It was apparent the genetic imperative was strong in all species.

Over time, the astronomers expanded the scope of their search to examine a larger volume of space. The staff of the observatory took turns checking out the many false alarms. It was a student who spotted an anomalous point of light and brought it to the head astronomer's attention. Upon careful examination and review of the data, they concluded the distant object would come close to their planet. Its absence of a tail convinced them it wasn't a comet. Their calculations showed it would arrive within one solar orbital revolution.

I had to read through many records for this period, for this discovery triggered much activity on the part of the humans. It is apparent they used this time to craft tools and weapons for their space station to greet the visitors. It was during this time the humans made another discovery—they spotted a second spaceship approaching their planet. So certain were they that the first object was the returning

Qu'uda spacecraft, they believed the second object was some kind of comet or a long period asteroid.

The humans launched a space platform to make the initial contact with the Hoo-Lii ship ... But I'm getting ahead of myself. This platform initially headed into an orbit near the moon before setting course toward the oncoming craft.

It was during this time the human astronomers finally realized the second approaching object was a threat to their planet. Their initial thought was it was an asteroid on a collision course with their planet. Whether natural or not, that would be a catastrophe. It would arrive about thirty planetary rotations after the first spacecraft.

The records show the human's space station contained many fusion obscenities mounted on primitive chemical rockets which they planned to use to divert the course of the asteroid that was on a collision course with their planet.

The humans have an account of what happened, which can be found elsewhere....

CHAPTER FORTY-ONE

As the Good-Child continued to decelerate, Not-Joh switched the holo-view back and forth between the navigation parameters and the view of the asteroid ship of the Others. It remained on the same course and drew steadily closer toward the Blue-Gem.

Not-Joh feared it might be pursuing them but said nothing. *If I show any sign of weakness, Har-Lih will assume leadership and that would be a disaster. I have my orders, both from the Council and those ones from Suh-Joh. I must fulfill my duty.*

As the Good-Child closed upon the Blue-Gem, it had shed most of its velocity. "Ion drive will shut down in eight squared seconds." The computer's voice echoed through the ship, warning the crew to prepare for a change in gravity vectors.

Har-Lih pushed her way forward in the command center. The walls of the compact room were filled with displays and control panels. "When will the Others' ship start its deceleration?" Icons flickered momentarily, several changing from the normal red to a warning yellow. The ventilation system sighed gently—the air carried aromas of many hives. Doors clanked shut.

Not-Joh waved a forelimb. "Ask it, for it knows the answer." She referred to the computer.

Har-Lih twitched her breathing flaps. "Show me projections of possible orbits for the Others' ship around the Blue-Gem."

A series of trajectories appeared in the holo-image, each weaving a web around the Blue-Gem, each indicated a slightly different course. Slowly, the surface of the planet's image became covered with trajectories until it was a shimmering mass of color.

Har-Lih pointed at the trajectories. "What does that mean?"

"The Others' ship has many options when it orbits the Blue-Gem." Not-Joh emitted a faint trace of the odor of frustration. "In other words, we don't know."

"When do you think the Others' ship must start its deceleration?" Har-Lih said.

"I can only guess. Logically, low acceleration rates make for easier maneuvering, which would be soon. But with these creatures, who knows?" Not-Joh closed her eyes and exhaled.

"How will we know when it happens?" Har-Lih moved about the command center, looking at the controls. "How close will they get to us?" Her breathing flaps flicked nervously.

"As soon as we detect radiation from their drive, we'll know. Even so, we'll arrive at the Blue-Gem before them. We must use that time to survey the planet before we hide behind its satellite. We must ready our weapon, just in case," Not-Joh's breathing flaps flared. "May the Spirit-of-the-Mother give us air." She invoked the traditional plea of all Hoo-Lii who traveled in the depths of space.

A tiny note sounded through the ship just before the ion drive shut down. Weightlessness followed. Systems changed automatically to operate in low gravity conditions. The living quarters of the Good-Child lurched gently as it began to spin up and induce rotational gravity.

Not-Joh ordered the forward scanning equipment activated. A new holo-image of the Blue-Gem appeared.

"Enhance image of all objects orbiting the Blue-Gem, use mass as the selection criterion. Plot a projection of their orbits," Not-Joh said.

Rings of circular orbits quickly painted multiple bands around the image of the Blue-Gem. "Mass of orbiting items, sort by size," she called. A table appeared in the holo-image and scrolled down. Most were small and showed no sign of life. "Show any orbiting debris emitting radiation."

Two objects flickered in the holo-image, indicating pinpoint sources of emitted radiation. One appeared to be in orbit about the planet. The smaller of the two was far from the planet and seemed to be stationary.

Not-Joh breathed deeply. "Computer, show the course vector of this object." She pointed to the smaller object in the holo-image.

A dotted green line extended toward the Good-Child.

"It's coming toward us." Not-Joh stared at it for a moment. "It must be a spaceship. Spirit-of-the-Mother, I fear the Others have found us." She glanced at the ship's status.

"Chosen-Male Warriors," she said. "To your stations. Unknown body approaching. Do not fire until so ordered."

Har-Lih glanced at the image. The second item too, emitted radiation. "What is that which glitters?" She indicated the something in orbit about the planet.

"Computer, enhance image of body emitting radiation. Provide analysis of radiation." Not-Joh ordered. The image grew larger until it showed a fuzzy shape that had two parallel sections with a central connection. As they watched, its rotation became apparent. "Spirit-of-the-Mother, that's a space station. Not only are the Others behind us, there are Others in front of us," she said, her voice pitched high with fear.

༄

Not-Joh watched the small object drift closer. *It's our velocity that makes us approach it*, she thought. The image flickered slightly. *Now*, she wondered. *What's happening?* She magnified the holo-image.

The indistinct image showed an irregular shape that gave the impression of having a small projection. Its spectral image revealed a mixture of aluminum and iron. A scale superimposed upon it indicated its size. *Spirit-of-the-Mother*, she thought. *It's too small to be a spacecraft with passengers. Not a spaceship, an object.*

Something flared brightly on the object.

"What is that?" Har-Lih asked.

"Spectral analysis," Not-Joh said.

"Low grade radiation, aneutronic fusion reaction of boron and hydrogen," the computer said. "It is a propulsion system. The object has negative acceleration on the same vector as the Good-Child. Relative velocity decreasing."

"So, it too, uses a fusion drive like the Others' ship that follows us. It is on the same course as us and makes no attempt at concealment. They are telling us they know we're here." Not-Joh stared at the holo-image. She hesitated. "Calculate time until object matches velocity with the Good-Child," she said. "Display countdown sequence."

A time display appeared in the holo-image.

"Will we need to use our weapons?"

"Not unless we have to. Its relative velocity is almost the same as ours. That makes it an easy target."

Something flashed in the holo-image.

"Object transmitting a low-power radio signal," the computer's softly impersonal voice said.

"Analyze the signal," Not-Joh said. "Chosen-Male Warriors, charge your weapons."

Lights dimmed momentarily as energy drained into the fast-discharge power cells of the Good-Child's heavy weapons. They were one step closer to battle.

Squiggling lines of spectral analysis appeared in the holo-image. A row of data appeared.

Not-Joh pointed. "See, this is an analog signal with a variable set of frequency ranges."

"Is it a weapon?"

"No." Not-Joh examined the spectral characteristics carefully. "Perhaps," she said. "It is an attempt to communicate with us."

In all their preparations, no one had given much thought to contacting the Others.

"Put it on audio."

A choppy sequence of unintelligible deep-toned sounds came from the speaker; followed by another sequence of even deeper sounds that was almost at the limit of Not-Joh's hearing range.

"What is that?" Har-Lih asked.

Not-Joh exhaled deeply, breathing flaps fully flared. "That, I believe, is the voice of the Others."

Har-Lih crouched lower, as if seeking to hide. "The Others. They have found us. Oh, Spirit-of-the-Mother, save this child ..." she began a prayer.

"Shut-up," Not-Joh said. Her breathing flaps shut noisily. "Shall I summon the priest for you?" she said. "Look, they start with words, not weapons. It seems, Mother willing, they seek an alternative to battle."

She silently prayed she was right.

"They match velocities with us. That is not a fighting tactic. So, that gives me reason to believe they are not about to attack. An object slowing to our relative velocity is much easier to hit than one moving fast."

She noted the display showed the Chosen-Male Warriors had brought the weapon up to full readiness. They were ready.

CHAPTER FORTY-TWO

At extreme magnification, the alien object had a lumpy, round shape. Several stick-like antennae protruded from its side. During the time it took for the planet to complete a rotation, the object repeated its transmission many times.

A vivid yellow line squirted across the other spectral lines hanging in the holo-image before them. Several lines of digits scrolled down explaining the nature of the disturbance.

"What is that?" asked Har-Lih.

"A pulse of electromagnetic energy."

"They're using a weapon?"

"It does not appear so." Not-Joh hesitated, reading the data in the holo-image. "It may be trying to obtain our size and configuration. If so, it is a primitive technology."

Long moments later, another yellow line—much fainter—appeared in the holo-image. More data appeared.

Not-Joh stared for a moment. "Distance to asteroid ship?" she asked.

The computer responded and gave the same distance as displayed in the holo-image.

"I think the burst of energy just reflected off the asteroid ship," Not-Joh said.

"Is it preparing to fire at us?" Har-Lih asked.

"I don't think so."

"What should we do?"

"Wait," said Not-Joh. "So far, it has not done anything to threaten us." *Other than approach us like a hunting maa-lii fly stalking an unsuspecting go-lik.*

She shivered at the thought of being a go-lik in the mandibles of a ravenous maa-lii. *And we get closer and closer to the space station that orbits the planet, as the asteroid ship approaches from behind. Are we in the jaws of a well-planned trap?*

࿉

"Look." Not-Joh pointed at a message that had just appeared in the holo-image. "There's single-frequency light reflecting off that object."

"Is it a weapon?" Har-Lih momentarily crouched lower.

"No. It's at a very low energy level."

"Then what is it?"

"It could be for communications."

"With whom?"

"It might come from the space station orbiting the Blue-Gem. Let us watch and see what else they do." Not-Joh turned toward a control panel and touched several keys, increasing power to the shielding. "Put ion engines on standby."

Har-Lih's breathing flaps flickered nervously. An aroma of fear hung about her like a garment.

The Good-Child continued to coast onward, closer and closer to the Blue-Gem. Time lay heavily on their limbs.

Not-Joh knew her orders were to stay hidden from the Others; she also knew they had been discovered. It was time to do something. "Har-Lih, I am going to send a greeting to the object in front of us," she said.

"We must not reveal our presence to the Others."

"They already know we're here. They know our size, our distance from them, and our exact location, for they have touched us several times with electromagnetic pulses. I want to try to communicate with them. It may be our only chance."

"Why?"

Not-Joh exhaled noisily. "If we try to flee, we can only defend ourselves from one of them. Since they approach from two directions, we can't align the ion drive laser at both of them. We would lose that fight."

"I see." Har-Lih's breathing flaps sank.

"We need to buy time. If the Others join forces, together, in the same vicinity, we would stand a chance in that fight, for we could then use our ion drive laser."

"You think it will come to a fight?"

"It would be far better if it did not."

"I don't understand these things, Not-Joh. You have command. Do as you think best. I will keep a record of your efforts." Har-Lih wagged her breathing flaps submissively.

"Computer, direct a standard hailing message to the alien object and orbiting space station in front of us. Tight-beam communication."

Blessed Spirit-of-the-Mother, Not-Joh thought. *I pray I am right.*

The message contained their identity and a request for the recipient to provide the same identification.

The computer flashed the message in a holo-image, confirming transmission of the standard greeting. Not-Joh watched the holo-image, wondering if there would be a response.

Time passed slowly. The holo-image flashed the icon that indicated reception of a radio signal. She ordered it played.

"Hoo-Lii." came the greeting, followed by the same low-pitched sounds they had previously heard.

"Spirit of the Mother. They are trying to communicate with us. Computer, start a detailed analysis of their language patterns. We must learn to understand them." She hesitated a moment. "Repeat their message back to them."

Moments later, the aliens transmitted more of their strange-sounding language.

The holo-image flashed a warning yellow.

Not-Joh stared at the rapidly scrolling display that showed the nearby object had started to move closer to them. Something was wrong, for there was no radiation from a fusion flame.

"Verify change in relative velocity."

The numbers disappeared momentarily. When they returned, they were the same as before—it was inching closer, very slowly. "Analyze for propulsion means."

A spectral analysis appeared in the holo-image. It was the same as before, except it now showed the presence of helium.

"Helium with no heat?" Not-Joh said. "What kind of drive is that?" The object was barely moving. "It has to be maneuvering with gas jets," she said.

The scrolling display became still. The object ceased closing upon the Good-Child. It was close enough for the optical scanners to show it was cylindrical object with several short quill-like antennae plus an object with a round shape. Weld marks scarred its surface. Wiring and metal tubing connected components.

"It is primitive," Not-Joh said. "It is made from many parts, crudely fashioned." As she spoke, a stubby mechanical arm unfolded and pointed a boxy device directly at the Good-Child.

"Amplify image on movement," she said. "Spectral analysis."

The image expanded to fill the holo-image. The shape appeared dark and grainy, and now looked like it was round and just barely reflected light. It wavered momentarily.

"What is it?" Har-Lih asked.

"I'm not sure." Not-Joh stared at the data scrolling across the bottom of the image. Aluminum, silicon, and oxygen, combined ... "It may be an optical scanner," she said. Or the sighting device of a weapon.

A yellow line flashed in the holo-image.

Not-Joh flinched, but the data showed it was only faint traces of laser light reflecting off the object. Something was sending messages to it.

The object hung motionless, its glass eye staring at them.

"Radio transmission received. Source is asteroid ship," the computer said.

"Put it on audio," Not-Joh said.

The frequency of the sounds emitted from the speakers was so low that it was almost at the limit of Not-Joh's hearing.

The noise ceased and then the sound came again.

"Spirit-of-the-Mother," Not-Joh said. "It must be."

"Why do they make such different sounds?" asked Har-Lih.

Not-Joh turned to stare at Har-Lih. *How did she rise so high in the Council of Hive-Mothers' esteem?* she thought. She must have talents not visible to one as humble as myself, other than her ability to report on the actions of others as she abases herself before the Hive-Mothers.

"Because they are aliens from two different Hives."

CHAPTER FORTY-THREE

"The Others are communicating," said Not-Joh.

"How do you know that?" Har-Lih's breathing flaps rose as though she smelled something dead.

"The Others' ship, the big one, just sent a radio transmission, perhaps to the space station orbiting the Blue-Gem." Not-Joh paused and touched the controls. In the holo-image, a red line extended from the asteroid ship's depiction in their direction. "Their course is similar to ours. They may be coordinating an attack on us."

The moment of hope the Others might try to communicate faded. Fear blossomed. It could be the jaws of a closing trap. "Warriors, prepare your weapon," she called. "Await my orders."

Throughout the ship, warriors squeaked acknowledgment.

Not-Joh watched the weapon system activate on the holo-image. One by one, the defense stations came to life. *Now*, she thought. *The Good-Child's spines are erect and ready.*

A solitary voice started a chant and echoed through the ship's communications web. It was the priest's traditional prayer for the warriors before they embarked into battle. The well-known words asked the Spirit-of-the-Mother for protection as they stepped forward to meet their foe.

"Will we attack the Others?" asked Har-Lih, nervous.

"No. We must be ready to defend ourselves. If these are the same Others who destroyed Chud-Loo without warning, we must be ready. We will watch and wait." Not-Joh felt exposed. Space lacked the security of life underground. There were no tunnels, no dark corners; there was no place to hide.

The holo-image flashed, indicating a change in status.

Not-Joh stared at the image of the Others' asteroid ship. It had just shed a small shard of light, another separate source of energy emissions. Had it launched a missile? Or was it another ship?

"The Others' ship no longer uses its fusion drive to decelerate," she said. "It launched something." *Now what?*

A point grew brighter, indicating a powerful source of radiation. "Computer, enhance image. Identify source of the radiation emissions."

"A separate craft, heading toward us."

"What's its velocity?" Not-Joh said. "Plot its course vectors."

The separate craft appeared in holo-image as a tiny yellow triangle and displayed its velocity as a small boxed number hovering to one side. The data showed it was accelerating toward them at about one gravity. Its energy emission, now small, was just barely detectable. The asteroid ship continued to decelerate as it approached them at a much lower velocity.

"Visual image of asteroid ship," Not-Joh said.

The Others' smaller ship grew large in the holo-image. It was a featureless dark mass, a backdrop for the plume of radiation from its drive. Its course would bring it toward the Good-Child. The computer listed its parameters in faintly glowing characters on its image.

"That craft is fusion drive powered. It's probably a piloted craft," Not-Joh said.

The holo-image flashed briefly to indicate a radio transmission had been received.

"Characteristics?" she asked. A faintly glowing message formed in the holo-image. "Its characteristics are similar to the signals sent by the orbiting spaceship. I don't think it's an attack." *Please, Spirit-of-the-Mother, make that true.*

"Why do you say that?" Har-Lih stared at her.

"If they intended to attack with fusion explosives, they would have launched a missile with high acceleration. The ship from the asteroid approaches at a rate more typical of piloted craft. That makes it an easy target," Not-Joh said.

"Warriors," she said. "Do not harm the approaching craft."

The deep voices of the aliens again filled the command center. It was more radio transmissions from the Blue-Gem and the orbiting space station. Icons flickered back and forth from safe red to warning yellow.

Not-Joh crouched lower, watching carefully.

An icon flashed insistently.

"Display changed parameter," she said.

A short table of values scrolled down the holo-image. They attached themselves to the bright red line describing the course of the small craft that had left the asteroid ship. Its course changed to point directly at them.

"Warriors," Not-Joh called. "The Others' craft approaches. Do not fire unless commanded."

Another icon began flashing insistently.

"Display," Not-Joh said.

The parameters listed showed subtle differences in the optical reflectance of the approaching craft. It had done something to change its form or shape. *Now what?* wondered Not-Joh. "Visual, maximum magnification."

A dark, slab-like craft appeared in the holo-image. It had no obvious openings, with two slender spines erected at right angles from its sides. It emitted little thermal radiation and gave off no radio transmissions. The course would bring it within four squared ship-lengths of the Good-Child.

It approaches slowly, thought Not-Joh. *We will have time to examine its form in detail. So close*, she thought. *We could almost reach out and touch it. Will it shed more velocity?*

Another icon began flashing.

"Display."

The data appeared immediately. It was an electromagnetic pulse from the approaching craft, but not a radio transmission. It was more typical of a large surge of electrical power. Nothing appeared different on its surface. The craft drew closer and closer. Seam lines on its surface became apparent. The projections at the ends of the stubby projections from the main part of the craft carried tubular sections. Tubular sections pointing directly at the Good-Child.

Fear swept over Not-Joh like a sandstorm. *Those look like weapons ...* She never finished the thought.

Two narrow tongues of energy flashed out. The Good-Child shook as a storm of relativistic particles raked the metallic ceramic composite guarding its nose. The shield's upper layer ablated off with actinic brilliance.

Alarms sounded. Shapes in the holo-image flashed green, registering damage to the forward shield. Damage assessment confirmed hull integrity. The shield had held.

Not-Joh stared at the holo-display. *Spirit-of-the-Mother, they'd struck without warning.*

"Warriors," she said, but the crack of the laser firing came at the same time. Lights inside the Good-Child dimmed momentarily from the power drain. The holo-image of the Others' ship showed it flashed briefly into incandescence under their lasers.

The entire outer layer of metal from the Others' craft had been volatilized, which gave it a smoother, shinier appearance. All of the surface protuberances on the ship had disappeared, including the weapons that had fired upon them.

Not-Joh stared at the Others' ship. "We clipped its spines. Its course is changed." *Yet*, she noted. *The ship still has the same shape and configuration.* The Others' craft continued to draw closer and closer. It would pass momentarily.

"Warriors, you have blunted the foe's spines," Not-Joh made an announcement to the ship. "All hail the Warriors of the Good-Child. Spirit-of-the-Mother bless you."

The crew repeated the cry.

Not-Joh flexed her breathing flaps and bellowed the cry again. She took her eyes off the holo-image of the Others' ship.

Claaang! The Good-Child shuddered. Lights flickered and dimmed. Air screamed and dust filled the air. Alarms squeaked.

The entire holo-image flashed green, warning the hull was breached. Wind picked up, carrying dust and loose items out of the command center. Air leaked out in prodigious quantities. The alarm squeaks became fainter as the air pressure dropped. The Good-Child vibrated as the emergency airlocks slammed shut throughout its length. The holo-image flickered, some of the alarm changed from green to warning yellow. Damage status and operational control messages rose in the holo-image. The Good-Child had been holed in several places. Several exterior compartments were open to space. Icons warned both shuttles were no longer attached.

The awful clanging sound repeated.

Spirit-of-the-Mother preserve us. Not-Joh prayed. *They've struck again.*

The holo-image blazed into the brilliant warning green.

Once more, the Good-Child clanged and shuddered under the fiery beams from the Others' weapons. The main lights failed. Pale orange emergency lighting panels brightened. Alarms squeaked continuously.

Not-Joh braced herself but no more attacks came.

She touched the controls, activating backup systems. "Computer, play recording of events that led up to the attack," she ordered. The Others' ship appeared in the holo-image. As she watched, new spines appeared to grow out of its smoothed exterior to replace those singed off. Without warning, fiery beams leapt from its spines. The holo-image collapsed as the tongues of energy reached the outside sensors.

It was not dead, Not-Joh realized. *Only stunned. Our weapon dazed it for but a moment. And, now ...*

CHAPTER FORTY-FOUR

"Status report." Not-Joh broadcast her order throughout the ship. The holo-image did not record the injuries the crew had suffered. As the reports came in, it was worse than she had initially believed. Har-Lih joined her in the command center, observing the data in the holo-image.

Har-Lih's voice interrupted her thoughts. "Not-Joh, you misjudged the Others. The Good-Child is badly damaged. Half our crew are nothing but fodder for the digesters."

Spirit-of-the-Mother, thought Not-Joh. *I erred and now Har-Lih wishes to assert dominance over me.* "You are right, I misjudged it. I did not expect its attack. When our lasers burned off its spines, I was sure we had killed it. I thought it was destroyed. It grew new spines, for its hide withstood our weapons." She reviewed the battle in her mind's eye. It was obviously a craft designed for war.

The computer showed the ship's drive system was still operable. However, the Good-Child had multiple ruptures in its outer shell. That meant the radiation shield, which was also their main water tank, had lost most of its water. They had lost a lot of air, and without water they could not make additional oxygen. The air reserves—when supplemented with oxygen from the remaining water—would only last for about eight-squared-sleep-periods, even if it was recycled constantly.

Not-Joh realized they would not have enough air and water to return to the transfer point for their trip back to Hool. There was no way to get water from the Blue-Gem planet since both shuttles had disappeared. No water, no oxygen.

Not-Joh flexed herself into a position of abasement as she reported the ship's status to the crew. *I failed*, she thought. *I should have anticipated the Others' attack.* She begged the crew's forgiveness.

"What do you propose to do now?" Har-Lih asked. Even though she could take command, she hesitated. She knew little about the ship's technical features. Under these circumstances, it was unlikely the crew would obey her orders.

"Repair the Good-Child, then wait and watch. If the Others approach, we fight with every spine."

The holo-image gave off a bright spark of light, indicating a powerful energy emission.

"Display source of energy," Not-Joh said. It was the Others' ship. "Replay events leading to energy discharge," she said. The Others' ship reappeared, larger and closer. As it retreated and grew smaller, it closed on the tiny object that had approached them earlier. Energy beams leapt from the Others' craft, the one that had attacked them. The beams sparkled on the front of the small object, which exploded into a geyser of expanding gas and debris.

"What?" Not-Joh stared at the image. "The Others attack one of their own? I don't understand this," she said. "Now it wages war on the object before us. Did that not also belong to them?"

"Then it must be from another Hive."

"Their Hives are not united. They, too, wage war among themselves. The Others are a warlike species and they're armed with terrible weapons."

The holo-image sported a flashing icon that called attention to a new radio transmission. The deep tones of the Others resonated through the command center.

Not-Joh looked up from the instrument unit that controlled a repair machine crawling over the surface of the Good-Child, laying down a new layer of skin. She watched the holo-image for a while, but nothing happened that seemed threatening. "I wonder what it means?" she said. She returned to the task of sealing the holes in the hull. In the background, the priest chanted the Cycle of Life prayer over the muted communication system, blessing those who died. Their bodies would be digested, and their water salvaged. Still, it wasn't enough for their return.

The computer sounded an alarm.

Not-Joh stared at the flashing yellow icon. The Others' ship—the one that had attacked them—had started its fusion drive. "Project vectors," she said.

A pale yellow line extended from the tiny point of light in the holo-image and wrapped around the blue and white globe that was the nearby watery planet. The line terminated at another point of light—it was the space station in orbit close to the Blue-Gem planet.

Har-Lih appeared silently at Not-Joh's side.

Not-Joh glanced at her. "Either it is a rendezvous or an attack," she said.

"Which do you think will be?" Har-Lih asked.

"I don't know."

Not-Joh opened her eyes and looked at the time measurer. Something clicked for attention. She had been asleep for only a short time. A message hung in the air before her.

Change in status of space station in orbit around Blue Gem. It has ceased rotation. And the nearby object that had attempted to communicate with them, and had been also attacked, had departed.

Odd, she thought. *Somehow it survived those terrible weapons.*

The sleeping alcove was a tiny replica of a cave. In many ways, Not-Joh found it the most comforting place on the Good-Child.

Familiar brown fabrics embossed with the crossed quill emblem of Suh-Joh's Hive covered the floor and sleeping mound. The metal walls had a texture reminiscent of the sandstone walls of her Hive. There was even a naat-jii lurking in the corner, scavenging stray organic material. Her paat-kli clawed its way from beneath her middle limbs and began to graze on her hide. She closed her eyes. She could almost imagine she was back in the safety of the Hive.

The message clicked insistently. The ship's computer risk assessment algorithm demanded she examine the data.

Not-Joh opened her eyes and the dream of safety evaporated. A wave of fear swept over her as reality returned. Almost no water and the Good-Child still leaked air. *Our days are numbered. Still, I must do my duty.* She arose and went to the command center.

The holo-image displayed the changed parameters of the space station. It had ceased rotation and had launched a large number of small objects in a radial pattern at very low velocity. They did not appear to be heading to any place in particular.

"Why did they launch them?" Har-Lih asked. "Do you know what these objects are?"

"No," Not-Joh said. "Perhaps they were sent out to protect the space station. If so, they use different tactics than us." She examined the holo-image. It showed the craft that had attacked them continued to shed speed. It was clear its course would take it close to the space station. The relative difference in velocity between them had dropped significantly. Both were now in orbit about the Blue-Gem; in one-eighth of its rotation they would meet.

"Sensors at maximum sensitivity."

In the holo-screen, she saw another tiny object, moving on the same course as the ship that had attacked them. She increased magnification and saw the course vectors that described its course.

It's the object that had earlier tried to communicate with us, she realized. A tiny blue glow extended from its rear. *So*, she thought. *It too, uses a fusion drive.*

It was small compared to the craft that had attacked them. It had moved away from the Good-Child, accelerating, and had built velocity almost like a missile. "Focus on departing object." She pointed at it.

The object appeared in the holo-image. Barely visible were jagged strands of metal at the front, evidence of the violence of the Others' attack. Yet it had an antenna hanging off one side, oriented in the direction it traveled. *It looks odd, like a ragged flower*, thought Not-Joh. "Plot course of the object."

The object she thought of as the "ragged flower" vanished from the holo-image. The Blue-Gem reappeared, along with the points of light that showed the space station and the Others' ship. The "ragged flower" was halfway between the Good-Child and the space station. A red line grew from it, tracing a curved course around the Blue-Gem toward the space station. It would reach it in about one-eighth of the planet's rotation.

"What's the Good-Child's status?" Har-Lih asked.

"Most of the repairs have been completed," Not-Joh said. "My initial estimate of air loss did not provide for continued leakage. Our situation is critical. We used most of our remaining water to make oxygen."

Since the attack, she had slipped into a role of reporting her actions to Har-Lih since she was the Council's representative. It was an acknowledgment of her failure to anticipate the Others' attack.

"What do you mean by critical?" Har-Lih asked.

"We have sufficient air for four squared sleep periods." Not-Joh knew repairs and water from the dead bodies would help. It didn't matter, for to get to the transfer point for the return to Hool, they needed more air than that, a lot more.

The holo-image flashed briefly. It was a warning the Others' craft had made a course change.

Not-Joh glanced at the image. "Computer, plot course vectors of the object," Not-Joh said. The image shrank until it again included the Blue-Gem. A red line etched itself toward the planet and joined a tiny sparkling point. Something didn't look right. "Enhance course destination," she said.

The holo-image expanded until it included the Others' ship that had attacked them. The course led directly to the Other's ship. A faintly glowing message scrolled across the image gave the time and velocity when the "ragged flower" would reach it.

"Consequences of contact?" Not-Joh asked. Another set of glowing symbols painted themselves over the image of the Others' ship. She wiggled her breathing flaps in amusement.

CHAPTER FORTY-FIVE

"Har-Lih," Not-Joh called. "Come to the command center."

The holo-image showed that the Others' ship was closing on the space station. A tiny sparkle of light appeared. Data scrolled down the image. High-energy particle beam discharge.

"Spirit-of-the-Mother," Har-Lih said in a low voice.

"Small wonder it sliced holes in us," Not-Joh said. *So, the Others' ship now attacks the space station. Perhaps*, she thought. *This outcome is not as obvious as it appears.*

The "ragged flower" craft continued its descent toward the space station and the Others' craft. The velocity differential between the "ragged flower" and the Others' craft had become large.

"What do you think will happen?" asked Har-Lih.

"Watch." Not-Joh increased the sensitivity of the visual sensors. The two hulls of the space station were barely visible. The tiny blue light of the drive system of the "ragged flower" was now only visible through maximum enhancement.

Flashes appeared on the surface of the space station. Data in the holo-image indicated metal volatilizing and confirmed the energy beams from the Others' ship were burning holes in the space station.

"See," Not-Joh said. "The Others' ship does to the space station what it did to us."

The "ragged flower" craft rapidly drew closer to the two ships. It caught up with the craft that had attacked the Good-Child. Something flashed brightly on the visual. Two pieces appeared, tumbling as they descended toward the surface of the planet. It wasn't long before they started to glow. Before long, they flared brightly and disappeared in the planet's atmosphere.

Not-Joh listened to the echoing voice of the priest as he chanted praise for the warriors' valor in their fight to preserve the Way-of-the-Mother.

It had taken one full sleep period for the crew of the Good-Child to gather up the dead and fatally injured and feed them to the digesters. For a few moments the ship became quiet, still after the priest finished the prayer. Once again, the priest's high twittering voice wove the melodious harmony that was a prayer of thanks to those who died and gave up their bodies' water as a gift to the living.

With power restored and the hull sealed, Not-Joh returned to the cramped control room. Deeply troubled by her failure to anticipate the attack and the strange unfolding of subsequent events, she activated the holographic display. She re-played the incident between the space station and the craft from the asteroid ship several times. The control room had an unusual glow that came from the many yellow and green warning icons.

It is a reflection of the degree of damage the Good-Child has suffered, Not-Joh thought.

Repair work continued so they could depart. However, the steps taken to conserve what little air remained had made the entire ship stuffy and its atmosphere more difficult to breathe. She knew the attack had damaged two of the three atmosphere recycling units and the water shortage precluded the manufacture of any more oxygen.

"I do not understand the Others," Not-Joh said. "They broadcast messages to the entire universe. They attack without warning. They use weak energy weapons but have heavily armored spacecraft. No two of their spacecrafts are alike. They fight among themselves like Chosen-Male warriors whose breathing flaps are filled with the scent of desire-to-mate. Who are they? What are they?"

She wondered if the small object that had rammed into the ship that had attacked them had possessed a crew. The collision had taken both vessels into the Blue-Gem's atmosphere where they'd burned up. That implied the Others might be a species that went willingly to death to defeat an enemy. She shivered at the thought.

"What happened? Why did they do it?" Har-Lih asked.

"Perhaps it's a dominance struggle between Hives."

"Do you think the small object destroyed itself to save the space-station ship?" Har-Lih asked.

"I don't know. There's much I do not understand."

Har-Lih pointed to the holo-display.

Not-Joh saw an icon blink into life. The holo-image flashed briefly and warned the status of nearby ships had changed.

"Display," she said.

It was the asteroid ship. Its drive had started. It was changing course.

Now what? she wondered. "Vectors on decelerating craft."

In the holo-display, a red line extended from the asteroid ship toward the Blue-Gem. "It looks as though it will orbit high above the planet," Not-Joh said.

A column of figures scrolled down. She saw it would take about two rotations of the Blue-Gem to arrive in orbit.

The crew of the Good-Child in the control room watched silently as the asteroid ship slowly curved in toward the Blue-Gem. Soon, the Good-Child would pass behind the planet's satellite and then settle into orbit around the planet. They would be almost one-quarter of an orbit behind the asteroid ship. It was still too close for comfort.

Not-Joh stared at it. That ship worried her—it was so big, it must be deadly. Red lines sprouted from the image that showed its course change and new velocity vectors. "Computer, display destination of ship."

The image of the asteroid ship shrank until the Blue-Gem

appeared. A faintly glowing red course vector extended to a point between the Blue-Gem and its moon. At this point, the line curved in a circle around the planet. The course vector passed close to a newly visible twinkle of radiance.

Har-Lih glanced at the pilot-navigator. "Now what will happen?"

"It appears the asteroid ship is on course for the space station. That asteroid has a formidable mass and a powerful drive. If it collides with the orbiting station, it will destroy it," she said.

"What's emerging from behind the Blue-Gem?" Har-Lih pointed to a new point of light in the holo-image. It flashed briefly to indicate a change in condition from the previous data file. It was the space station.

"Enhance image of orbiting space station," Not-Joh ordered. It grew large in the holo-image, floating, suspended against the complex patterns of the Blue-Gem. Something seemed different, but she could not smell it out.

"Why does the space station not rotate anymore?"

Ah, that's it. "Perhaps it is in preparation for the coming battle." Not-Joh saw many objects near the orbiting craft. A light flickered into existence within the holo-image.

"Computer, enlarge image of orbiting craft." Not-Joh pointed to the orbiting space station.

The Blue-Gem disappeared. A tiny flare appeared in the holo-display. A small, slender vehicle that left a faint white trail had just departed from the orbiting space station.

"Computer, course and velocity vectors of accelerating craft. Show destination." Not-Joh had a premonition. The image in the holo-image expanded until the asteroid ship appeared. The course vector extended directly toward it. Something was odd about the accelerating craft.

"Spectral analysis." Not-Joh pointed at the accelerating craft.

Faintly glowing data painted across the slender craft's image. Its velocity continued to increase.

Not-Joh stared. *This cannot be*, she thought. "Computer, repeat analysis. Verify components in drive system."

"What is it?" It was obvious the symbols in the holo-image meant nothing to Har-Lih.

The faintly glowing data readout winked out and reappeared.

"That is a chemically-powered rocket," Not-Joh said.

"What's that?" Har-Lih asked.

"It's a very primitive means of propulsion. We used something like it in the very first days of our space travel. It's slow, inefficient and has a very short range. It must be a ceremonial device, or a signal." Not-Joh paused.

The chemically-powered rocket reached a high velocity. The visible plume ceased from the rocket and it coasted onward. Just before it reached the asteroid, there was a brief flash. The glowing symbols in the holo-display flickered and changed.

Not-Joh examined the new data intently. "It appears the asteroid ship destroyed the primitive rocket." As she watched, the spectral analysis data changed abruptly. As she read the symbols, her breathing flaps flared.

That's not possible, she thought. *I dare not say anything until I'm sure.* A feeling of horror rippled through her and her last meal threatened to come up.

"Why?" Har-Lih asked.

With difficulty, Not-Joh dragged herself back to Har-Lih's question. "Perhaps they believed it to be a weapon. I don't understand these Others. Why do they attack each other?" She turned her attention to the other small objects near the orbiting spacecraft. "Enhance image of orbiting space station."

The image expanded to show two long smoothly-rounded cylinders that lay parallel to each other. They were connected at their centers by a tube at right angles. Several additional slender strands appeared to run between the cylinders. One cylinder of the spacecraft was oriented toward the approaching asteroid ship, held out as though a shield.

Perhaps it was a mistake, Not-Joh thought. *Maybe ...* "Search for objects near the space station," she said to the computer.

The image shrank until the space station was only a tiny dot of red light. Tiny red lights winked into existence around it.

More, Not-Joh thought, *but are they the same?*

"Enlarge an image of one of those objects indicated in red," she said.

The space station faded to be replaced by a slender dart. It was identical to the primitive chemical rocket recently destroyed by the asteroid ship. "Spirit-of-the-Mother save us," she said.

Another icon in the holo-image winked briefly into existence and demanded attention.

"Display," Not-Joh said.

The holo-image went blank for a moment. Another slender dart, except this streamed a tail of hot chemical combustion similar to the previous rocket.

"Course vectors, enlarge to show destination," she said.

The image dissolved. The asteroid ship floated into the holo-image along with a symbol for the chemical rocket. A red line representing its course vector reached out and then went past the asteroid ship.

"Image of chemical-powered spacecraft," Not-Joh ordered.

The holo-image vanished and the dart appeared. It moved forward, again leaving its faint white trail. Across the image faintly glowing symbols described the vehicle's parameters. *For such a primitive craft*, she thought, *it accelerates rapidly*.

The tail abruptly disappeared. Something flashed brightly. The holo-image blackened.

A seed of fear germinated in Not-Joh and threatened her control. "Diagnostics of image failure, replay record and show cause." She needed a different system to bring back the image.

Lines of symbols appeared in the holo-display, which stated broad-band radiation overload caused the image failure. The symbols faded.

"Replay image," she said. *No, please*, she thought. *Let it not be true.*

The holo-image darkened and two position-indicating lights winked on. The point of light representing the dart sparked and grew monstrously bright. Light washed over the now-visible image of the asteroid ship before the holo-image faded into blackness.

Fear in her gut grew into a giant, all-consuming monster.

CHAPTER FORTY-SIX

"What is that?" Har-Lih's breathing flaps flared.

Not-Joh was too busy to answer. She called up records, for she had this terrible, terrible feeling about what she had just seen. Data scrolled rapidly through the holo-image. It confirmed her suspicions.

She closed her breathing flaps and eyes. *It cannot be.* She wanted to be away from this place; it was like being in a nightmare. Her fear blossomed fully. "Spirit-of-the-Mother save us," she said. For just an instant, she crouched low in a position of total submission.

Har-Lih stared at Not-Joh. "What is it? Tell me, what is it?" Her breathing flaps flared.

"That was a fusion explosion." Not-Joh almost gagged on the words. "The Others, the terrible Others, are here. That was one of their obscene fusion bombs." She abased herself and began to pray. "Oh, Spirit-of-the-Mother, preserver of the Way, save us—"

Ping.

The computer issued an imperative warning. Within the holo-display was an image of a cluster, no, it was hordes of chemical rockets flaming toward the asteroid ship. Each of the tiny darts was approaching from a different direction.

"They have more." Not-Joh watched almost like a voyeur seeing something forbidden, something awful. Her spines erected as her fear grew.

She stared, horrified, as one rocket after another accelerated to a high velocity. Their engines ceased, and they coasted onward. The holo-display continued to show them, indicating their positions by small points of red. The number of points in the holo-display suddenly multiplied into a sea of tiny red lights, which looked like a swarm of tiny red glo-lik flies converging upon a summer blossom.

They're missiles, Not-Joh told herself. *Not insects, but missiles with fusion obscenities.*

They had multiplied at least eight-fold and were now diving on the asteroid ship from many different directions. It was like getting a hint of the existence of a malevolent spirit, no, it was more like seeing the face of evil.

An icon in the holo-display flashed briefly, indicating a change in status. A visible picture of the asteroid ship grew in the holo-display as beams of energy flicked from its surface. Each beam caused a tiny red fly to flare and die. The swarm of red lights continued to draw closer and closer to the asteroid ship until they seemed to merge with it.

A point of light spiked. The holo-display darkened. Another point of light appeared, to coalesce and grow into a gigantic sphere of incandescence, filling the control room with brilliant yellow light.

The holo-display blackened abruptly. Columns of figures scrolled through the air.

Not-Joh felt she had seen the face of the ultimate evil. It was almost a religious experience.

"Spirit-of-the-Mother save us," she cried. "The Others use fusion obscenities like they're sand from the desert. What kind of monsters are they?" Fearful but fascinated, she wanted to see what had happened.

It is still my duty, she thought as she worked to recover a recording of the event. "Ah, I've got it," she said. "Replay at slow speed. Filter out the bright light."

The asteroid ship grew large in the holo-image. Tiny dark flechettes sank down like a flock of hunting maa-li flies about to feed upon maggots in carrion. One by one, the missiles closed on the mass of the asteroid ship, only to disappear with tiny actinic flashes when touched by the flickering beam of energy.

The asteroid ship's defenses are good, Not-Joh realized dispassionately.

One flechette appeared to close with the surface of the asteroid ship. A point of light started and continued to grow, filling the holo-image with a star-like intensity. It grew ever-more brilliant, lighting up the control room like a new sun. The light slowly faded, until the holo-display was again black, empty.

Not-Joh was overcome with fear and awe. She felt the urge to crawl into the deepest, darkest cave of her Hive. She wanted to hide as far away as possible from these violators of the Way. But the flashing yellow and green icons forced her back.

"Computer, show the ship approaching the Blue-Gem." She wanted to see what was left of the asteroid ship.

A soft, plaintive sound came from the holo-display. It remained dark. It could not comply.

"Show volume of space where fusion explosions occurred," Not-Joh said. After that, all she expected to see were rock fragments. The holo-display brightened.

The asteroid ship appeared. Its forward section looked different, as though it were smoother, more rounded. No longer did any of the tiny spiky weapons protrude from its surface. A set of faintly glowing symbols scrolled across the holo-display to show its course. It no longer was heading toward the Blue-Gem. Its course led past the planet in the direction of the system's star.

An icon in the holo-image flashed to indicate a change of status of a nearby object.

"Display," Not-Joh said.

The orbiting space station appeared. A small triangular shaped spacecraft slowly moved away from it and then accelerated.

"Course vectors for the spacecraft under power," Not-Joh demanded. The holo-display showed a large dark area. A tiny twinkling point of light, identified as the accelerating spacecraft, occupied one side. On the other, a point of light indicated it was the asteroid ship. A faint red course vector extended from both to a point in space.

"They are going to the asteroid ship," said Har-Lih. "Why?" Her breathing flaps flared.

"That I cannot answer," Not-Joh said. "This may be time to leave. Prepare the Good-Child for departure. Start the ion engines. Warriors, arm the ion drive laser." The sight of a fusion explosion had been a moving experience. She was filled with fear, or was it terror? Even without oxygen and water, she wanted to flee into the depths of space rather than face those who would use such weapons.

A bright yellow icon flared in the holo-display. The main ion engines would not start.

CHAPTER FORTY-SEVEN

It wasn't until much later that I, Kot-Nih, learned the true reason for the violent battle that took place high above the Blue-Gem. It seems those we called the Others are the alien Qu'uda, which of course, you already know. Even though the humans of the planet Earth were fighting to prevent the total destruction of their civilization, we know the Way-of-the-Mother does not condone the use of fusion bombs against life under any conditions.

Yes, yes, I know we use them to power the lasers used in our planetary defense system, but we Hoo-Lii never use them directly on planets or people.

Forgive me, but I'm getting off my main tunnel of thought. It seems the humans sent something with communications capability to contact the Good-Child, a communications pod. That communications pod was attacked immediately after the Qu'uda craft crippled the Good-Child. Now that we understand the nature of the Qu'uda intentions, it is clear why the humans subsequently used the communications pod to destroy the Qu'uda craft, which was attacking the orbiting space station.

As for the human's use of fusion bombs on the asteroid ship, well, it must be viewed as an act of desperation. Even so, according to most priests who serve the Spirit-of-the-Mother, the humans committed a sacrilege. However, there are a few who point out they did not use those weapons on the surface of any habitable planet.

Yes, yes, I know it is a fine distinction, nevertheless it does offer them an argument should they eventually come to understand the universality of the Way-of-the-Mother and seek enlightenment.

I'm wandering again.

What they did after they used fusion weapons on the asteroid ship caused the greatest internal debate within our society. However, I, Kot-Nih, having read their records, now know the humans had no evil intentions directed toward we Hoo-Lii. It was their curiosity about us that compelled them to make the controversial gesture, which was an attempt to communicate with us....

"Hoo-Lii," came from the communicator. The greeting had come many times. It had become hard to ignore.

Not-Joh stared silently at Har-Lih for a moment. "Well, what do we do? They know our greeting; they have communicated numbers to us. They make no overt hostile gestures. Do we die like cowards gasping for oxygen in the depths of space? Or do we face them with Hoo-Lii courage?"

Four eight-day cycles of the Mother-of-the-Sky had passed since they tried to start the main ion engines and discovered they were also damaged in the attack. It had taken until now to get them repaired. The air was malodorous with the scent of many hives. The air reserves had dwindled; less than four squared days' supply remained—even if they used all the water obtained from the dead warriors to make oxygen.

"Well," Not-Joh asked. "Do we respond to their greeting?"

"We cannot tell them about Hool," Har-Lih said.

"I agree. Do we have anything to lose by communicating?"

"No, but I'm afraid."

"I, too. I do not know if these are the ones who destroyed Chud-Loo. If they are, we must destroy them in our departure."

Har-Lih flexed her torso toward the floor in a faint motion of abasement that signified her acquiescence. "Attempt communications, Not-Joh," she said.

"Computer, start the learning sequence. Transmit in the teaching mode," Not-Joh said.

That would start the carefully thought-out process to simultaneously decode the alien language, while at the same time instructing them in the structure and basic form of the Hoo-Lii language. It was a task that occupied their time for several cycles.

ॐ

"What is it?" Har-Lih had asked the same question several times previously. She stared at the icon that had just started flashing in the holo-display.

Not-Joh continued to ignore the question. "Computer, full scan of radiation emissions from approaching object." They had watched the aliens carefully and none had approached the Good-Child during the last four squared sleep periods.

Until now.

It was the delta-winged craft from the orbiting space station. Its course led directly toward the Good-Child.

This was the craft that had traveled between the space station and the asteroid ship several times. Careful analysis of data collected by their sensors had revealed that its long, boxy body was fragile and thin-skinned. Its delta wings and tall fin at the rear suggested it was an atmospheric shuttle. With large windows at its front, it was ill suited for war. Further scanning did not reveal any apparent weapons. In addition, careful review of the records showed it had not fired any weapons during the battle over the Blue-Gem.

As it got closer, it slowed and adjusted its velocity to almost match that of the Good-Child. Long doors opened along the axis of its body. A tiny cylindrical object rose out of its interior. For a short while, both delta-winged craft and small cylinder continued to drift closer. The delta-winged craft rotated to face away from the Good-Child. Faint blue cones of fire appeared in its three engines. It accelerated in the direction of the orbiting space station, away from the Good-Child. The small cylinder continued drifting onward.

"Scan approaching object with all sensors," Not-Joh said.

The spectral characteristics of the approaching cylinder filled the holo-display. Not-Joh read the data carefully and called up several reference programs to analyze the data further.

She breathed a sigh of relief. It showed no radiation characteristic of weapons or fusion reactors. Its emissions were low-level heat and traces of electromagnetic activity. So low, the approaching cylinder appeared almost derelict. Its infrared signal suggested a low-temperature heat reservoir. The computer had no similar radiation profile in its memory banks.

"Computer, probability of hostile weapon," Not-Joh asked. *It's small*, she thought. *Too small to carry a passenger and life support system. Too cold, too.*

Not-Joh examined the computer's answer in the holo-display. It was negative with wide error bars. In frustration, she flapped her breathing flaps. "Go to visual image of object, up close." She did not know what else to do.

The stubby cylinder appeared in the holo-display, revealing tiny plumes of gas from maneuvering jets were slowing the cylinder's approach. There were other items on its exterior that Not-Joh did not understand immediately what their role was.

"Greater magnification," Not-Joh said.

As the cylinder expanded in the image, something flickering drew her attention.

"Focus on source of visible radiation."

The holo-display enlarged the image and showed the boxy cylinder had a screen which had a sequence of images. It took only moments for her to realize it was instructions to operate controls on a cylinder.

The picture sequence finished with liquid flowing out of the cylinder. The screen went blank. It started over again and showed the same picture sequence. She noted the cylinder's velocity relative to the Good-Child dropped almost to zero. Its gas jets ceased operation.

It was two ship-lengths from the Good-Child, stationary.

Every able warrior had a weapon trained upon it.

Time crawled by. The cylinder's temperature continued to slowly decline. The screen played the same sequence of images over and over again.

We must do something, Not-Joh thought. The section of the holo-display remained focused upon the cylinder's flickering screen. She had memorized it. "Shrink image of object," she ordered.

All at once, she realized the object in the screen was the cylinder. Her breathing flaps flared. *Is it? Could it be it contains water?* "That object on the screen is the cylinder." Her nose flaps flared. "It shows the cylinder holds a liquid—"

"Are they telling us what to do?" Har-Lih snorted her breathing flaps. "Is the liquid water? Can they know we need water?"

Not-Joh rose up on her hind limbs. "If it is water, we're saved." Every tiny quill on her body quivered. "Get that alien object in here. No, wait. Get a warrior into a space suit. Get the priest to bless him." Her breathing flaps vibrated, and her spines erected, now stiff with excitement.

"You're going to bring that thing in here?"

"Yes. Have the priest bless the remote manipulator too and send it out to retrieve the alien device," Not-Joh said.

It's a risk, she thought. *No, it's not. We're already as good as dead. So, what do we have to lose?*

"Maybe it's not water, but a trap? What if it's a fusion explosive?"

"There is no fusion source on or near the device. It uses such primitive technology it should not even be in space. I think I know what it is."

"Tell me, what is it?" Har-Lih flared her breathing flaps as if to smell-out a predator seeking to ambush her. "What if it isn't water?" She closed her eyes, lowered her head, and silently prayed.

Not-Joh did not respond.

The holo-display changed to show the remote manipulator slowly closing on the ungainly cylinder. When the manipulator's mechanical mandible obtained a firm grip on the alien cylinder, it towed it back to the Good-Child. For a moment, the cylinder disappeared from the holo-display as it slid inside the hull.

The holo-display brightened again to show the cylinder within the air lock. The screen on the cylinder continued to show the same sequence of pictures repeatedly, how to operate its controls. The sequence again ended with a liquid flowing, which if it were water, would give them the means to get home.

Inside the airlock, the higher light levels revealed the screen had a visual sensor with an attached transmitter.

"So," said Not-Joh, "They're watching us, too."

"Perhaps we should destroy it, so they cannot learn how badly we're damaged." The tone of Har-Lih's voice lacked any authority to cause any Chosen-Male warrior to respond.

"It doesn't matter," Not-Joh said. "They saw how we suffered on the spines of the craft that passed us. They have known of our condition for some time." She watched the holo-display carefully. "Yes," she said. "Get a sample."

The warrior, who had received a special blessing from the priest, followed the directions on the screen and collected a sample of the liquid from the cylinder in a sample container, which he sealed tightly before opening the airlock. Once he passed through a hastily erected decontamination chamber, he brought it into the Good-Child.

"Quick," Not-Joh said. "Get it tested."

A small unripened female skilled in the operation of analytical tools put the container in an isolation chamber before drawing a sample of the liquid. The analytical tool responded almost instantly. She repeated the test.

Not-Joh stared at the results of the analysis of the liquid from the tank. "It is water, pure, with no contaminants. More than enough to get us back to Hool, praise be to the Mother."

She hesitated for only a moment. "Transfer the water from the cylinder into the Good-Child's system. Keep it isolated from the existing water supplies," she said. "Use the analytical tool to test it as it transfers. Make sure all of it is water." It was a gift from the aliens. They had sent water.

"Oh, Blessed Spirit-of-the-Mother, Savior of these unworthy children ..." Har-Lih began to pray loudly.

"Har-Lih, let the priest recite the prayers," Not-Joh said. "There's work to be done."

Once the crew transferred the water, the warrior, once again blessed by the priest, moved the cylinder—now much lower in mass—out of the air lock. Floating free off the Good-Child, he attached a device that contained a recording of the language-training program. It also included a copy of the Holy Scriptures that would show the aliens how to achieve enlightenment through the Way-of-the-Mother.

When we return, Not-Joh thought, *it is better they speak our language, for they gave us the gift of water.*

All on the Good-Child, especially those who had fought with Suh-Joh, understood the significance of the gift of water. Now it did not matter if these aliens had used fusion weapons, for they had indicated they were willing to accept direction, Hoo-Lii direction.

They would bend to the Way-of-the-Mother now they had agreed to become new servants.

"Priest," Har-Lih called. "It is time for a prayer."

The priest began the chant that was the special prayer of thanks for surviving battle. As it echoed through the Good-Child, first the Chosen-Male warriors joined in, soon followed by the crew, their voices pitched high in sincere thanks for the gift of life and salvation.

"Open a link to the aliens and send them this message: Hoo-Lii! We shall return to lead you, this we promise," said Not-Joh. "Computer, prepare the Good-Child for departure from this system. Set the course for the Lin-Fed transfer point. Advise me when the Good-Child is ready."

The Good-Child's engines coughed into life. Soon, the low vibration from the ion engines provided its comforting sound to the crew as the ship accelerated away from the planet of the aliens into the darkness and safety of space. It was their first step on the way home.

Not-Joh watched the holo-display for signs of pursuit. No radiation flared; no craft followed.

We are safe, she thought. *We are on our way back to Hool.*

Inside the privacy of her sleeping alcove, Not-Joh prayed and gave thanks to the Spirit-of-the-Mother for protecting them and gave special thanks for letting them find a new world for her Hive-Mother, Suh-Joh.

CHAPTER FORTY-EIGHT

The Good-Child never reached Hool.

It was only after I, Kot-Nih interrogated an unripened one, who had been secretly placed aboard as a crewmember of the Good-Child by the priests from the Shrine-of-the-Mother. The unripened female fled the ship and hid in Suh-Joh's mining facility in the asteroid belt. Her signal summoned us, and she told us of what had happened on board the ship. It seems that Son-Nih, Suh-Joh's counselor, still lived, neither had he forgotten his skills of battle and duplicity.

"Are the aliens following us?" Har-Lih asked. Even after several cycles of the Mother-of-the-sky, she feared the aliens would seek to follow them home.

"No." Not-Joh stared at the hologram. A web of colored lines surrounded the blue orb that represented the Blue-Gem. "They swarmed after the asteroid ship like naat-jii after dung. It is again under power and now heads toward the Blue-Gem."

"Praise the Mother." Har-Lih vented out aromas of satisfaction and relief. "We have a clear tunnel before us."

Not-Joh turned away from the controls and rocked back on her two rear hind limbs. It was time.

"Yes," she said softly. "We, as leaders of this ship, have reason to give special thanks to the Spirit-of-the-Mother for our escape. For without her divine intervention, we would not have survived. Priest," she called. "We need your services."

"The priest?" Har-Lih's breathing flaps flared. "Why do you call for the priest?"

"I want the priest to give a prayer, a special prayer of thanks only he can give. And you, as representative of the Council of Hive-Mothers, should join in this prayer of thanks. For we are not the only ones who have reason to celebrate."

Har-Lih vented an aroma of agreement.

"Just the two of us, a special prayer."

"Just us?"

"Yes," said Not-Joh. "After all, we have been through a lot together, haven't we?"

Har-Lih rippled her breathing flaps in agreement. She turned and spoke to her two Chosen-Male warriors that were her guards. "Allow me," she said. "A few moments of private piety."

The two warriors flexed their torsos in a motion of abasement, acknowledging her authority. They turned and left the control center as the old priest entered.

"You called?" the priest asked, head bowed.

"It is time," Not-Joh said. "For the special prayer ..." she hesitated. "It is time, yes."

"Ah." The priest made the gesture used at the beginning of prayers and moved closer to the two females. "Children of the Spirit-of-the-Mother, let us show our humble gratitude."

Not-Joh and Har-Lih assumed the position of abasement, flexed, exposing vulnerable openings in their carapaces before the priest.

"For delivering us from the mandibles of death, let us first take a moment to think about all the death we have experienced together. It is time for us to recite the Cycle of Life ..." He began the prayer of death.

Not-Joh and Har-Lih joined in the prayer.

"... From Life to Death." As the priest uttered those words of the prayer, he dropped onto Har-Lih like a hunting Maa-lii, spines extended. With three slashes, Har-Lih lay gasping in a pool of blood on the deck, her life expiring.

"It is done," the priest said, his breathing flaps flaring in unison as he exhaled heavily.

Not-Joh flexed in abasement. "Honored counselor, Son-Nih."

The priest turned toward Not-Joh. "Are you ready to do the rest of what is required for our Hive-Mother?" He wiped the blood from his spines with great care.

"Of course." Not-Joh raised her head. "Computer, emergency activation of internal defenses. Sedate all occupants except those in this control room. Do it now."

"Releasing soporific. It will require one-eighth of a cycle of the Mother-of-the-Sky to clear air of soporific."

"Good," Son-Nih said. "Once I feed the remaining Chosen-Male-warriors to the digesters, there will no trouble with the rest of the crew. They will make the gift of water to me, or I shall take their water after they visit the digester."

ↄ
ↄ

Once Son-Nih had removed all Chosen-Male warriors from the Good-Child, Not-Joh guided the ship to the odd distortion in space-time and activated the resonator to open the transfer point. The Good-Child made the jump through space-time to emerge at the transfer point at the outer limit of the Hool system.

Instead of broadcasting its presence, the ship slipped quietly into the most distant part of the asteroid belt to one of Suh-Joh's mining operations.

It was there she saw the dim light from Hool's star reflect with a metallic brilliance off Suh-Joh's massive ship, the Mother's Servant.

It was a bulky ring attached by four spokes to a central stem that dominated the craft's appearance. The ring rotated slowly about the craft, providing gravity for the crew and passenger living quarters. One end of the central stem held a cluster of engines that would drive the

Mother's Servant through interplanetary space. The other end of the stem grew into a giant, spherical fuel tank. It was almost the diameter of the craft's ring.

In the shadow of the largest asteroid of Suh-Joh's mining operation, was a pale, icy, cometary body that had been retrieved from the outer planetary belt. Tiny shuttles, lights flashing, moved back and forth between the asteroid, ice-ball, and the Mother's Servant. Fusion torches flickered on the aft end of the giant fuel tank.

"Most gracious Hive-Mother Suh-Joh." Not-Joh unconsciously flexed as she spoke. "The Good-Child has returned home."

The hologram flickered and Suh-Joh's visage appeared. "It pleases me that you have returned. What did you learn?"

Son-Nih stepped forward. "It is better that we tell you in person what we have learned and what has transpired."

"Ah," Suh-Joh said. Her breathing flaps rose. "I think I understand. Please, come to my quarters in the Mother's Servant as soon as possible."

"Most gracious Hive-Mother, the Good-Child no longer has its shuttles," Not-Joh said. "We have no transportation."

"I will send a craft."

"... in retrospect, we know the aliens on the Blue-Gem planet made no hostile or aggressive act toward us." Son-Nih shifted uneasily. "It seems these aliens were defending themselves from attack by the Others on the asteroid ship. We may have misunderstood them." Son-Nih said. "They used the fusion weapons only after their orbital space station was attacked. Seeing those fusion bombs explode was horrible. It was obscene. It was worse than obscene. It was pure evil." He lowered his head as if in prayer.

"They did not attack you and then after some time, attempted to communicate with you?" Suh-Joh raised herself onto her two hind limbs and turned toward Not-Joh. "Is that right?"

"Yes, they sent us water. We tested it. It was pure and safe for consumption. We put the object that contained the water outside the ship, along with instructions to learn our language and a copy of the Holy Scriptures. As servants, we expect they will study it and learn the Way-of-the-Mother."

"Perhaps you should have brought that object back with you. Our scientist could have learned much about their technology from it," Suh-Joh said softly.

Not-Joh flexed into a position of abasement she held rigidly. "Forgive me, most gracious Hive-Mother, I did not think to do that. However, we do have a good visual record—"

"It really isn't that important." Suh-Joh beckoned with a forelimb. "Rise," she said. "The important thing is they made the gift of water and acknowledged their submission to us."

"It also allowed us to return safely."

"Did they follow you?"

"They made no attempt to follow."

Suh-Joh lowered herself as though uncomfortable. "I cannot return to Hool. If I do, the priests at the Shrine-of-the-Mother will force me to ripen my successor, which I do not wish." She raised herself to her full height. "So, I must leave." She turned to Son-Nih. "Which is it?" she said. "Invade Kamah and carve out a domain, or accept the invitation of the Others?"

Son-Nih lowered himself. "I cannot make that decision for you. I can only advise you on the facts as I see them. The Blue-Gem world is rich beyond our wildest dreams. And the conquest of Kamah would be bloody, very bloody ... With no guarantee of success."

I, Kot-Nih, can tell you that Suh-Joh's ships never appeared in the Kamah system. It took some time to find this out. When she fled, she took only the Mother's Servant and the Good-Child. When a combined force under the command of the Council of Hive-Mothers arrived and attempted to take her into custody, the battle of the mining station took place. It was not much of a battle, since Suh-Joh's craft fled from us. The Hive-Mothers' forces gave up pursuit after Suh-Joh's craft generated a powerful laser beam from their ship's ion engines and destroyed several of the Hive-Mothers' ships. They realized it would be futile to close upon such a powerful weapon. Nevertheless, our forces did inflict some damage upon her ships, which then disappeared toward the transfer point for the world of the Others.

We discovered she had removed much of the manufacturing equipment from her asteroid ship building facility. That slowed our efforts to build more interstellar spacecraft. Consequently, our pursuit of Suh-Joh was long delayed.

As you know, by the time we found her, many strange events had occurred in our system and those of the alien Others, which of course, is another story....

EPILOGUE

The Mother's Servant, carrying much of Suh-Joh's Hive, including its Chosen-Male warriors, fled the Hool system. The Council of Hive-Mothers' fleet of battle craft pursued them. As they closed upon Suh-Joh's ship, they launched missiles at it. Laser beams, fired from the rim of the dwelling-quarters ring of the Mother's Servant, destroyed most of the incoming missiles.

Yet the Hive-Mothers' fleet continued to draw closer to the fleeing ship. Without warning, the Mother's Servant's ion engines generated a monstrously powerful laser beam and aimed it at the pursuing battle craft. The closest of the Hive-Mothers' craft flashed into incandescence and volatilized. The remaining battle craft dispersed into a circular pursuit formation.

The Mother's Servant altered course and fired its ion engine laser again, destroying yet another battle craft. This happened two more times before the remaining four battle craft broke off pursuit and returned to Hool.

Not-Joh piloted the Mother's Servant, Suh-Joh's ship, to the transfer point and reduced velocity in preparation to enter.

"Are you sure this will lead us to the system of the Blue-Gem?" Suh-Joh asked. The pursuing fleet had inflicted more wounds upon the Mother's Servant than the pursuers knew. One-fourth of the Chosen-Male warriors in hibernation would never awake. The ship's engineers issued warnings about damage to the structural integrity of the spokes holding the rim. "What kind of stresses will the transfer impose? Can the Mother's Servant make the jump safely?"

"Most gracious Hive-Mother, I'm sure of my navigation," Not-Joh said, flexing slightly with a hint of abasement. "I can only say the Good-Child came through without damage. Perhaps the engineers should examine its data banks."

"Yes," said Suh-Joh. "Engineers, do it."

ౖ

The engineers used the data from the Good-Child to design and reinforce the Mother's Servant. During the time the engineers did this work, the crew strove to repair the living quarters on the ship's rim. They took the dead and nearly dead to the digesters, recovering their water, and concentrated their protein into feed for the food-insects.

Suh-Joh grew increasingly nervous as time went by. She knew they were vulnerable while they hung motionless in space. One high-speed missile could destroy the Mother's Servant before they even saw it coming. There was no good defense against a coordinated orthogonal attack. But nothing came out of the dark.

"Most gracious Hive-Mother." It was her counselor.

"Yes, Son-Nih?"

"In two cycles of the Mother-of-the-Sky, we shall be ready."

Suh-Joh rose up from her resting mound. The quickness of her movement made her paat-kli scurry for the safety of her mating-flap. "So, the ship is ready?"

"Yes, most gracious Hive-Mother."

"Are engineers sure the ship will survive the transfer?"

Son-Nih hesitated. "They have done all that is possible with the equipment and materials at mandible."

"Which means?"

He hesitated again. "In terms of probabilities, seven-eighths sure. There is always a chance something will go wrong."

Suh-Joh's breathing flaps flared. "Better than my chances should I return to Hool. Enter the transfer point when ready."

PERSONAE

HOO-LII AND THEIR EQUIPMENT

Kot-Nih: The Priest-Narrator.

Lok-Nih: A powerful and warlike Hive-Mother.

Zak-Joh: Counselor (deceased) to Lok-Nih, known for his patience and negotiating skills. War leader of the army raised to confront the Disobedient.

Suh-Joh*: The Hive-Mother that sponsors the expedition to investigate the radio anomalies, daughter of Lok-Nih.

Bok-Nih: Senior priest at Lok-Nih's funeral.

Son-Nih*: Chosen-Male warrior, ripened by Lok-Nih and favored by Suh-Joh. First the strong arm of Suh-Joh, then her counselor.

Sad-Loh: Scholar recruited by Suh-Joh.

Lil-Tih: Scholar recruited by Suh-Joh.

Buk-Tar: Has the title "Oldest" Hive-Mother; leads Council of Hive-Mothers.

Nah-Kih: Young Hive-Mother with political aspirations.

Disobedient: The sect of Hoo-Lii who rejected the traditional way and ripened all members to sexual maturity.

Wod-Jur: Leader of the Disobedient who preached universal ripening; exiled to Chud-Loo.

Di-Nah: Exiled to Chud-Loo and becomes its first and last Hive-Mother.

Tuh-Kar: A Disobedient who becomes Di-Nah's first Chosen-Male.

"Good Child": A deep-space craft having faster-than-light (FTL) capabilities; carries a standard crew of eight squared (64) Hoo-Lii.

Vin-Boh: Unripened-Male pilot-navigator on the voyage to investigate Chud-Loo.

Pun-Tih: Co-pilot on the voyage to investigate Chud-Loo.

Gat-Sun: Hive-Mother's representative on the investigation of Chud-Loo.

Not-Joh*: Pilot-navigator on Good-Child on the voyage to the Blue-Gem (Earth).

Har-Lih: Hive-Mothers' representative the Good-Child on the voyage to the Blue-Gem.

QU'UDA AND THEIR EQUIPMENT

MingLik TuKan: A Defender of Qu'uda, or combat officer on board the "Star-Seeker."

ChaKut DuJutu: Astrogator and spokesperson for the crew of the "Star-Seeker."

Star-Seeker: The interstellar space craft sent to investigate the pulsing radio signals in the nearby star system.

Mata ChaLik BuMaru*: Spokesperson for the Deli Qu'uda committee on the Egg-that-Flies, which is known as the Keepers-of-the-Egg.

DalChik DuJuga: Principal archivist for the Keepers-of-the-Egg and leader of the "Home-Seeker" faction.

Egg-that-Flies: The massive fusion-powered spacecraft made from an asteroid with interstellar range belonging to the Deli Qu'uda.

Bird-that-Soars: Fusion-powered atmospheric space shuttle, interplanetary range; belongs to the Deli Qu'uda.

Little-Egg-that-Flies: The ship made from a small asteroid and fitted with a fusion drive; used by the Deli Qu'uda for their return to Earth.

Bird-of-War: Fusion-powered battle craft, heavily armored and possesses powerful particle beam weapons; also carries a squad of armed Deli Qu'uda.

HUMANS

Taylor MacPherson*: First leader of the Clan. Also Elder representing the Hill District.

ABOUT THE AUTHOR

Malcolm Wood, born in England, came to the USA at age 14 and graduated from Aurora, Ohio High School and Kent State University with a degree in chemistry while working full-time. Three years later, he fulfilled a self-made promise and spent two years traveling around the world. After resuming a career in chemistry, he obtained a MA in economics. About thirty years ago, he became a registered professional engineer in two disciplines (petroleum and environmental engineering), leading to a career in finance, and later, environmental consulting.

It was about this time he resumed writing fiction while working for a company that prepared economic analyzes on specific industry sectors. Since these publications contained a significant element of fiction, it motivated him to start writing fiction. He attended numerous writing workshops and joined the Cleveland Science Fiction Critiquing group (also known as the Cajun Sushi Hamsters from Hell), which had such writers as Geoff Landis, S. Andrew Swann, Charles Oberndorf, and Maureen McHugh. Their critiques and comments pushed Malcolm hard to improve his craft. Almost twenty years ago, he formed the West Side Writers Fiction critiquing group, dedicated to writing at a professional level. During this time, he finished twelve novels and a biography of his travels.

His activities include obtaining a private pilot's license and a competition driver's license. In addition to writing, he has found time to ski, hunt, taste wine, and enjoy gourmet food.

IF YOU LIKED ...

If you liked The Blue Gem, you might also enjoy:

Stranger
by M.B. Wood

Arcana
by Paul Kane

Assemblers of Infinity
by Kevin J Anderson & Doug Beason

OTHER WORDFIRE PRESS TITLES BY M.B. WOOD

Collapse

Stranger

Coming Soon:

New Star

Dawn

Our list of other WordFire Press authors and titles is always growing. To find out more and to see our selection of titles, visit us at:

wordfirepress.com